ALSO BY CATHRYN GRANT

THE ARTIST

A PSYCHOLOGICAL THRILLER

CATHRYN GRANT

PROLOGUE

I stabbed her with a palette knife.

Repeatedly. Until she was dead.

I know I'm not a killer at heart. But sometimes you do what has to be done to escape the prison you've found yourself in. And that was my only way out.

The lies had piled up until I was suffocating. There were so many lies, my whole life was a lie. What were a few more?

The way I look at things, even now, it was her or me.

1

NOW: MORGAN

The Spanish-style villa glowed like a painting as the sun settled into the desert horizon behind it. Standing alone as far as my eyes could see in any direction, the house managed to look both welcoming and desolate.

Jade sped up the long driveway. She was giddy with excitement to introduce me to the artist she'd commissioned to paint my portrait. The painting was a gift she'd given to me when Tyler and I had announced our engagement. During the long drive to the artist's estate, Jade had behaved as if she and I were lifelong girl-friends on our way to my bachelorette party. Easing myself out of the passenger seat of her Mercedes, I had to remind myself for the twentieth time in two hours—she was my future mother-in-law.

Becoming closer to my fiancé's mother was the entire reason I'd agreed to have my portrait painted. It was the reason I was spending ten days in the desert, which the artist demanded of all her portrait subjects so she could get to know them intimately. It was impossible to capture a person's true nature if the artist didn't establish an inti-mate connection. That's what Jade had said. It sounded a little grandiose to me, but I kept that thought to myself.

I wanted to love Jade. And I wanted her to adore me. I wanted to build a lifelong relationship. Not a typical mother-in-law and daughter-in-law jaw-clenching tolerance, but something really special. Genuine love and affection. I didn't think that was too much to hope for.

Jade's excitement was contagious, but after two hours in her sublimely comfortable car, I didn't feel any closer than I had during the previous eight months that I'd known her. She was a difficult person to get close to, even though I'd put a lot of effort into it. When you've lost your own mother at the age of twelve, the chance to find an almost mother in your mother-in-law is deeply, almost desperately compelling. At least it was to me.

There was no doubt she liked me, but there was a distance. As if she didn't quite consider me part of her family.

We approached the entrance to the villa through a long, tiled courtyard nestled between the two wings of the house with a fountain in the center. The windows of the rooms facing the courtyard were shielded by small flowering trees and lush, leafy plants. Before we could ring the bell, the enormous oak door opened.

Ember West stood facing us, the look on her face decidedly uninviting. She had shoulder-length dark hair that was piled on top of her head. Loose strands fell around her thin face which was completely free of makeup. Her eyes were large—dark brown with long, dark lashes. Her eyes were beautiful, but looked tired, almost haunted.

She wore faded jeans and a long white T-shirt. Her feet were bare, with rings on the second toes of both feet.

I suppose I'd expected her hands to be covered with paint, but they were clean, her nails beautifully shaped and colorless.

I felt I was being inspected, as if she wanted to be sure I was suitable for a portrait that would enhance the critical and commercial acclaim she enjoyed. She studied my face, staring into my eyes without blinking, her gaze moving methodically across every feature, then slowly down my body as if deconstructing each bone, holding it up to the light.

"It's so good to see you again." Jade's voice was half an octave higher than usual.

Ember gave her a cool smile and held out her hand, silver rings on every finger. Her hand drooped slightly at the end of her wrist and I couldn't help thinking the extravagant amounts of silver weighed it down.

Jade ignored the extended hand and rushed in for a generous hug. After releasing Ember from her embrace, she turned toward me. "This is Morgan."

With the barest whisper of a smile, Ember said it was a pleasure to meet me. She turned and drifted toward the interior of her home. We followed into the enormous entryway featuring a vaulted ceiling.

The house was cold after the warmth of the late afternoon May sunshine. So cold, I felt I was inside a tomb. The thought was likely prompted by the cemetery we'd driven past with its aging mausoleums. For some reason, the chalk white plaster walls of the house reminded me of those structures.

I rubbed my arms, but it did no good. My body felt colder with each breath.

A man in his thirties with shoulder-length light brown hair joined us. He also wore faded jeans, but with nice-looking leather shoes and a button-down shirt. He seemed to appear out of thin air since I hadn't noticed from what direction he'd come.

"I'm Bryce," he said. "Ember's assistant. I'll show you around and then help you with your luggage. You'll have time to freshen up before dinner at eight."

We followed Bryce on a tour that began in the living room across from the entryway. The large, comfortable room had bifold doors opening onto a patio with a swimming pool, hot tub, and fire pit. Beside the living room to the left was a formal dining room, and to the right was a good-sized room devoted to a pool table. He showed us a large kitchen with pale gray granite counters, a bar, breakfast nook, and a sitting area. The left wing of the house had three spacious bedroom suites, one of which Jade and I would share. He didn't show us the master suite and home office, or his own small apartment with a separate entrance in the other wing flanking the courtyard.

Next, he led us across the patio, through a spectacular walled cactus garden and along a pathway to another, ancient-looking Spanish-style building that housed Ember's studio. In addition to a bathroom, there were four rooms—the studio itself, a workroom, a supply room with storage cabinets, and a small gallery with a separate entrance. On display in the tiny gallery was a selection of Ember's work, spanning the entire twenty-plus years of her career.

"I love finishing the tour in the gallery," Bryce said. "Viewing Ember's work is inspiring. Clients begin dreaming about their own portraits. Sitting for a portrait can be draining, but having a vision of the finished work is energizing." He smiled, holding my gaze until I smiled back.

"As you look around the gallery, really take your time. An outstanding portrait is all about the eyes. Our eyes reveal our individuality. Our souls. Without the talent to capture a person's eyes, that spark of life, a portrait lacks vitality." He looked at me with such intensity, I felt so uncomfortable I ached to look away, but I felt that doing so would indicate some kind of weakness on my part.

"You have extremely evocative eyes," he said.

Jade had had her portrait done by Ember, so I knew how breathtakingly talented she was. I wasn't sure I needed to view the gallery for a sales pitch on her talent. But I followed his instructions.

We moved slowly around the room. The paintings were unbelievably lifelike. It almost seemed as if each frame were a window through which I looked at someone who was gazing back at me, inviting me with their eyes to come inside and speak to them.

Finally, I came to a small alcove. I stepped inside and looked at the narrow wall opposite. The painting was of a woman in her forties. She had dark hair and wore a black silk top with thin straps. Her hair was swept up, exposing her elegant neck.

As my attention settled on her face, I gasped.

There was something wrong with her eyes. They looked … glazed. Vacant. Almost as if she were dead.

2

NOW: MORGAN

*D*inner was as formal as the eight o'clock hour had suggested.

Bryce knocked on our door a few minutes before to escort us to the dining room. When I saw his coffee-colored silk shirt, black slacks, and dress shoes, followed by his pointed but friendly glance at my denim skirt and tank top, I wondered out loud if I was dressed too casually. Without directly answering, he said we had a few minutes to spare if I wanted to change my clothes.

Now wearing a black dress that caused Bryce's eyes to widen with approval, Jade and I walked behind him to the dining room. Jade had also chosen black, and I realized I should have followed her lead when I saw the style of her dress and watched as she stepped into high heels. As we paused before entering the dining room, she gushed over the flattering cut of my dress. Bryce took my arm, and I walked into the room feeling like the guest of honor.

There were eight of us at a table large enough for twice that number, although the additional chairs had been removed, giving us plenty of space. The table was lavishly decorated with fairy lights and small crystal bowls of flowers. The plates were southwestern in style but still looked like fine china.

Dinner was a ranch style feast—gazpacho to start, followed by a green salad, and then thick, tender steaks, baked potatoes with butter swimming inside, and roasted vegetables.

Despite having started off feeling like the guest of honor, I quickly realized that vision had existed only inside my head. I'd been caught up in Bryce and Jade's approval of my dress and the grandeur of the dining room. Instead, the evening quickly turned into a family reunion of sorts, with Jade and Colin West, Ember's husband, doing all the talking. Colin was Jade's godson. When he married, she embraced Ember as part of her virtual family as well. She gushed repeatedly that Ember was her *virtual* daughter. I wasn't sure what she meant by that, but she'd emphasized it to me during the drive here as well. More than once.

Jade and Colin took turns telling stories about his childhood, remembering his parents, who had taken on the forms of a god and goddess now that they'd been dead for nearly ten years. As we made our way through the cold soup, the salad, and then carved into the meat, I felt more and more like an audience to their storytelling. I wondered if the others felt the same.

Bryce kept a pleasant expression on his face, seeming to enjoy the stories of the past, anecdotes about people he'd never met. He glanced at me often, giving me friendly smiles, but he did nothing to try to change the subject away from a topic that was impossible for anyone but Jade or Colin to participate in.

Ember's sister, Olivia, who had been living with them since her divorce, seemed less fascinated. "You had an idyllic childhood, Colin. A golden life." She placed a thin slice of steak on her tongue, closed her mouth over it, then held it there, not chewing.

I watched, waiting to see if she might try to talk around it.

She noticed me looking at her, grinned, then chewed it quickly. "Doesn't Ember have a lovely family, Morgan? And such a beautiful home?"

"It's gorgeous," I said.

Olivia gave me a wicked grin. "The house? Or the family?"

I felt my face get hot. I welcomed the warmth after the coldness that had settled into my core and remained since the moment I'd stepped through the front door. Not even a hot shower had stopped the occasional shivers rippling through my body. "Both."

"She thinks you're gorgeous, Avery."

Ember and Colin's twelve-year-old son turned red, as if a colored light had been shone on his face. He looked at his plate, pressing his fork into the baked potato.

"Ember has done well for herself, that's for sure." Olivia batted her eyelashes. "A son that anyone would be proud of. A charming, devoted husband. And her magnificent career."

I wasn't sure how to interpret that. It sounded … not genuine. Was she jealous? Blatantly trying to make her sister uncomfortable?

Ember hadn't spoken much at all. She sat at the head of the table like a ruling monarch, watching everyone, seeming to be in control of the room with her silent looks and her sweeping gestures that sometimes interrupted the chatter between Colin and Jade, causing everyone to look in her direction.

"The food is delicious," I said. "You're an amazing cook, as well as an artist."

Olivia laughed. "Ember didn't make dinner. She doesn't have time for bodily needs, do you Ember?"

"I don't enjoy cooking," Ember said. "Colin does a fabulous job."

"Oh. Sorry," I said. "I shouldn't have assumed …"

Colin laughed. "No worries. It happens all the time. People assume women do the cooking."

"It's outstanding," I said.

"Thank you." Colin gave me a warm smile. "That's high praise coming from someone who makes her living preparing food."

"You can see that Ember has some kind of magic, doesn't she?" Olivia said, as if no one had spoken. "A man who *cooks* for her. How many women would kill for that? Am I right?"

No one said anything.

I thought I should comment that Ember was lucky, but I didn't know her. I felt strange making judgments about her life, essentially telling her she should appreciate her good fortune. She obviously wasn't inclined to give public appreciation to her husband, or to dispel the awkward mood that was growing more intense.

Every social instinct in me wanted to fill the space with something—a question to Avery, an inquiry about Bryce's background, an expression of interest in Colin's construction company. But the longer the silence continued, the more ridiculous and staged anything I came up with would sound.

"Ember really does have it all," Olivia said softly. "Especially the spectacular career. So much notoriety, thanks to poor, pathetic Derek."

"Ugh," Avery said. "You talk too much, Olivia. Put a cork in it for a few. 'K?"

Olivia laughed.

No one explained who Derek was. They all continued eating as if we were supposed to know who she was talking about and how he'd impacted her career.

Colin stood. "Gelato for dessert. How many want coffee?"

Olivia stood and began clearing plates. Colin picked up the wine bottle and topped off his own glass, gave me a questioning look, and before I could shake my head, refilled my glass as well. He made his way around the table, filling glasses until the bottle was empty.

Before the gelato was served, Ember left the table, saying she had work to do. No one objected. The conversation over dessert was a continuation of Jade and Colin's shared memories.

Following dessert, two cups of coffee, and after-dinner drinks, I went outside and sat in one of the chairs by the swimming pool. From there, I could see the faint glow in the distance of the lights in Ember's studio. I wondered what she was doing. Was she making sketches of me from memory?

When Jade had announced that her engagement gift to me was a portrait, my immediate reaction was to say *no*. There had never been a single moment in my life when I imagined or wished for an oil painting of myself. Where were Tyler and I going to hang a forty-by-fifty painting of me? But the expression on Jade's face had made it clear that she'd selected this gift after a great deal of thought, that she wanted to please me, that it was an act of incredible generosity. How could I turn down a gift like that?

It was clearly expensive, although I couldn't even guess how much. Ember's website didn't provide pricing. I suppose it was one of those situations that fit the truism—if you have to ask the price, you can't afford it. My future mother-in-law was financially secure. Her first marriage to the father of her two children—Grace and Tyler—had left her feeling isolated and alone, even while married. But she was well-cared for when her husband left her for a woman more to his liking. A woman who also considered children nothing but roadblocks to a global travel and entertainment-rich lifestyle.

So I'd accepted her gift.

But I was a little nervous, possibly truly scared of what it meant to sit for a portrait with a woman who wanted to establish intimacy with me but so far had been so cool and aloof, I couldn't stop shivering.

A coyote howled somewhere in the darkness, close by or miles away, I couldn't tell, but I slid off the chair and hurried toward the lights of the house.

3

NOW: BRYCE

I started every day but Sunday the same way—with a sunrise run in the desert. At this time of year, it was pleasant, and I didn't mind getting up to meet the sun at five-thirty a.m. In the winter, the temperatures dropped close to freezing and running was brutal, but it offered a different kind of pleasure. In the winter, I was reminded of how resilient I was. Winter reminded me that I was strong and young. My future was filled with potential. But for now, working as Ember's assistant felt like the right thing. It *was* the right thing. The only thing.

Working for Ember offered a lot of perks. I lived in a luxurious Spanish villa with a swimming pool and hot tub. Despite her grueling work schedule, I had a decent amount of time off. I was never assigned menial tasks just because my title was *assistant*. My rooms were spacious and quiet, with a separate entrance. I had a lot of freedom.

I considered myself lucky that I could go running in such stunning terrain without another human being in sight. It was a natural high every morning. The quiet of the desert at sunrise, the orange glow as the sun spread across the earth, backlighting the cacti and the low hills in the distance, grounded me. It made me feel as if I belonged there, even if it wasn't exactly a hot career, and even if it meant never having anyone hang out at my place, especially girls.

I did have Sundays off. Once upon a time, I'd spent Sundays at Claire's house, but she and I had quietly ended things two years ago without really explaining to each other why, because probably, neither of us could really explain why, even to ourselves. There hadn't been anyone serious since then. My living situation wasn't always conducive to meeting women, but I did try to get away from the villa most Sundays. I sometimes played a little golf or went to hear local musicians playing at clubs where I met other music lovers. Mostly, I tried not to think about it. That's usually when stuff like that happens. When you're not thinking too much about it.

This Sunday, I was staying around the house because Morgan and Jade had only just arrived, and part of my job was making them comfortable. Ember never wanted our guests, the subjects of her portraits, to feel they had to ask permission to get snacks or a glass of wine, to feel that they couldn't go for a swim or play a game of pool whenever they felt like it.

I want them to feel at home.

She told me this, not them. My job was to tell them. She liked to be the artist, not the logistics person. I got it.

I made southwestern omelettes for breakfast. I'd asked what they wanted when I found them sitting on the patio drinking the coffee I'd brewed before leaving for my run. Jade, who was not at all shy about asking for what she wanted, probably because she felt like she was Colin's mother on some level, suggested the omelettes when I said I would make them whatever they wanted.

I served the eggs on the patio with sliced strawberries and mimosas. Jade loved that. Morgan was grateful. She thanked me multiple times for everything I did. It was going to take some work for her to feel at home, no matter how Ember wanted her to feel.

"Why don't you and I go for a walk after your breakfast settles?"

Morgan looked at me. "A walk? To where?"

"To enjoy the landscape. I can tell you about Ember's process, so you'll know what to expect."

"That sounds like a lovely idea." Jade splashed orange juice into her flute and filled the rest of the glass with champagne.

"It's getting hot," Morgan said.

"It won't hit ninety until about noon. If we take it easy, we'll be fine. Just wear a hat. And bring water."

"Are there snakes?"

I laughed. "Some. But they fear you more than you fear them. You'll be fine."

"What about scorpions?"

"I've never seen one."

"Tarantulas?"

She had quite a list of phobias. I wondered if I should pass this information on to Ember, or let her stumble upon it herself.

"You should honestly be more concerned about black widows than tarantulas. But I'll keep an eye out while we're walking. Most creatures prefer to avoid humans as much as we want to keep away from them. You won't regret the views."

I began clearing the dishes, and she left to get ready for our walk.

We started out on one of the pathways leading to a gate at the back left corner of the property, one of several in the wall surrounding Ember and Colin's villa. All of them were operated electronically, kept unlocked during the day, then automatically secured at night. I lifted the latch, and we stepped out onto a path that wound in a loop for about a mile past some magnificent saguaro cacti.

"Are you excited about having your portrait done by Ember?" I asked.

"Yes. I ..."

"You seem hesitant."

"It's not something I ever thought about. Until Jade offered it."

"You're lucky Ember accepted you."

"Accepted me?"

13

"Her waiting list is years long."

"I had no idea. What did Olivia mean about her notoriety? And Derek. Who's Derek?"

I wanted to tell her about Derek. She had a right to know, but I didn't want to frighten her. I kicked a rock off the path that didn't need to be moved, but it gave me something to concentrate on. I needed to give her an answer. She was obviously feeling skittish, but hearing the entire story would be upsetting. Still—

"Who is he?"

"He sat for a portrait with Ember. And he—"

"Is it in the gallery?"

"No. Those are older works, from before she was so well-known," I said.

"I guess she's notorious because she's so demanding?"

"That's part of it. Sometimes—"

"I didn't know that many people had portraits done nowadays."

"Enough do." I decided to let the conversation follow her lead for now, rather than rushing to explain who Derek was. "It's expensive though."

"It was a gift. From Jade, if you didn't know."

I wondered if I should tell her. It seemed crass, but it also seemed like she could be more appreciative of what she was getting. "You don't seem thrilled with it. For such a generous gift."

"How generous?" she asked.

Well, she'd asked. I wanted her to know. I wanted her to know she was fortunate. It's an uncomfortable feeling, having people do things for you when you don't know all the details, when you don't know what you're getting into. I hoped I was doing her a favor. "Thirty-five thousand."

She made a sound like she was being strangled, stumbling slightly. She stopped walking.

I paused.

Her hand was on her throat, as if she were truly strangling when she repeated what I'd said. "Thirty-five *thousand* dollars?" Her voice was a hoarse, raw croak.

"You didn't realize how well-known she is?"

"I—"

"Don't let it intimidate you. I didn't tell you to make you feel self-conscious. I thought you should know. You are lucky. It's an honor, but don't let it mess with your head. Some people do, but you shouldn't. It's just a painting."

She moved her hand away from her throat. "Thanks for telling me. It's not as if my mother-in-law can't afford that. But it's … a lot."

I nodded. "Should we keep going?"

We started walking.

"What's her thing with intimacy? Jade said she likes to be intimate with her subjects." Morgan was slightly behind me, so I couldn't read her expression.

"Ember has her method. All art is seduction. Right? Music seduces us through our ears, literature seduces us through our minds, and visual arts seduces our eyes. So doesn't it make sense that she has to seduce the subjects of her paintings? Don't you think maybe film directors do the same with actors?"

"It makes me feel—"

"Don't read too much into it. Enjoy the experience. Let yourself go. It's a once-in-a-lifetime opportunity. Who else do you know with a life-sized oil painting of themselves?"

She laughed, her voice tinged with a suggestion of hysteria.

I turned, but she looked happy, not hysterical, as I'd imagined.

"No one," she said.

"That's right. So enjoy. And she's not out to seduce your body. Just your soul."

She didn't ask any more questions after that and I wasn't sure if I'd made her feel more relaxed, or if I'd completely freaked her out.

4

NOW: MORGAN

The cost of the portrait that Jade had commissioned sat like a thick ball of dough in my stomach. I couldn't think about anything else for the rest of our walk. As a result, I couldn't enjoy the raw beauty surrounding us, the endless open space, stark and brutal, so untamed it made my heart ache.

I wanted to rush back to our room and tell Jade I couldn't accept her gift.

I'd known within months of falling in love with Tyler that his mom was quite well-off. In fact, she kind of oozed money, which she spent freely to support artists and charities. She enjoyed a home in Los Angeles, as well as a condo at Lake Tahoe. Even though she would pay for our wedding and had made it clear that whatever wild girlhood dreams I'd had for my wedding were up for consideration, the cost of this painting was decadent, and it made me uncomfortable.

It seemed frivolous and almost embarrassing. And where would we hang it? I hadn't given any serious thought to that. There wasn't a single wall or room in the small house Tyler and I owned that was suitable.

But no matter what conversation I imagined having with Jade, they all came out sounding ungrateful or excessively vain, as if I were overthinking the idea of having my image captured in oil paint. I couldn't get it sorted out in my thoughts and I knew it would be worse if I tried to speak any of them out loud. Besides, I couldn't imagine that someone who charged that kind of money for a painting would hand out refunds. I was trapped.

Was it worth it? Thirty-five thousand dollars? Jade sure seemed to think so. She thought Ember was a genius, that her talent was borderline supernatural. She'd actually used that word. I agreed her work was mesmerizing. Although, when I closed my eyes, that painting of the woman who looked like she was dead came into my mind. I'd wanted to ask Bryce about it, but Jade had been talking so much during our tour, I hadn't had a chance. When he revealed the cost of my portrait, it had shocked the question right out of my head.

Tyler would laugh and tell me not to worry for a single second about the cost because his mom loved to spend money on all kinds of unique things and I should just enjoy the experience. Almost exactly what Bryce had said. So I tried to ignore that ball of dough still sitting in my belly and tried to decide what to wear for my first sitting.

Bryce had said I needed to be sure my clothes were comfortable so I could sit without moving for long periods of time.

The temperature in the house continued to feel unnaturally cold to me, so all the summery tops I'd brought made me think I'd be sitting in the studio, goose bumps running up my arms and down my back. I finally chose a pink T-shirt with a scooped neck and yoga pants. Bryce said the outfit wasn't important because initially, Ember would just be doing sketches. Comfort was all that mattered.

Walking into Ember's studio for my first sitting was not at all like it had been when I'd entered the space during our tour. Now, the room seemed fraught with mystery. It was simple and, at the same time, slightly intimidating. There were three large windows, several plants in large pots, a few potted succulents hanging from the ceiling, and an armchair with a small table beside it. A large easel stood in the back corner with a wicker chair beside it.

What was going to happen while I sat in that armchair that would allow her to become so intimate with me, she felt as if she knew who I was in a way that would allow her to capture me and display not only my likeness, but my personality, my very soul, for eternity? Because that's what her virtual gallery, and Bryce, claimed.

Bryce was already in the room. He told me to take a seat. He left, returning a few minutes later with a tray holding a pitcher of water and a glass. "Would you rather have herbal tea? We don't allow coffee because it plays havoc with your pupils. Not to mention making you jittery."

"Water is fine."

"Just relax." He gave me a warm, sympathetic smile. "This will be fun. You'll love it."

"I'm relaxed."

He laughed. "You are anything *but!*" He filled the glass and handed it to me. "Take a few sips and try to breathe deeply and slowly. I can feel your tension without even touching your shoulders."

I took a sip of water.

I glanced toward the easel and saw that Ember was standing there. "Hi. I didn't even know you were here," I said.

"Pretend I'm not," Ember said.

That seemed like an impossible request. I took another sip of water. Bryce walked across the room and sat in the wicker chair. He took a notebook off the wide windowsill, opened it, and placed it on his lap.

"I want you to look out the window behind Bryce," Ember said. "Please don't talk unless I ask you a question. Keep your mind focused on something other than the portrait. And relax."

I nodded. If someone told me to relax again, I was sure I was going to get a foot cramp or my fingers were going to start twitching on my lap. It was like someone telling me not to blink or not to swallow. It's all I could think about and it was making my shoulders and neck feel like the twisted branches of the Joshua trees we'd seen on our walk.

The next hour seemed to expand until it felt like three hours.

Ember was constantly telling me to shift my head by a quarter inch this way and that, to open my eyes wider, to shift my gaze from one side of the window frame to the other, and in between, she told me to relax. I couldn't relax. The more she instructed me how to sit, and the more the silence stretched between her commands, giving me time to think about how expensive this was, how lucky I was to have this opportunity, the more tense I became.

She seemed irritated with me, as if I were a squirmy child who was refusing to do what she'd asked.

I was trying to relax. I was trying to keep my thoughts on calming images, but doing that sometimes made me want to close my eyes, and that really annoyed her.

During those achingly long silences, I also wondered what she meant by intimacy. Was she going to ask me personal questions? How personal? What else was going to happen? When was I going to see what she was working on? When would she stop sketching and start painting? When would I wear the clothes that would be in the painting and did I get to choose my clothing, or was that her decision?

The questions spilled over in my mind and I wondered why I hadn't asked a single one of them before hopping into the car with my suitcase packed for a ten-day visit to the middle of nowhere with my future mother-in-law.

How was this really helping us to grow closer?

Maybe she should have commissioned a painting of Tyler and me together. That would have been so much more fun and something we might actually want in our home. I was feeling like I'd been so agreeable simply because I wanted to be close to her and now I was stuck alone in this room, tormented by questions and utterly failing to sit in a way that was pleasing to the artist.

Never in my life had I felt I needed a break from *sitting*. But I desperately wanted to stand, to stretch, and walk out the door. I wanted to go for a three-mile hike through the desert, feeling my skin perspire and my muscles burn. Or eat a giant roast beef sandwich and wash it down with a beer. Anything to acknowledge my body was alive and in need of something beyond sitting in a chair and being stared at like a porcelain doll.

"You're doing great," Bryce said. "People don't realize that sitting still is grueling work."

I smiled. It felt as if he'd read my mind.

"Please don't smile," Ember said.

I let the smile linger, then slowly dissolve, still grateful to Bryce. I wondered what he was making notes about. But I couldn't glance in his direction or Ember would really get annoyed.

"Only another twenty minutes or so," Bryce said. "Then we'll be done for the day. The next sitting will be longer, but you'll be more relaxed, now that you know what to expect."

"A lot longer," Ember said. "So you need to steel yourself."

I didn't smile. I didn't nod. Instead, I wondered what Jade saw in her. She was a cold person as far as I could see so far. Maybe all her passion and warmth were reserved for her painting. Maybe I was just an object for her art and despite her promise to reveal my essence, I was nothing but a still life to her.

5

NOW: MORGAN

*W*hen I was excused from the chair that had felt like a torture device, I leaped up and hurried out of the studio with a quick goodbye. I didn't look at Bryce or meet Ember's gaze. I doubt she would have peered around her easel at me anyway. I wanted to run.

Instead, I walked back to the house, taking long strides, wishing it was farther than the fifty yards I had to cover along the curving pathway. I hardly admired the rocks and succulents lining the pavement. I didn't bother to look out toward the horizon. I beelined to the house, went to the guest room I was sharing with Jade, and changed into my swimsuit.

I went out to the pool, sparkling like a sapphire under the cloudless sky, and dove in without testing the temperature of the water. It felt heavenly. The water was warm enough that it didn't shock my system, but refreshing. I surfaced and swam ten laps without stopping, my feet kicking furiously, my arms stretching as far as possible with each stroke, as if I were reaching into a tree trying to grab a piece of fruit just beyond the tips of my fingers.

Finally, I stopped and wiped the water off my face. I rested my arms on the edge of the pool and squinted toward the lounge chairs.

Jade was stretched out on the one closest to the pool, a large white floppy straw hat covering most of her face. She waved as if we hadn't seen each other for days. I swam five more laps and climbed out of the pool. I grabbed my towel, dried off, and spread it on the chair next to Jade's. As I settled beside her, I put on my sunglasses and hat. "That felt amazing," I said.

"You looked like you were in a race. Did you ever swim competitively?"

I laughed. "No. I just needed to get rid of some pent-up energy. Sitting for the portrait made me a little jumpy."

"I'm sure you'll relax once you get used to it."

I didn't enjoy hearing her suggest I needed to relax. For half a second, I wondered if Ember had told her to pass this message along to me. I shook off the paranoid thought. "I'm sure I will. It's an interesting process. She only did some sketches today. I wonder when I'll get to see how it's progressing."

"I doubt she'll let you see anything until it's complete."

"Really?"

"She's a brilliant artist, Morgan. They can be territorial with their work. They don't let anyone into their creative space."

"Is she doing my portrait because Colin's your godson? As some kind of favor?"

"Why do you think that?"

"She seems ... I don't know ... annoyed, I guess."

"She's very serious. Very focused. Don't take it personally."

"You think a lot of her. And Colin."

"I adore them." She tipped her head back, gazing up at the sky. "Colin is like my own son. Not that Tyler isn't my boy." She turned and gave me a glowing, sentimental smile. "It's not at all the same, but I do feel like Colin's second mother, which is what a godmother is. And Ember is so perfect for him. They've blossomed together."

"Are Tyler and Colin close?" I was pretty sure I knew the answer, because I'd only heard Tyler mention him once or twice.

"Not really." She sighed. "Colin is so much older. They never had a chance to really connect. Colin and Grace played together as kids, but they didn't stay in touch. I was hoping when she came for her portrait, they would become friendly again. But ..." She shrugged.

"Grace had her portrait done by Ember?" In the year Tyler and I had been together, I'd never met his sister. She'd been traveling in Asia on a spiritual quest of some kind for over a year. According to Tyler, he and his sister had been close as kids, but when she'd left for college, they hadn't done a great job of keeping in touch, seeing each other only during short holiday breaks, rarely communicating in between. When Grace broke off her engagement and took off overseas, they hadn't had any contact at all. Her choice, he'd said.

He didn't seem as bothered by that as I would have been in his position, but I didn't have siblings and I knew it could be complicated, so maybe being bothered depended upon a lot of things. Maybe I had no idea how often siblings stayed in touch. Because I didn't have any of my own, and I'd lost my mom when I was only twelve, and basically lost my dad when he pawned me off on my grandparents to give me *stability*, I tended to get a little obsessive about the importance of family. I knew that about myself. So if Tyler ignored his sister, and she did the same, or they took each other for granted, I wasn't going to judge them for that.

Jade sighed deeply. "Grace's portrait was never completed."

"Why not?"

"Grace walked out on Ember ... before the painting was finished. It was so embarrassing. And hurtful, to be honest." She put her hand on my wrist. "I know you well enough now, I think I can tell you this." She squeezed my wrist gently. "I almost wondered if she did it deliberately to humiliate me. She's a little jealous of Colin ... maybe." She let go of my arm and fiddled with the gold hoop in her ear.

"Was she uncomfortable with the process? Or—"

"I have no idea what that girl was thinking. And I still don't. She took off, and she hasn't spoken to me. Or her brother. She hasn't been in touch with her father either. And it took a lot for me to contact him and humiliate myself further by asking if he'd heard from the daughter he'd shown almost no interest in for decades."

"You don't know where she is?"

"No."

"Aren't you worried? Did you call the police?"

She laughed sharply. "What on earth for? This is Grace. She does what she wants, when she wants."

"What if something happened to her?"

"I have no reason to think that. She told her fiancé she was too young to make such a serious decision. Choosing a life partner. That her *experiences* here made her think about the entirety of her life … or something to that effect. She needed to clear her head. Without him in her life, with no commitments."

The sun had burned all the water off my skin and I was getting hot, but it felt so good after the constant chill inside the house, I decided to soak it up for a few more minutes. Then I would go for another swim. I was unsettled by Jade's revelation. It felt shocking, somehow. I wasn't sure if it was my distorted perspective on the importance of family relationships or something about her lack of concern.

I wasn't sure if I felt closer to her because she'd told me something about her daughter, or if I felt deeply alienated because I couldn't understand her reaction to not hearing from her daughter for over a year. No matter how much someone wanted to sort out her life, didn't she at least call her mother on one of the major holidays? Or her birthday? Wouldn't she send a text message?

It felt slightly disturbing that Jade had commissioned a painting for me without telling me about her daughter's experience with this so-called genius. Did Grace leave because Ember's attempt at intimacy, whatever that was, had upset her? Or was it something else entirely?

Jade didn't seem worried about where her daughter might be. Tyler wasn't worried either. Was that normal? For families to not speak to each other for a year? I tried to imagine it. I had friends from high school I hadn't communicated with for a few years and I still considered them friends. If I heard from them, and I had no doubt I would some day, or I would get in touch with them, it would feel as if that time hadn't elapsed.

If I didn't make the effort to contact my father once a week, it would probably be months between phone calls from him. Neither of us were off exploring the world, so maybe it wasn't completely outside the realm of normality.

"Don't fret about Ember," Jade said. "You've only just met her. And her work speaks for itself. Your painting will be stunning. I'm absolutely certain."

"I'm so grateful for your gift," I said.

"Maybe what you're picking up on with Ember is that she might be a bit hesitant after Grace was so rude. Because you're another person from my family. Maybe it's not that at all, but it's possible. At the end of the day, she's so incredibly talented, she's not like us. So don't judge her by the same standards."

Knowing that Jade already considered me a member of her family gave me a sense of belonging. Maybe trying to understand her feelings about her daughter would bring us closer. But I didn't think Ember got to live by different rules, just because she was talented. On what planet was that true?

6

BEFORE: DEREK

*E*mber West was a sadist.

If I said that to anyone in her house—her devoted wuss of a husband, her entitled son, her jealous, flirty sister, or her attentive, somewhat co-dependent assistant, they would say I didn't *understand*. I needed to *trust the process*. I was simply feeling *the strain of sitting*. It was *hard work*. Oh, how they had patronized me with the assurance that sitting in a chair was *such* hard work.

There was nothing hard about it, but Ember had transformed that armchair into a torture chamber.

My neck ached from keeping my head in a position that she seemed to measure with a sextant she was so precise about the angle she wanted. My joints were locked from being immobilized for hours at a time. No matter how many YouTube videos I watched on yoga for office workers, trying to stretch out in my room at night, parts of my body felt like they were being fused into a permanent position.

Swimming didn't always help either, although Bryce assured me it was like magic.

Now, my stomach growled, ravenous for a steak dinner though it was only four in the afternoon. It was the sitting. Nothing like doing nothing to make every part of your body start exercising demands even when it's not the right time. My body wanted to sleep, scratch wildly, eat, pee, fuck anyone I could find. But there was no one. Just me and the chair. Bryce and Ember. And Ember was one person my body was taking a hard pass on.

I truly was starting to believe she might be a sadist. I didn't think I was exaggerating. This wasn't a time lapse photograph where a movement would screw it up. It was a painting. I could move a hundred times and she could still work around it. I could get up and go for a five-mile run and return to the same position and her oil paints wouldn't be dry. The demand to remain motionless yet relaxed was sounding like bullshit. Despite her brilliant work, which I had to admit was brilliant, I wondered if she enjoyed the power she wielded over me almost as much as the art.

Because now she'd come up with a new way to torture me.

"I need you to look at the window, Derek."

"I am."

"Without blinking. I asked you not to blink."

"It's not possible to avoid blinking."

"It can be done for a few seconds. It's really important if I'm going to get your eyes right. The eyes are everything. Without capturing the depth of your eyes, getting the color absolutely right, the portrait will be a failure."

"I have to blink."

"You don't. Please stop repeating that to yourself. You're only cementing that belief in your subconscious. You don't have to blink. It's one reflex that can be controlled by the conscious mind. Like the breath."

I stared at the window. I felt my eyes start to burn. Then the tears started to spread across the surface. I blinked.

"Derek. Please."

"I can't keep my eyes from blinking indefinitely."

"I know you can do it for a few seconds. This is really important."

I stared. Within four seconds, I blinked.

I stared.

I couldn't imagine this was how other portrait painters worked. It was a power play. She wanted to exert her will over me. That's why she demanded I stay at her home. Although, she lived hours from anywhere, so there really wasn't a choice, I suppose.

I felt Bryce standing beside me. His hand was on my shoulder. "Do you need a quick break?"

I laughed. "For blinking?"

"You're really tense."

"I'm fine."

"Anything I can do to help?"

"Nope. It's all good." I cracked my neck, closed my eyes for a few seconds, then let them open slowly. "Let me know when you want to start up again," I said.

"Whenever you think you can control your impulses," Ember said.

I stared at the window. I thought about strangling her. I continued staring, widening my eyes, wondering if it made her feel as if she had some kind of mystique if she made her clients suffer. My eyes burned and watered, but I kept staring. She was not going to win. I would stare until my eyeballs dropped out of my head.

If I thought hard enough about how sick it was that she was deliberately trying to torture me, probably so she could capture some weak, vulnerable side of me in the portrait, I could stare out that window forever. I could spend the rest of my life staring, unseeing, letting my focus drift to nothing.

7

NOW: MORGAN

*L*unch on Monday was another elaborate meal in the dining room. It was all fancy salads and fruit which would have been delicious in the warmth of the sun-drenched patio, but in the eternally chilly house, I found myself craving a bowl of soup.

Once again, Ember reigned like a silent queen at the head of the table. And it was clearly the head—she sat in the so-called captain's chair, her forearms resting on the arms of the chair when she wasn't eating, which wasn't much. She mostly stabbed her fork at the tiny portions of food on her plate, lifted the morsels of food, inspected them, then returned the fork to her plate. I wasn't staring at her constantly, but I never once saw her actually chew a bite of food.

Colin was at the foot of the table, his attention centered on his wife, a worried expression on his face. I wondered if it was because she wasn't eating, or there was something else. I hadn't noticed whether she'd left most of her food untouched during our previous meals. I'd been so overwhelmed by the mildly uncomfortable atmosphere which echoed that first formal dinner, I'd barely paid attention to the food on my plate.

Avery kept glancing at his lap, where I was pretty sure he had his phone wedged between his knees, but no one else seemed to notice. Or if they did, they weren't bothered by it.

"How was your first sitting?" Olivia asked. "Was it thrilling to be the center of attention, to have Ember focus all of her passion on you?"

I felt my face grow warm. No one seemed to react, so maybe the heat was only inside, not spreading across my skin, making me look naïve and inexperienced. "It's hard to know how to answer that," I said. "Since I've never had a portrait done before, I have nothing to compare it to."

"But you've surely been admired by a lover," Olivia said.

Now I knew my face was flushed. The smirk on Olivia's face confirmed it.

"It wasn't like that." I regretted the words the moment I spoke them. Maybe I'd insulted Ember. Maybe it was supposed to be exactly like that. Was I supposed to feel flattered and admired? Was that what Bryce meant by seduction? What had I gotten myself into here? I wondered if Jade knew about all of this. She'd had her portrait done. Was it always the same, or did it depend upon the person who was being painted? It seemed as if the moment I had one question answered, four more arose in its place. "It is flattering," I said. "Absolutely. But since I can't see anything, and I was focused on my posture …" I had no idea what I was supposed to say. It almost felt as if Olivia's questions were a trap, that she was waiting for me to trip myself up in some way, but I couldn't see where the trap might be. The longer I spent trying to answer her question, the more her smirk deepened.

"Don't be embarrassed," she said. "You'll get into it. Ember will make sure of that." She looked at Colin and gave him a friendly smile.

I took a bite of potato salad, aching for someone else to talk. No one did. I took a sip of water.

"I didn't mean to put you on the spot," Olivia said. "Just relax. It's only a portrait. Right? We take selfies every day. No big deal."

I glanced at Ember. She was staring at her sister. She didn't look upset that her incredibly expensive and well-regarded portraits had been compared to cell phone selfies. She looked aloof, as if the words coming out of Olivia's mouth were in the realm of nonsense.

Finally, Colin began talking about baseball. Jade and Bryce joined him and I felt myself fade into the background, although every time I looked up from my plate, I found Olivia staring at me. Her smirk hardening into something less friendly.

When I tried to clear my lunch plate, Olivia insisted I was a guest who shouldn't be working. Glad for the chance to escape, I left the dining room as fast as I could. I crossed the entryway and went into the poolroom, closing the door behind me. The shutters were closed, so I left them, turning on the recessed lights.

I took a cue off the rack, chalked it, and broke the balls.

It had been a few years since I'd played pool and I'd never been remarkable at it, but I did alright with straightforward shots. I moved around the table, knocking first the solids, then the striped balls into the pockets. It was calming, hearing the click of the balls against each other, and the thump of them falling into the pockets, watching them disappear from the table.

As I knocked the green striped ball into the far corner, I heard the door open, followed by Colin's startled voice. "Oh."

I turned.

"I didn't see you come in here," he said.

"Am I not supposed to?"

"No. Of course. It's fine. I usually play after lunch."

"I'm finished," I said.

"But you're not."

I put the cue on the rack. I felt scrutinized enough around these people. I wasn't in the mood to have my pool skills, or lack thereof, observed and critiqued by someone who played every day.

"How about a game?" he asked.

"I think I'll go take a nap. Like everyone keeps saying, it's surprising how sitting in a chair for a portrait can be so exhausting."

"Most of us aren't used to having someone stare at us and pick apart our features for the purpose of recreating them," he said.

I felt myself relax, possibly because he was the first one who hadn't demanded it.

"Apologies if Olivia put you on the spot."

"No worries," I said.

"Really?"

I laughed. "It is a little uncomfortable."

"Everyone reacts differently. There's a surprising amount of psychological pressure. Having a portrait painted is not a normal experience. And when you do experience it, most likely it will be a once in a lifetime event."

"Has she painted your portrait?"

"Sadly, no."

"Why not?"

He shrugged.

It seemed strange that he thought it was sad. That implied he wanted her to. Had he asked, and she'd declined?

He took a pool cue off the rack. He chalked it. Without asking, he shot the eight-ball into one of the side pockets. "The intensity might be too much for us," he said, finally.

"Was it too much for Derek? Is that why Olivia said he was pathetic?"

He began pulling balls out of the pockets. "Derek was not a happy person. Ember is incredibly talented. You've seen her work. Yes, she's unconventional in her methods of capturing the essence of her subjects, but she's brilliant. And you've seen the evidence of that."

"What's the issue with Derek? Why does—"

He interrupted me so aggressively I felt as if I'd been punched in the mouth. "It's inappropriate to be talking about Ember's other clients. Do you want us to talk to future clients about your experiences?"

"Of course not. But Olivia—"

"Then don't be so inquisitive. It's crude."

"I didn't know it was a secret. Olivia said—"

"Olivia shouldn't have said anything. Care for a game of pool? Or not?"

"I'll let you keep your usual routine." I gave him the friendliest smile I could manage.

By the time I'd crossed the entryway and walked down the hallway to the guest room, I was so tired, I truly wanted nothing but a nap. Luckily for me, Jade was not in our room. I closed the shutters, pulled back the comforter on my bed, and slid between the sheets, eager for my body to warm the bedding so it would provide a cocoon for sleep.

8

NOW: MORGAN

*M*y nap transformed me into a new person, or rather returned me to my usual self, as sleep always does. I suppose there's a reason we need to devote nearly a third of our lives to it in order to maintain sanity.

It was three-thirty in the afternoon. I was shocked that I'd slept so long since I'd had a full eight hours the night before. But I felt alert and as refreshed as if it were seven in the morning, instead of dull and disoriented as I sometimes did after a nap.

I made the bed, took a shower, put on makeup, a backless dress that would be comfortable on the sun-drenched patio, and brought a sweater in case I decided to stay inside the house.

As I opened the door, the house seemed deathly quiet. I wondered if the other occupants had also taken siestas. Walking down the hallway, I heard the faint sound of people talking.

From the living room, I could see the deserted patio. I walked toward the kitchen, where the voices became more distinct. Without stepping into the doorway, I could see Avery and a girl his age sitting on the couches near the windows. Both of them were looking at their phones, talking to each other in low voices.

I couldn't figure out where Jade might have gone. It was possible she was playing pool with Colin, since the doors to the poolroom were closed, but I had no desire to see him again so soon after he'd chastised me for asking a simple question about a guy that both Olivia and Bryce had made cryptic comments about.

I wandered out to the front courtyard and sat on the lip surrounding the fountain. The air was hot, but the courtyard was shaded by the two wings of the house, and the small flowering trees made the air feel soft. I dipped my fingertips into the water and pulled them out, watching the water turn to beads on my burgundy nail polish. Before we'd made the drive to Ember and Colin's house, Jade and I had spent the morning at a salon getting mani-pedis, and I liked looking at my exotic fingernails and toenails.

Kicking off my flip-flops, I wiggled my toes. I wanted to dip my feet into the fountain, but there was a swimming pool for that, so I restrained myself. I sat there for ten or fifteen minutes, trailing my fingers through the water, letting my mind drift over the events of the day.

"Care for a glass of wine?"

I glanced up and saw Olivia standing in the front doorway. She looked nothing like her sister. With wavy, very light brown hair, eyes that sparkled as if she were privy to an inside joke, and a much curvier body, she seemed more full of life than Ember. She was in her mid-forties, seemingly content to live aimlessly in her sister's luxurious desert home.

She held a glass of white wine in each hand. Clearly she'd brought one just for me, making it difficult to say no.

"Sure." I pulled my hand out of the water and dried my fingers on the hem of my dress.

"Isn't it peaceful out here?" Olivia handed me one of the glasses and clicked hers against mine. "Cheers."

I wished her the same and took a sip, glad that I'd accepted. She wasn't the type to tell me I was too inquisitive. And she was the one who had mentioned Derek to begin with. I wasn't sure why I hadn't gotten the full story from Bryce. Somehow we'd gotten off the subject. Maybe it hadn't seemed like such a big deal until after I'd had my first sitting and realized how oppressive it was going to be.

She sat beside me. "I hope you're enjoying yourself."

"I think so."

She laughed. "Is that something you have to think about? Don't you just know?"

I took a sip of wine. "It's not like anything I've ever experienced."

"I imagine not."

"Has your sister ever painted your portrait?"

"Absolutely not."

"You don't want her to?"

"No. I don't need an enormous oil painting of myself staring me in the face."

"Do you live here permanently?"

"For the time being. After my divorce, we sold the house, obviously. Then, I was the victim of layoffs and things were quite gloomy in my life. Poor pathetic me. Right?" She laughed. "My generous sister invited me to stay, and it's so beautiful here, I can't leave."

I wasn't sure if she was mocking her sister's generosity, or her compliment was genuine. But there was that word again—*pathetic*. Just like Derek.

"It is beautiful. I could get used to it. I haven't spent much time in the desert. It has a lot of appeal."

She nodded and took a sip of wine.

"Tell me about Derek," I said.

She placed her glass on the lip of the fountain and crossed her legs. "Why?"

"There seems to be some secret about him. Why did you say he was pathetic?"

"Is there a secret? Who says?"

"Just an impression."

"Hmm."

"It seemed like no one wanted you to mention him."

"Well, it is a little dark."

I took a sip of wine. "Ember painted his portrait?"

"She started it. But he died. He hung himself."

I felt the wineglass start to slide out of my hand, my fingers weakening as her words sank into my head. "He ... *here?*" I grabbed the base of the glass to steady it.

She nodded.

"In ..." I cleared my throat, but my voice came out rough and strangled. "In the room where we're staying?"

"Oh, god. No! That would be too much. Wouldn't it?"

"Where?"

"In her studio."

I gasped. I took a long swallow of wine, then held onto my glass with both hands. "That's so awful."

"It gave my sister a lot of notoriety, that's for sure. Her career really exploded after that. It's kind of sick." She looked up from her phone. "But it is what it is, right? People are drawn to the macabre. We can't help ourselves. At least some of us can't. And Ember's portraits became a hot commodity."

"How can she work in her studio after that?"

"The floor was re-finished. The walls got a fresh coat of paint. She put in new shutters and bought a new chair. So ..." She shrugged. She stood and looked at her phone again. "I have some things to take care of. Enjoy the wine." She wiggled her fingers at me, turned, and walked back into the house.

I took a sip of wine and closed my eyes. The courtyard was completely silent except for the splash of water in the fountain. I couldn't begin to imagine why knowing a previous subject of one of her paintings had killed himself would make people desire a portrait of their own. My stomach heaved slightly as I thought about returning to her studio, sitting in the room where he'd died.

Was he suicidal before he'd arrived at Ember's home, or had

something happened while he was here that made him want to end his life? The thought was too much. I drank the rest of my wine so fast, I felt light-headed when I stood up.

9

NOW: BRYCE

I was cleaning Ember's paintbrushes. After Morgan had rushed out of the studio that morning, Ember spent some time testing colors that would be the right hues to capture Morgan's hair color. Ember was strict about wanting her brushes cleaned immediately, but I hadn't done it. Watching Morgan's obvious tension had made me tense, and I needed to escape the claustrophobic feeling in the studio. I'd shoved the brushes into the cabinet where Ember wouldn't see they were still thick with paint. I knew there wouldn't be any problem getting them so clean she would never have a clue that I hadn't followed her instructions.

Despite the sometimes oppressive feeling I had in the studio, working alone in the supply room was always nice. I could move at my own pace. Although Ember was good about showing appreciation, she was fussy about how she wanted things done. She didn't trust that the end result was what mattered. Working alone was almost meditative because I didn't think. When Ember was there, even if she wasn't talking, I still heard her voice in my mind, giving instructions, correcting the most minor errors.

When the brushes were cleaned and drying, I organized her tubes of paint in the trays, making sure they were in the color groupings she preferred, squeezing the bottoms to adjust the contents, which ensured the paint would flow smoothly the next time she used it.

I never went into her workroom. It belonged only to her, and she considered it a terrible violation of her creative energy if anyone entered that space. All my work was confined to the studio and the supply room. Occasionally I spent time in the gallery, hanging newer paintings, making sure I displayed everything to its best advantage.

I heard the door to the studio open and footsteps on the hardwood floor.

"Bryce?"

I stepped out of the storage room and closed the door behind me. Morgan was standing in the center of the studio.

"You shouldn't be here. Ember likes …"

She had a defiant expression on her face and I could see that she didn't care about Ember's idiosyncrasies right now. "What's wrong?"

"Why didn't anyone tell me that someone who had his portrait painted by Ember killed himself? Right here?!" She swept her arm around the room. "You let me sit here and—"

"Okay." I took a deep breath. I should have told her. I'd known it was a mistake. "Okay. Calm down. It's … No one likes to talk about that. It was really upsetting. I wasn't sure … what would be the point in telling you?"

"Because I have a right to know!"

"Ember was extremely upset. We all were."

"Why didn't you tell me?"

"I was going to, and I would have, at the right time. But sometimes, it's healthier not to relive horrible experiences in conversation, you know? It brings it all to life again."

"If that was true, we'd never talk about anything." She looked around the room, studying the corners, tipping her head back to gaze up at the ceiling.

"Don't try to *picture* it," I said. "Imagining the details will mess with your head. It will interfere with your portrait."

"My head is already messed up."

I moved closer to the armchair. "How did you find out?"

"Olivia told me. And I think it's a little ... I don't know ... strange that no one mentioned it."

"Ember wants you to feel comfortable."

"Does she?"

"Sitting can be awkward, and some of it will be awkward, for sure. But she honestly wants you to feel comfortable. She wants to give you a piece of art that will thrill you for the rest of your life. Her vision is an incredible challenge, and she takes it seriously. So do I."

She backed away from me. Again, she looked up toward the ceiling.

I don't know if she expected to see the remnants of a rope, or if she wanted to figure out how he'd done it. I knew I should have mentioned it right away, but she'd been so jumpy about the possibility of even seeing a large spider, I hadn't wanted to freak her out. "I'm sorry if you feel betrayed in some way."

"It seems secretive."

"It wasn't meant that way."

"Olivia said Ember's career took off because of it. That people have some weird fascination. Doesn't that bother her?"

"Please don't ask her about it. Okay? I really advise you not to talk to her about this at all. She was so upset and that's probably why no one mentioned it."

She took a few more steps away from me.

"It was a horrifying tragedy, but we've tried to move past it."

She stared at me.

"I really think it's better not to talk about things like that, reliving them over and over in your memory. When my brother ..."

"What happened to your brother?"

I was pissed at myself for mentioning him. I wasn't sure why that

41

had slipped out. More than pissed. My brother was a private thing with me. Something that hurt in a way that I sometimes couldn't deal with. And it was true, talking about his situation too much made it seem bigger, worse.

But I'd wanted so much to calm Morgan down, to get her to stop thinking about Derek, to realize that fixating on something ugly wasn't conducive to creating a beautiful work of art. Adam managed to burst to the surface because he had a way of doing that when I least expected it.

"He's had health problems … his life hasn't gone the way he'd hoped. And it's just … it's hard." I did not want to be talking about this. Not now, not with her, not ever.

"I'm really sorry," she said. "You seem—"

"Yeah. Anyway. Nothing to do with Derek. And it was an awful thing, but the studio's been completely re-done. New flooring, fresh paint. A new chair, obviously. Even new windows. You can't let it preoccupy you. Okay? And please, please, don't ask Ember about it. The best thing is to put it out of your head. Can you do that?"

She was standing by the door now, gripping the frame. She glanced at the ceiling, then back at me. "Why does that painting in the gallery look like the woman is dead?"

I laughed. "She's not *dead*. Ember likes to keep that as a sample of her early work. It reminds her how important the eyes are to a portrait. It illustrates that so well, don't you agree?"

"It's creepy."

"That's why it's hung separately from the others. But she treasures it. As a reminder." I crossed the room and stood next to her. "You seem very uncertain about being here, about having your portrait painted. It feels like you don't trust Ember. Or me. Are you going to be able to see this through?"

She turned her head, looking at the armchair where she'd been sitting that morning. "It's different from what I expected. And knowing he …" She looked up at the ceiling.

I touched her arm gently. "Relax into it. This truly is a once in a lifetime experience. Try not to be so tense, so worried. I promise, you'll love the end result."

"How can you promise that?"

"Because everyone does."

"Derek didn't."

"He didn't give it a chance, did he?"

"It's so … sad." Her voice trembled on the last word.

"It is, but he was troubled. And now, he's at peace. Why don't we go outside and enjoy the sun? Have you spent much time in the cactus garden?"

She shook her head.

I opened the door, and we stepped outside. I took a deep breath and asked her to tell me all about her catering business. She seemed eager to talk, eager to turn her attention from death to her love of preparing celebratory food. I hoped that was the end of it. I hoped she would take my advice to avoid bringing it up with Ember.

10

NOW: MORGAN

*B*efore I ever met Jade, I knew I would love her. There were two reasons for this. The first was her son.

I met Tyler when I catered a team-building event for his company. He told me it was the first time he'd eaten catered food that tasted like actual food. I asked him what fake food tasted like and he said it tasted like it came out of a vacuum-sealed package instead of a skillet or out of the oven.

Giving me a detailed answer made me feel as if he meant what he'd said, that he wasn't just flirting or trying to get an extra chocolate chip cookie for dessert.

After that, he ditched the team-building scavenger hunt and other games he was supposed to be involved with. He spent the entire day hanging out in the kitchen of the farmhouse they'd rented for the week, sitting on the counter talking to me.

What I found out about him in those first few minutes was the truth. He was the same when we started going out and the same when we fell in love. Genuine. He noticed what I cared about. He paid attention. And it hadn't taken long for me to fall in love. Because it felt as if he knew me inside and out and that he liked everything he saw.

He treated me like a princess without making it seem as if I were precious or fragile or a prima donna.

I'd learned that some of those traits had come from his mother.

His father hadn't been around much, traveling all the time, until he wasn't around at all. He started a new life with another woman before Tyler and his sister Grace started school. Jade had raised her children by herself until they were pre-teens, when she'd married the love of her life. She and Thomas had *ten sweet, perfect years together* until his heart stopped on a Sunday afternoon. Since then, she'd poured her love and energy, as well as the money from her first marriage, into other things.

The second reason I'd known I would love Jade was because the first time she invited me to dinner, she'd asked Tyler for a list of my favorite foods so she could prepare a meal that I would love from start to finish. And she didn't serve the meal in a way that made me feel as if she wanted a big show of gratitude for her thoughtfulness. She brushed it off as if that was what any woman would do for her son's new girlfriend.

No one could ask for a better mother-in-law, but I wanted more than that. I wanted to take the *in-law* out of our relationship. I felt cared about when I was with her. I felt noticed. I wanted her to feel the same from me. And some deep, orphaned part of me wanted a sliver of the mother I'd lost. I couldn't wait to start planning my wedding with Jade beside me.

Hearing her slightly disconnected feelings for Grace had bothered me. I couldn't decide if she was the most gracious mother in existence, giving her daughter enormous amounts of respect and freedom from expectation and obligation, or if she was blinded by the glow that emanated from Colin and Ember in her mind. I wasn't sure if it was abnormal to not hear a word from your daughter for over a year, or if that was something that happened all the time. The whole situation was confusing and felt slightly off. Maybe more than slightly.

While Bryce tried to distract me with gorgeous cacti and sculpture, pottery and meditative sitting areas, as well as thoughtful questions about my catering business, I kept my eyes on the back patio of the house in the distance. I needed to talk to Jade. I needed to know if she knew about Derek's horrible death. I wasn't even sure why I was being so polite to Bryce, allowing him to keep me occupied with a friendly chat.

After about fifteen minutes, I couldn't take it anymore. "I'm going to head back to the house," I said. "Olivia gave me a glass of wine earlier and I'm really thirsty."

"Sure." He followed me out of the garden as if he were now responsible for keeping tabs on me.

I walked quickly, Bryce trailing behind. He'd seemed genuinely interested in my catering business and I'd enjoyed telling him how I got started, why I loved what I did, how I believed food connected people at their most basic level. At the same time, I'd felt a queasy sensation in my stomach as I talked. The awareness of a man dying in the room where I would spend hours every day for the next week and a half sickened me. Replacing the floor and repainting did nothing to wipe the image from my mind.

The back patio was deserted. I went into the house with Bryce still close on my heels. I'd thought I might find Jade sitting in the living room, but, it too, was deserted. The sounds of dinner being prepared came from the kitchen. As I started toward the dining room, Bryce grabbed my wrist.

"Are you sure you're going to be okay? I know this is really upsetting. It was ... how can I help? I want the portrait to be a great experience for you. I'm really sorry if you think I, or anyone, tried to hide something from you."

I looked at the obvious worry in his eyes. Hearing him mention his brother, then change the subject as fast as he possibly could, had made me wonder if he and I had had similar experiences of pain at a young age. He was only in his late twenties, but his eyes seemed older, more concerned than most guys his age.

I had felt as if he'd lied to me by not telling me about Derek. But why? How does someone communicate a story like that? It's not as if Ember would announce it on her website. I thought back over the things he'd said to prepare me for the sitting and dinner the evening before. There really hadn't been an appropriate moment. "I'm ... it's a shock. Thinking about sitting in that room is—"

"Hopefully, once we get going, you can put it out of your mind. Think about other things. While Ember is doing her sketches, and then painting the portrait, you should think about your fiancé, your future. How much you love him. It is an engagement portrait."

I smiled, although it felt like it required a lot of effort. "Yes." I placed my right hand over my left and felt the diamond on my ring finger. I ran my finger along the edge. "I think I'll go for a swim before dinner."

He grinned, almost triumphantly, as if he'd finally succeeded in clearing thoughts of Derek out of my head.

11

NOW: MORGAN

*J*ade was in our bedroom, sitting in one of the armchairs by the windows. She was holding her phone, texting madly. She spoke without looking up. "How was your nap earlier?"

"It was nice. How did you know I was napping?"

"I peeked in on you."

It made my skin crawl to think about someone watching me while I slept. I regretted not locking the door, although at the time, it had seemed slightly rude to lock the door to our shared room.

"When is your next sitting?" she asked.

I settled into the other armchair. "I'm a little tense about that right now."

"Oh?" She looked up from her phone.

"I just found out that a guy who had his portrait painted by Ember killed himself. Right here! He hung himself in her *studio*!" I shivered. Saying the words made it feel worse.

She placed her phone on the table between us. She ran her fingers through her hair, moving the highlighted blonde and brown curls off her face. She looked tired. She sighed.

"You knew," I said, my voice flat and cold.

She nodded.

"Why didn't you tell me?"

She covered her face with her hands for a moment, then lowered them to her lap.

"Did Grace know?" I asked.

She shook her head.

"Why did you let her come here? Maybe that's why she took off. Because she found out ... it's really upsetting. Maybe she couldn't sit in that room, knowing what happened."

"I didn't tell you ... or Grace, because it was *so* upsetting for Ember and Colin. Imagine how they felt. What a horrible person that man was to do that to them. If Derek was feeling so awful about his life, why did he come here? Why would he even want to have his portrait painted? It made no sense, and it was so unfair to inflict all his pain on them, especially Ember."

"But didn't you think Grace would be upset?"

"She's not a morbid person. I don't think it would have bothered her. I really don't think that's why she left. She broke up with her fiancé. She was very clear about why she left. She shared some of her feelings with Colin. She was confused. She was worried she was cutting off all the choices in her life too soon, when she was too young."

"Well, it makes me really uncomfortable."

"Try not to think about the morbid aspects. Try to think about the beauty that Ember creates. Think about how wonderful it will be to have her capture something about you that you'll have for the rest of your life. Something that you possibly don't even recognize yourself. You can't let a disturbed young man who took out his rage on someone else destroy all of this for you. Why would you let a stranger have that kind of power over you?"

I laced my fingers together and looked at my hands. Studying them on my lap made me wonder if Ember had sketched them. If she'd made sketches of every part of me or if she'd only focused on my face, the general outline of my body. I longed to see what she'd done so far. It was going to drive me insane with curiosity, waiting to see my portrait. And I was disappointed I wouldn't get to see it each step along the way.

"Do you hear what I'm saying?" Jade asked.

I unlaced my fingers and looked up at her.

"Ember is incredibly talented. She wants to share her gift with you. It's terribly unfair to let someone with so much darkness inside of him ruin all of that—for you, and for her. He could have destroyed her career."

"Olivia made it sound like some people, a lot of people, were fascinated by it. That it brought her quite a bit of attention and her work started selling more because of it."

Jade's face tightened into a scowl that seemed to pull every muscle toward the center. "How awful."

I nodded.

"You need to put this out of your head. Can you do that? For me? For my godson? For Ember? I realize you hardly know them, but you will. They're part of our family. We can't let a tragic but selfish act damage them permanently."

I stood. "I was thinking of going for another swim." Being inside, I had less desire because once again, I was cold, but my body still felt the desire to move, and I knew the rhythm of it would help me clear my mind.

Jade seemed to feel as if Colin and Ember were her children. Maybe because Tyler had spent several years traveling and now Grace obviously had a similar wanderlust, she'd taken them on as surrogate children. Maybe she and I were more alike than I'd realized—trying to fill holes in our lives with other people. But Tyler was done with his traveling now. And she had me. Maybe she was still undecided about me.

12

NOW: MORGAN

By the time I was supposed to walk over to Ember's studio for my second sitting, I felt as if I was ready to enter the room with a clear mind. It seemed as if all the things I'd pictured taking place in that room hadn't really happened, or had happened in a room that no longer existed.

The building was beautiful with its ancient adobe walls and red-tiled roof. The hundred-twenty-five-year-old structure had been remodeled to accommodate large, modern windows that looked out on the garden and the endless expanse of the desert visible over the walls that surrounded the estate. Inside, it smelled clean, as if fresh air were constantly drifting through the rooms. The new hardwood floor was pale ash with a soft finish that had made me want to take off my shoes and walk across the room barefoot.

The armchair, except when I was told how to position my head and turn my neck, was quite comfortable. The room was filled with light.

It was only my imagination, and Olivia's macabre story, made worse by suggesting the suicide had brought customers flocking to Ember's work, that cast a shadow over the building. There was no reason I couldn't turn my imagination in another direction. And

Jade was right. Derek had obviously arrived at their home deeply troubled. It wasn't fair to let his despair infect this beautiful place and tarnish the generous gift my mother-in-law had given me.

When I entered the studio, there was a bouquet of eight yellow roses sitting on the table beside the armchair. The extra effort that someone—Bryce? Ember herself?—had put into welcoming me, made me feel even better. The aroma made the air smell sweeter, which went a long way to brushing the sour feelings further from my mind.

I stood by the window and looked out at the cactus garden, waiting for Bryce to arrive. I'd expected him to already be here and was surprised to find the building deserted. I watched a jackrabbit hop around the garden, leaping from one shaded spot to another, raising his sensitive nose to the sky, constantly sniffing out threats.

When the rabbit disappeared from view, I turned from the window and went to the chair. I wasn't ready to sit, knowing I would have more than enough time in that chair.

The door opened, and Bryce stepped inside. His hair was still wet from the shower and he hadn't shaved. I hadn't seen him at breakfast, which made me think he was the one who had been busy getting fresh flowers.

"Change of plans. My bad to keep you waiting. Ember's gallery owner popped by."

It was hard to think of someone *popping by* when the house was an hour's drive from Palm Springs. It was also difficult to picture anyone popping in on Ember. She didn't strike me as a person who liked surprises. I wasn't sure why I'd come to that conclusion. I hadn't spoken to her for more than fifteen minutes, but it was a gut feeling. "Okay."

"Ember said to give you her apologies."

"When should I come back?"

"I guess we'll decide that later. After Hendrix leaves."

"He's the gallery owner?"

"Yes." Bryce stepped out of the doorway onto the patio. "So, you're all good?"

"Sure."

"Okay. Cool. Gotta go." He hesitated. "She doesn't like anyone hanging out in the studio when she's not around. So ..."

I nodded and followed him out. He locked the door. A moment later, he was hurrying along the path and then he disappeared from view. I sat on a bench in the garden. It was made of concrete without a back, so after a few minutes of trying to relax and quiet my curiosity about Hendrix, I gave up and returned to the house.

13

NOW: MORGAN

*B*ryce, Ember, and Hendrix were seated in the dining room with papers and brochures spread out, covering half the enormous table. There was no sign of Olivia.

I'd learned that Colin drove Avery to his high school every morning and often stayed in town, even though he no longer worked full time running his construction company. He worked more in a consulting capacity since his wife's career had taken off so that he could devote more attention to their son. He'd hired a general manager to run the construction company for him.

After spending so much time psyching myself up, I was frustrated about the cancellation of my sitting. I wondered how long it would be until Ember rescheduled. Although I'd talked myself into putting thoughts of her troubled client out of my mind, I still wanted to ask Ember about him. I didn't care about Bryce's warning. I wanted to hear directly from her. And I thought she owed me that. I thought it would make me feel better to hear from her exactly what had happened.

With the sitting canceled, I wasn't sure what to do with myself. I'd realized that between sittings, ten days at Ember's home might start feeling confining. There wasn't a lot to do besides swimming and playing pool. There was a TV in our room, but I usually only watched TV a few evenings a week.

I'd thought I would spend more time with Jade, but it wasn't as if we could go out to lunch or shopping without a long drive to Palm Springs. Anywhere we sat around the house, even for a cup of tea or a glass of wine, meant we were in spaces used by Ember and her family. All the bedrooms but ours had private patios. Ours was the only one that opened directly into the courtyard.

Not wanting to miss meeting Hendrix, I took my laptop into the living room to catch up on work emails so there would be less backlog when I returned from vacation. When Hendrix left, at least I would get an introduction. I settled on one of the couches and positioned myself to face the entrance to the dining room.

They remained at the table, talking in low voices, for over two hours. It sounded like a very intense meeting, with lots of conversations that were more like debates than simple updates from Hendrix.

Finally, Ember pushed her chair away from the table and stood. With her voice raised, allowing me to hear more clearly, she thanked him for keeping everything on track and told him she would see him at the reception. I wondered what this referred to and if it was anything taking place while Jade and I were around.

Ember left the dining room without seeming to notice I was sitting there. She crossed the entryway and went into the wing that housed her bedroom, Colin's home office, and a private sitting room, closing the door firmly behind her. Bryce left the room immediately after. He passed through the entryway, raised his hand in a wave to acknowledge me, and headed out to the courtyard toward his suite of rooms.

It didn't look like my sitting was going to be rescheduled any time soon.

I closed my laptop and stood.

Hendrix came out of the dining room. He was a slim guy, about forty, with short, stylish black hair and thick but carefully shaped eyebrows. He had a self-conscious two-day growth of facial hair, a thick gold chain on his right wrist, and a gold smart watch on his left.

"You must be Morgan Hayes." He moved toward me, almost gliding across the floor in his leather ankle boots with sharply pointed toes. He extended his hand.

I shook it. "Yes. And you're Hendrix?"

"I am he! Introductions made." He took a step back and tipped his head to the side. I almost expected him to extend his arm and hold up his thumb as if he were measuring the space between my eyes. "Your portrait will be exquisite."

"That's what everyone keeps saying. How do they know?"

"Because *you* are exquisite. And Ember is brilliant. Because Ember is brilliant, and you are exquisite. No other outcome is possible."

I wondered if he always spoke in this weird, theatrical way or if this was for my benefit. Maybe it was required to own a gallery and sell expensive art to collectors. I'd never bought a piece of original artwork in my life, so I did no know how it was sold or what kind of style they felt was needed to convince people to purchase expensive art.

"How is the painting progressing?" Hendrix asked.

"I have no idea. I'm not allowed to see it."

"Of course, of course." He smiled sadly. "But soon. You'll get your chance, won't you?"

"I suppose."

He lowered his chin slightly and spoke in a low, conspiratorial tone. "Do tell me what the occasion is."

"It's for my engagement."

"Oh. Oh how nice. Of course you're engaged. A beautiful creature like you." He moved toward me. "Let me see your ring."

Before I could give him my hand, he took it. He held it in both of his, turning it slightly to examine the diamond. "It's quite large."

I felt my skin grow hot—my hand from his hot fingers, and my neck and face from what he'd said. There was no response I could think of that had an ounce of class.

"But it's not a surprise, since your mother-in-law can afford a painting, several paintings in fact, by the sublimely talented Ember West."

The pressure of his fingers grew firmer. Then he stroked the top of my fingers with his thumb. I tried to pull my hand out of his grasp, but he refused to let go.

He ran his thumb down the webbing between my fingers. "Are you insecure, Morgan? Just relax, give yourself over to the feeling of the moment."

"Let go of my hand."

He dropped my hand. He raised both of his beside his face. "Didn't mean to offend. My deepest apologies."

I heard the door leading to Ember and Colin's wing of the house open.

"Hendrix!" Ember's voice was loud and commanding. "You forgot to go over the first quarter inventory."

"You're so right. Let me get my tablet. The reception took over my mind." He scurried toward the dining room.

Ember stepped back into the hallway leading to her rooms, disappearing from my line of sight.

I returned to my spot on the couch in the living room. I wasn't done with Hendrix. After his slimy behavior, he owed me answers to my questions.

14

BEFORE: DEREK

*T*he room was darker than last night. I turned from side to side for what seemed like an hour, but it was probably ten minutes, trying to figure out why. It was darker than dark in my room. Pitch black. Finally, I realized the decorative lights in the courtyard that had been lit all night every night since I'd arrived had been turned off.

I twisted around in the sheets for another fifteen-minute hour, trying to decide if I should try to locate the switch to turn them on. I thought about turning on my bathroom light and leaving the door partially open, but that would be too much light, making it impossible to sleep, which I was already finding difficult.

I just didn't like it so dark.

I didn't use to be like this. Anxious because it was too dark, so dark I couldn't see the shapes of the furniture or even tell where the bed ended. It made me feel as if I were five years old. Four years old. The oldest, most primal memory of fear I could recall.

Because that's what it was. Fear.

She did this to me. With her sadistic attempt to control my eyes, with her questions designed to make me squirm, to make me question every single thing in my life, every facet of myself. She stripped me down until there was nothing left but whatever that thing is that slips out of our bodies with our last breath. Something we can't define or describe, a piece that sometimes feels as if it exists only in our imaginations.

And now, I couldn't sleep because I thought someone was in the room with me. I could feel them. I couldn't see, obviously, but it seemed as if the temperature had shifted slightly.

First, I heard a sound. A metallic click. A creak.

I was certain it was the door opening. I lifted my head off the pillow, straining to see, trying to sense whether the room had grown cooler. When I reached for the light switch, I couldn't find it. My fingers shook as I fumbled around the cord, groping for the toggle. Finally, they touched the switch, and I pressed it. Nothing. I flicked it back and tried again. The room remained dark.

Had the power gone out? That would explain why the ambient light I was used to from the courtyard was no longer there.

I moved my hand around the nightstand, feeling for my phone. My fingers touched nothing but smooth, polished wood. I ran my fingers across the surface, sweeping wider and wider, leaning up on my elbow now.

"Who's there? Is someone here?"

There was no response.

Someone was in my room. Someone had taken my phone off the nightstand before I'd woken, although I thought I'd been awake for hours, reliving the strain of that day. It had been torture, forced to keep my eyes from blinking for what seemed like hours.

"Who is it? What do you want?" My voice was hoarse and high pitched.

I pushed the covers off and sat up. I swung my legs over the side of the bed, and moved my feet around the floor, feeling for my phone, hoping I'd knocked it off in the fit of a dream, even though I couldn't recall sleeping. It wasn't there.

Keeping one hand on the bed to guide me, I stood.

Suddenly, there was a hand on my chest, pushing me back onto the bed.

"What are you doing? Who ... turn on the light."

"Shh."

I fell back onto the bed.

I felt the press of a cool, metal blade against my throat. I cried out.

"Shh."

The blade disappeared, and a hand was across my throat, pressing my body more firmly into the mattress, my head into the pillow. I lay there, stiff, wanting to fight, knowing I should fight, but terrified of what might happen because I couldn't see anything. I couldn't know if the blade was still inches from my neck. How did my attacker see? But of course, the aggressor has the advantage.

Hands pressed against my head. A cloth was tied around my eyes and I realized I hadn't been in absolute darkness after all. Now, I was.

15

NOW: MORGAN

I couldn't concentrate on work, but I wanted to stay where I was. Despite talking myself into thinking I needed to put Derek's suicide out of my mind, I couldn't. The idea of someone paying so much money for a portrait, then choosing that moment to kill himself, was not only sad and upsetting, it was bizarre.

Maybe he'd wanted to hurt Ember. Was it possible there was a history between Derek and Ember? Or had something happened during one of the sittings? Even so, it still suggested he was already considering taking his life when he'd arrived at Ember's, for anything to cause so much upset that he would decide to end his life right then and there.

I pulled out my phone and sent a message to Tyler. So far, all I'd sent him were two selfies of his mom and me—one in the courtyard and one beside the pool, a picture of our room, and a few breathtaking photos of the desert. I'd also sent a few emojis and *I love you's*.

Morgan: *Are you busy?*

Tyler responded immediately. Another thing I loved about my fiancé. Unless he was in a meeting or driving, he always responded to my messages as if he were sitting there waiting for them to pop up.

Tyler: *Just got out of a meeting. What's up?*

Morgan: *I found out that a guy that came here about a year and a half ago to have his portrait done killed himself. Right in Ember's studio. He hung himself!!!*

Tyler: *Shit!*

Morgan: *So you didn't know?*

Tyler: *How would I know?*

Morgan: *Your mom did.*

Tyler: *Wow. She never mentioned it.*

Morgan: *Did you know your sister had her portrait done here, but it was never finished because she disappeared?*

He replied with an emoji rolling its eyes and a laughing with tears emoji.

Tyler: *She didn't DISAPPEAR.*

Morgan: *It's creeping me out that he hung himself. And I have to sit in that room where he died.*

Tyler: *Try not to think about it.*

Morgan: *How can I not?*

Tyler: *By thinking about your portrait. By thinking about me.*

He made it sound simple. He made everything sound that way. And often, he was right. I tended to overthink things, but some things require overthinking.

Morgan: *It bothers me that your mom didn't tell me.*

Tyler: *She probably didn't want you to do what you're doing right now. Get upset. Feel weird sitting in the studio.*

Morgan: *Do you think it's creepy that she commissioned a painting for your sister? And now for me, knowing that?*

I felt disloyal texting that thought, but I had to ask. At the same time, it made no sense to ask. What did I think he was going to say? Call his mother a creep? Agree that I shouldn't be here and that she'd done something weird and disturbing for her daughter, and now, for her future daughter-in-law?

Tyler: *No. It has nothing to do with the portrait. Or with Ember. It's not her fault some guy couldn't cope any more. It's not creepy at all. It's sad, that's for sure. But not creepy.*

I sent him a blue heart emoji.

Morgan: *The vibe here is a little ... strange. Intense.*

Tyler: *What do you mean?*

Morgan: *It's hard to explain. It feels like there are things not being said. Underlying conflicts or something. I don't know. Secrets, maybe.*

He sent a laughing emoji, followed by one with a sharply raised eyebrow.

Tyler: *I really think you're reading into it. Try to enjoy the luxury and pampering and having your portrait painted. How awesome is that? We'll have a giant you in our living room.*

Morgan: *Will we?*

Tyler: *Unless you want it across from our bed, so I can admire you every morning as soon as I wake up.*

I sent all the laughing emojis, two of each.

Tyler: *They probably want to forget about it. I bet they asked my mom not to talk about it because they don't want to be reminded of it. Relax. Enjoy the pool and the amazing food. Hang out with my mom. She can be fun, as moms go.*

Morgan: *I know.*

Tyler: *Cool.*

Morgan: *I'm curious. And nosey. You know that.*

Tyler: *I do.*

Tyler: *Get it? I do.*

He sent a bride and groom emoji.

I sent him some kisses. He told me someone had stopped by his office. We texted goodbye, and I let my phone go dark. I wondered how long Hendrix would be with Ember. No matter how much Tyler made me smile and laugh and relax, I still had questions I wanted to ask him. It wouldn't hurt to ask.

I was curious.

16

NOW: MORGAN

It was another hour before Hendrix emerged from the door leading to the wing of the house that remained a mystery to me. The door opened quickly, and he closed it behind him just as fast. He started toward the front door, turning sharply when he heard my voice.

"Were you waiting for me all this time?" He glanced at his watch.

"Yes."

"I feel stalked."

I wanted to roll my eyes. Was he serious? He wasn't smiling.

"We were interrupted."

"Were we? I'm here to meet with my number one client, so I don't think you could say you and I were *interrupted* by any stretch of the imagination."

"Do you meet everyone who sits for portraits with Ember?"

"Absolutely. I make a point of it."

"Is that why you came over today?"

"I'm here to discuss the reception, and the rest of her career, obviously. I'm out here at least once a week, so it happens without planning. Not everything needs to be planned, Morgan. Don't you know that?"

"So you met Derek? The guy who killed himself?"

He folded his arms across his chest. "You're quite blunt."

"I just wondered if you knew him."

"I did. So sad, what happened." He paused for half a second. "But fabulous for her career."

His sad smile didn't communicate what he seemed to hope it would. It was obvious he was thrilled with what had happened to Ember's career after Derek killed himself. The sadness was a word he threw into the sentence. He spoke about it as if a man's suicide was some kind of accident—*what happened*.

"How can a man killing himself be good for an artist's career? That's really disturbing."

"Are you uncomfortable?"

"Isn't that normal?"

"Define normal. It's a meaningless word."

"It's how most people would react." I didn't like his attitude. I wasn't sure if he was cold or if he was worried I was going to convince Jade to ask for her money back. He made me nervous. I didn't like how he'd touched me. I wasn't sure if he'd been coming on to me or he wanted to make me squirm or he was socially awkward. He said a lot of strange things.

"I wondered if you knew he was depressed, or disturbed in some way before he started sitting for his portrait."

"I have no idea what his mental state was. But I do know his choice of a suicide venue was fabulous for Ember's career. As I said, so very sad. Tragic that he had to take his life, but so generous to give such a gift to Ember. It was a fabulous apology to her for darkening her beautiful studio and damaging the aura of her work space."

"No one kills himself as a *gift*. That's disgusting."

"It doesn't matter what he intended. That's what it was."

"What happened to her career?"

"You are a curious little bug, aren't you?"

I glared at him. "Will you answer the question?"

"It blew up. Big time. She was doing well before that, but the demand for portraits skyrocketed. She's booked over a year in advance. Her rates nearly tripled. And they'll probably go up again. We'll raise them to manage some of the demand. I'm worried she's getting exhausted."

"I don't understand why someone's suicide would do that. It's so … ugly. So …"

"People are drawn to the macabre. Don't you know that?"

"Not me."

"Not everyone can admit it. Not everyone *likes* to admit it, they don't like knowing it's the truth."

He looked excited. The more he talked, the more his eyes almost glittered with happiness, as if he loved believing that most people were so dark they wanted to think about things like this. I wondered if he was telling me what Ember believed, or if this was all his idea.

"Knowing that Ember was one of the last people to speak to him, knowing that she'd spent time alone with him, that she may have heard his darkest secrets, made other people want to be in her presence," he said. "They wanted her to capture their essence in paint. It makes them think she has some kind of power to make them larger than themselves, to make them immortal."

I felt sick again. I couldn't believe it was true. How could a man's suicide make people think an artist was more talented, or that she had some kind of ability to paint a portrait that would make them famous? Maybe that was it. Maybe it was the desire for attention or notoriety and because of the horrible story around her work, it fed on itself? Any way I looked at it, I felt ashamed to be part of the human race.

"Are you worried everyone will think you're a sicko?" Hendrix gave me a wicked smile as if he hoped I was worried, as if he wasn't smiling in sympathy, but was laughing at me.

"No. Jade has known Colin all his life. She knew Ember for years before … I didn't come here because—"

"You don't need to explain it to me."

"I'm not explaining."

Now his smile was full of pity. I wanted to smack his face.

"Any more questions?" Hendrix asked.

"No."

"I won't tell Ember about our conversation."

"Tell her whatever you want. It's not a secret."

"Really? Are you sure that's wise?" He raised his eyebrows slightly, then turned and walked through the entryway and out the front door.

I stood there for a moment, hyperaware of the silence inside the house, wondering if Ember had been listening to us. Did I care if she'd heard our conversation? I glanced at the door. It was closed, but that didn't mean she wasn't right on the other side. It didn't mean the door hadn't been cracked open and closed softly when I was caught up in my feelings of disgust. I hadn't been paying attention to anything but the horrifying words coming out of Hendrix's mouth.

I grabbed my laptop off the couch and went into the guest room. I sat on my bed and opened a browser on my laptop. I typed in Derek's name, suicide, and Ember's name. Several blogs and news articles popped up.

Starting with the news articles, I read everything I could find.

Derek Shaw was found dead in Ember's studio. He'd left a short note, although none of the articles mentioned what was in it. I supposed that was good. It was the most intimate thing he'd ever written. Maybe it had even been addressed to a single person. But I longed to know what it had said. Had he mentioned Ember? And who found it? Who read it?

There'd been a brief investigation. The articles mentioned only that he was staying at the West home while his portrait was painted, naming Ember and Colin.

One article noted his fiancé had asked for a deeper investigation, claiming that Derek never would have killed himself. That the last conversation she'd had with him gave no hint that he was suicidal. The police spokeswoman said that it was a common reaction to grief to disbelieve the facts.

After the news articles, I moved on to the blogs. There were two. One that covered local scandals and one that focused on controversial artists.

The art blog analyzed the effect his death had had on Ember's career. It read as if Hendrix had provided some background material because some phrases sounded as if they'd come directly out of his mouth.

The blog discussing local scandals had two posts about his death. Both were guest posts from Derek's fiancé—Zoe Ellis. She claimed that the four-word suicide note didn't sound like Derek's words. She said their conversations leading up to his death had been cheerful and upbeat. He'd never said a word about feeling despondent or suggested he didn't want to continue living. In fact, they'd been making detailed plans for their wedding and an extensive honeymoon trip to South America. She insisted he'd been murdered.

The second post followed up on her initial claim, but she'd clearly grown frustrated because rather than laying out the facts about his state of mind, she railed against the police department, their lack of intelligence, their stubbornness, their blindness to anything outside their own opinions. She ranted about Ember and Colin West, their privilege and money, and how the entire art community was stonewalling her. She concluded by going so far as to suggest that her fiancé had been murdered in the ugliest way possible in order to promote Ember's career—to give her name recognition and to cast some intrigue and darkness around her artwork.

17

BEFORE: COLIN

*E*mber will do anything for her art, and I will do anything for Ember.

It's been that way from the beginning. During those first moments, when we exchanged our stories the night we met in that bar, I knew I wanted to help her achieve her dreams.

We were both waiting for drink orders for the friends we were with. She, for vodka tonics, me for two beers.

"What do you do?" I asked her.

"I'm a painter," she said. "Not buildings, canvases." She smiled.

I liked that she didn't seem pretentious about being an artist, and that she seemed to have a sense of humor.

"You make a living at it?" It was a rude question, but it slipped out before I could stop it. She didn't seem to mind.

"Almost. I also teach, but I'll probably be able to give that up soon."

My beers were placed on the bar, but I didn't pick them up. "I've never met an artist. It's kind of a thrill."

She gave me a coy smile. "What do you do?"

"Nothing that classy or creative. I own a construction company."

"Making buildings is art."

"Nice of you to say but—"

"I'm not lying," she said. "It's absolutely true. Anyone who creates something is making art."

I think I fell in love with her right then.

Her drinks were placed on the bar, but she didn't leave. We talked until the vodka tonics started to sweat. Finally, she wiped them down with a cocktail napkin, reached into the tiny little purse hanging from her shoulder, and handed me a red business card with white printing. "Text me." She picked up the drinks.

I watched her walk all the way across the bar to her friend. When I returned to the guy I was with, he laughed at me until his beer glass was half empty. He told me I was paying for the next round as well, because I'd taken so long, the beer was lukewarm.

By the time Ember and I were engaged, she'd given up teaching and was making a solid income from her portraits. The company I'd started was also doing a whole lot better. Building luxury homes in Palm Springs was satisfying and lucrative. When we got married, one of the architects I worked with designed our secluded villa in the desert. We bought land miles outside the city limits that included an old adobe house. There was already water and electricity running to the property. We surrounded our place with stucco walls to give it privacy, and to keep out the coyotes and most of the rattlesnakes.

I never dreamed the venom that would destroy us would come from inside our own walls. It came from something insidious and unseen that sank its fangs into Ember. Something I couldn't make sense of.

At first, I thought it was because she hired that guy as her assistant. After Bryce moved in, it was no longer our private space, just the three of us. Even though Bryce had a suite with a tiny kitchen and a separate entrance, I could always feel his presence. And Ember spent most of the day with him.

It wasn't that I was jealous because he was a young, good-looking kid. It wasn't even that they shared painting and the details of her work, binding them together. It was simply his presence.

He changed the atmosphere of the house.

But that wasn't what got into Ember.

She wasn't happy. The more successful she became, the more she withdrew from Avery and me. She made excuses for that because Avery was a boy and needed his dad more than his mom as he got older. She insisted I was a more nurturing parent.

And she made other excuses. She had to be available whenever the *muse* struck. If that meant going out to her studio at night instead of lying in my arms, that's what she had to do. If it meant our sex life began to dissolve into the ether, she couldn't help it. Of course she still wanted me, she said. And then she would prove it. But the next week and the next month, she would work until just before dawn. Again.

At dinnertime, she would often sit through an entire meal without talking. Avery or I would ask her a question, and she seemed not to hear us. We would repeat the question and she would stare at us as if we were speaking a language she didn't understand.

When I asked her what was wrong, she insisted everything was fine.

"Why do you think something is wrong?" she asked.

"You seem unhappy."

"How can I *seem* unhappy?"

"You don't smile."

"Is smiling proof of happiness? Men are always telling women to smile because it makes them feel better."

"I don't think that's what I'm doing. You used to smile a lot."

"I'm thinking about my work."

"Doesn't your work make you happy?"

"Yes. But not giddy. It's a different kind of happiness."

"You don't seem happy," I said.

"Stop saying that. You can't possibly know how I feel."

"Are you happy?"

"Are you?"

"Not when you're not."

"That's not healthy, Colin."

I was tired. The conversation was going nowhere and I could feel it had the potential to turn into an argument. My gut told me she wasn't happy. She'd dodged the question, several times. "Are you pleased with the work you're doing? Are you excited about your success?"

"I try not to fixate on success. I try to focus on the work."

I sighed. I tried to suppress it, but she heard me.

"Are we finished?" she asked.

"Sure."

She walked out of the room. She was not happy. And I had no idea why. I didn't think it was me. It felt like she wasn't happy with her work. Maybe she was afraid of success. Maybe she didn't like the attention. It could be overwhelming at times, and it was getting more intense.

I vowed I would do whatever I could to support her career. I was awed by her talent and I wanted her to enjoy her success. She deserved it. But she was so tense, her mood so dark sometimes, she seemed almost angry.

18

NOW: MORGAN

*J*ade and I were playing a board game in the lounge area off the kitchen. It was beastly hot outside, too hot for sitting beside the pool, even under an umbrella, even with a dip into the cool water every ten minutes. The water sizzled off my skin within seconds of leaving the pool. For once, I welcomed the icy cold air inside the house.

We were sipping strawberry-infused water loaded with ice and nibbling cashews.

Bryce stepped into the kitchen and waved across the room. "Morgan. Time for your sitting."

I'd assumed, since nothing had been said, that it wasn't happening until the following morning. After Hendrix left, we'd eaten lunch and played three games of pool. I'd vowed not to talk or allow myself to even think about Derek, despite how uncomfortable I'd felt after my encounter with Hendrix, despite the blog posts from Derek's former fiancé.

Zoe Ellis was absolutely certain that someone associated with Ember, if not Ember herself, had murdered her fiancé. Every time the thought returned, my chest got so tight I stopped breathing for half a second. I wasn't sure what to think, and part of me wished I'd never read what she'd written. I wanted to go back to the feeling I'd had the day we'd arrived, when I'd first glimpsed that beautiful villa —slightly nervous, but excited about having my portrait done. Looking forward to this chance to form a lifelong connection with Jade.

Now, I felt I was living in a waking nightmare.

I couldn't stop thinking about Derek, but I didn't want to think about him at all.

And since part of the reason I was here was to get closer to my future mother-in-law, I'd decided that was where I would put all my attention.

Forcing myself to keep my thoughts on pleasant topics was working. Jade and I had talked about my wedding, a trip to Paris she was planning with two friends in September, and Tyler's job. He was the executive director of a non-profit that connected people in need of organizations with resources. It sounded fluffy, but it was a vital link in a massive, disconnected network of social services.

Seeing Bryce, hearing his voice, thinking about sitting for the portrait, punctured the fragile shell I'd managed to construct in the past hour.

"Right now?" I touched my hair, pulled into a messy ponytail.

"Don't worry about your hair. Or your clothes. She wants to do more sketches of your face, to make sure she has your bone structure right. What you're wearing, with your hair back, is actually perfect—without the sweater."

I stood, glancing down at my cut-off shorts and flimsy tank top covered by a long sweater to fend off the chill. "It's cold in the studio. I should—"

"We'll raise the temp for you. Let's go."

He seemed oddly impatient.

Once I was seated in the forest green armchair facing Ember's easel, Bryce left the room. Ember was nowhere to be seen. I crossed my legs, even though I'd been told not to, because it threw my body out of alignment. Until she was in the room and sketching, I couldn't see that it mattered what my body alignment was.

Because I'd been told to leave my phone in my room and there was no clock in the studio, I couldn't tell how much time was passing, but it felt like I sat there for fifteen or twenty minutes.

During the entire time, I didn't hear voices from any of the other rooms. It felt as if I were all alone in the small building. If they wanted me in a relaxed state of mind, avoiding thoughts of the man who had died here, abandoning me in this slightly too cold room with nothing to do but think, was not the best choice.

Finally, Ember came into the room. She greeted me, stepped behind her easel, and a moment later I heard the soft scratch of charcoal on paper. We only had ten days. I wondered how long she would spend sketching before she actually began painting.

There was no point in asking her permission to speak. She would say no, since it would surely affect the alignment of my bones. "I heard about the guy who killed himself here."

"Please don't talk while I'm working. Unless I ask you a question."

"I just wondered how that made you feel."

"Exactly how you might think it would make me feel. Now, please stop obsessing over someone you don't know."

I felt my jaw tighten. I curled my hands into fists.

"Lift your chin, please. And relax."

Bryce came into the room. "Are you comfortable?"

I ignored him. "I asked a simple question. I'm not obsessing."

"What?" Bryce said.

"I asked you to please stop talking," Ember said softly.

"I just don't appreciate the accusation."

Ember stepped away from her easel. "I can't sketch you when your jaw is moving all over the place. Do you understand that?"

"I wanted to clarify that I'm not obsessed. I wanted to know how you felt. That's all."

"I've moved on. You should too. Please stop talking if you want me to paint your portrait. I have to lay the groundwork and we're losing time."

Bryce walked toward me. He stood beside the chair and rested his hand on the top of my head. The heat from his fingers spread across my scalp. It was soothing and comforting to my body, but I was irritated. I wasn't a puppy or a toddler that he needed to calm down. "Please move your hand," I said.

To his credit, he removed it immediately and took a step away from me. "I thought it might help. It's usually calming. I developed it with my … anyway. Apologies if you don't find it centering."

"Did you do that with Derek?"

"Ember asked you to stop talking. Please try to relax." He crossed the room to the wicker chair, sat down, and picked up his notebook.

The room was silent for a while, except for the sound of the charcoal moving across the paper. I ached to see what I looked like through her eyes, in charcoal. It felt as if they were torturing me, refusing to let me see the progress. I'd never had even a sketch made of me and I was beyond curious to know how it looked, to know whether there was only a vague resemblance to me, or if it looked exactly like me. Ember's painting of Jade was a brilliant representation of her. It looked as if Jade might stand up from the chair and step out of the painting. It was eery to look at, especially now that it had been a few years and Jade had aged slightly. It was still a perfect reflection of her. As if Ember truly had captured some essence beyond Jade's physical appearance.

"Relax, Morgan," Bryce said.

"I am."

"You weren't."

"But I was."

Ember stepped out from behind her easel and walked out of the room.

"Just relax. No need to discuss."

I had been relaxed. But if I told him that, he would tell me again to stop talking, and remind me a third time to relax. "Where's Ember?"

"She'll be back," he said.

I sighed.

After seven or eight minutes had passed, she returned. The scratch of charcoal resumed.

Bryce spoke again. "Just relax."

"I am."

"You don't need to argue each time. I can see when you tense slightly."

"But I—"

"I can see it. Just listen and when I say relax, remind yourself to relax. Okay?"

I clenched my teeth.

"Morgan."

I relaxed my jaw. I closed my eyes for half a second, then let them pop open, anxious that one of them would start harping about that.

Once again, Ember moved away from the easel and left the studio. Again, I asked where she was going. Bryce assured me she would return. We sat in silence. Talking wouldn't have disrupted the sketching, obviously, but there didn't seem to be anything to talk about. Tension filled every molecule in the air. Bryce was probably correct in accusing me of failing to relax. There was nothing about the situation that invited me to feel comfortable.

When we resumed, Bryce had a new complaint.

"You're blinking too much."

I sighed. I hadn't been aware of my blinking. I held my eyelids steady. My eyes began to burn. Tears started to pool. I blinked. Once. Then twice.

"Don't get self-conscious about it," Bryce said.

"You made me self-conscious."

Ember left the room.

I wanted to scream.

Were they playing some kind of game? Did she leave the room to signal him what to say to me, or to tell me I wasn't sitting properly? I wasn't sure if her leaving had anything to do with me at all. It seemed random, and she said nothing. Bryce didn't comment on it in relationship to my failure to relax or my propensity to blink.

"This is really difficult," I said.

"Try to relax."

It was now utterly impossible to relax, and the two of them had created that situation.

Ember returned. She sketched furiously for another twenty or thirty minutes, and then we were finished.

I was exhausted and angry. I wanted to cry. I felt like a child who couldn't sit still in school. A child who had been punished, but she wasn't sure what rule she had broken.

19

NOW: BRYCE

*M*organ was so upset after her second sitting she bolted from the studio like a horse breaking out of its corral. I hurried after her, but she was nearly running, despite the hundred-and-five degree reading on the thermometer outside the studio door. I didn't catch up to her until we were near the swimming pool. The ground felt like it was on fire, heat coming through the soles of my shoes.

"Hey, Morgan. Let's do a debrief."

She laughed sharply. "I feel like I'm being tortured. That's my debrief."

"I told you sitting can be hard work. I'm sorry if I didn't set your expectation at the right level."

"Sitting still is hard work. Being told not to blink is impossible work." She began walking toward the house.

"It's emotionally draining, and can stir up some … slightly para-noid thoughts."

She stopped and whirled around to face me. "I'm not *obsessing*, as Ember accused me of. And I'm not paranoid. Being told to correct the pace of your blinking is a perfect way to make someone think too much about their blinking. It's a normal reaction. Just as being upset about a man hanging himself in a room where you're spending hours a day is a normal reaction. It's *normal*."

I moved closer. "Let me give you a hug."

"I don't need a hug. I need a swim. Or a drink. Probably both."

"It's hard work sitting for Ember. She's such a perfectionist. It's harder sitting for her than other artists. But you've seen her portraits." I studied the combative look in her eyes, the stubborn expression on her face. "How about this? Why don't we go for a drive? We can head into Palm Springs and visit her gallery. It's nothing like the little gallery attached to her studio. It'll blow your mind. I promise. And we'll get a drink."

She looked like she was more inclined to shove me into the swimming pool than she was to get into a car with me for an hour or two. She rubbed her hands across her face, then reached back and yanked out the elastic that was holding her hair in a ponytail. Her hair fell around her neck and shoulders, emphasizing the perspiration that caused the tiny hairs around the sides of her forehead to curl.

"It would be great to get away from here for a few hours. But Hendrix is ... I'd rather not spend a lot of time around him."

I nodded. "He knows art. And he understands how to sell it. But he's a strange dude, I know."

"Even if he has to toss ethics in the trash."

"It's ... you give customers what they desire. Right? Anyway, he can be a piece of work, I agree. But we don't have to stand around talking to Hendrix. We can look at the gallery, admire her work, and grab a drink."

She glanced at the swimming pool, then up at the sky—the sun blazing without a cloud in sight. "I need a shower."

"I'll meet you in the courtyard in half an hour."

She left without saying anything more, so I assumed that meant agreement. I supposed I would find out in half an hour.

When she stepped out the front door thirty minutes later, Morgan was wearing a white dress, navy blue flip-flops, and her hair was woven into a single braid, still damp from the shower. During the hour-long drive, I kept the conversation focused on her work, asking more questions about how she'd gotten started as a caterer and about her long-term plans. I asked how she'd met her fiancé and followed up with questions about his career. I was good at having a constantly running list of topics in my mind with which to distract the people who came to have their portraits painted.

I'd become skilled at the art of asking distracting questions with my brother, guiding him away from uncomfortable subjects when I didn't want to hear the things he longed to impress upon me with so much passion. Controlling the conversation helped Adam and me get along better. That ability also helped me manage Ember when she was moody.

Knowing how Hendrix was about his appointment schedule, determined to roll out the red carpet for art buyers, I'd texted to let him know we were coming. I'd told him since Morgan wasn't a buyer, we didn't need to occupy his time. It wasn't typical for him, but he seemed to take the hint. Even through a text.

Hendrix: *I'll keep myself busy. You can have the place to yourselves to do your own pitch.*

He kept his word. We spent nearly an hour studying Ember's work. I was surprised that Morgan took her time. The shower, talking about more calming topics on our drive, must have soothed her. She was mesmerized by the colors and the lifelike portrayals around her.

"Who are these people?" she asked.

"Some are local celebrities. Quite a few of the paintings are on loan. They're rotated out on a regular basis. Some are subjects she found intriguing and were hired to sit for her."

We looked at portraits of children gazing into their futures, older people who might very well be looking into another realm. We saw couples with their eyes filled with love, and people whose faces displayed every emotion, from utter heartache to absolute bliss.

She stopped in front of one, standing motionless with her eyes wide, unblinking, her lips slowly parting. She gasped softly. "Is this a woman having ..."

"Yes."

She moved closer, unable to look away. She shivered slightly. "It's ... I don't think I could have anyone besides my fiancé look at my face ... much less paint it."

I didn't say anything. She didn't have to tell me that, it was obvious from her discomfort. I began talking about the next painting and we moved on.

After we were finished, we went to a wine bar, sitting on an air-conditioned, glass-walled patio.

We both ordered Chardonnay. We sat on wide, low chairs with large cotton cushions. I rested my feet on the table, tired from standing so long on the painted concrete floor of the gallery.

I raised my glass toward Morgan. "To suffering for art."

She laughed.

I grinned and took a sip of wine.

"Why does it have to be such torture?" she asked.

"Don't the results speak for themselves? Don't you want her to look into your eyes and think about who you are, to imagine your thoughts and capture every sliver of light and shadow she sees there?"

"But she's not even painting. She's sketching."

"Don't second-guess her process."

Morgan took a long swallow of wine. She gazed into her glass, then looked around the room. Without meeting my eyes, she said softly, "If you say so."

She took a few more sips of wine. "How did you become Ember's assistant?"

I shrugged. "I admired her work. And I was at a crossroads in my life. It was a good fit for my—"

"What crossroads?"

I didn't want to tell her my life story. I kept all that to myself. My job was to ensure that Morgan was relaxed and comfortable for the painting, not to be friends. I'd had other clients of Ember's who wanted to be friends, but I liked keeping to myself. If I got too friendly, the next thing I knew, they were trying to compromise my job and what I was hired to do.

She was fun to talk to, and kind of hot, but she was also four years older than me. Not that four years is the end of the world. And I really shouldn't have been thinking that way about a client. Definitely not. But it was hard not to sometimes. Besides, she was engaged.

It had been almost a year since Claire and I split. I wanted someone new, but at the same time, my job and living situation made that difficult. This was a great job financially, and not so great lifestyle-wise. It couldn't last forever, but for now, it had to do.

20

NOW: MORGAN

*W*hen I'd first stood up from the chair in the studio, blinking as if my eyelids had turned into mechanical devices that had malfunctioned and lost control, sweating from the effort of *relaxing*, I was certain I would tell Jade I just couldn't accept her gift.

The minute I had that thought, I felt terrible. Rejecting her gift would be a rejection of her. She loved art. She loved all the artists she supported, and she adored Ember. She was in awe of her talent, and she adored Ember as a person. If for no other reason than because she'd loved Colin since he was an infant.

We'd come all this way. and she was relishing her time in the desert, lying around in the sun, reconnecting with people she considered part of her extended family, drinking in the raw beauty of vast stretches of dry earth and curiously beautiful cacti against brilliant blue skies and flaming sunsets.

After my gallery tour and a glass of wine, I felt better. Escaping the inexplicably claustrophobic feeling of being in a very large house on property that stretched for acres, yet sometimes felt very confining, probably helped.

Simply having a normal conversation, sitting in a car, looking at art, and going out to a restaurant went a long way toward getting my brain dislodged from thoughts of death and the torture of being observed.

Ember's artwork was truly extraordinary. It was almost impossible to take my eyes off the people she'd painted. Every single one of them touched me in a way that made me feel as if I'd known them all my life, or maybe as if I longed to know them. It made me wildly excited to see what she would do with my portrait. It made all the discomfort that had truly felt like torture seem worth it. Getting away from the studio, the house, had allowed me to laugh at myself. Had I really thought that being asked to sit still and relax my shoulders was *torture*? It was a ridiculous exaggeration.

Whatever had happened with Derek was not Ember's fault. No one sat for a portrait and decided to commit suicide. No matter what his former fiancé said, the police were right. It had been her grief talking. Something had been troubling him long before he arrived at Ember and Colin's estate. She just hadn't seen it. The more likely explanation for her feelings was that she felt incredibly guilty for not recognizing he'd lost the desire to go on with his life. She was lashing out.

It was possible that Ember's repeated disappearances from the studio while she was sketching me had been her need to center her own thoughts. Maybe she was terse and aloof, because she was trying to keep her feelings in check. How awful it must have been for her to find her subject's body hanging in her studio. I couldn't imagine what that must have felt like.

And to have her career explode as a result? What kind of feelings might that stir up? Guilt and shame that I couldn't begin to comprehend. I'd misread the entire situation. Just because her gallery owner was an opportunist with unsavory ethics didn't mean she was the same.

The wine and our drive back through the breathtaking landscape, listening to country music streamed from Bryce's phone, put me in a mellow frame of mind. I couldn't wait for a nice dinner with

Jade and her friends. I was eager to approach Ember with a different attitude, and consider what an amazing gift she was giving me, even if it had cost Jade a fortune.

When we arrived at the house, it was close to six. Bryce went immediately to his suite. I continued through the courtyard and into the house alone. The living room and the patio beyond were unoccupied. I didn't hear any voices or even the sounds of Colin preparing dinner.

I walked toward the kitchen, aware that I was incredibly thirsty after the large glass of wine.

Avery and the girl I'd seen him with once before were seated in the lounge area. They were bent over the coffee table, working on a jigsaw puzzle. Their voices were low. Neither one looked up when I walked into the room.

I took a glass from the cabinet and began filling it at the fridge. I raised my voice so they could hear me over the sound of water gushing. "Hi."

There was no response. The water must have been louder than I'd realized. I took a sip and moved toward the lounge. "What are you working on?"

The girl looked at me. She stared at me as if I'd asked the most idiotic question she'd ever heard. I got it that it was clearly a jigsaw puzzle. I'd only been making conversation, asking about the image. Was it that difficult to interpret my meaning?

She said something to Avery that I couldn't make out.

He murmured a response.

I sipped my water, wondering if I should give up or persist. I took a few more steps toward them. "How many pieces in your puzzle?" The question sounded stilted in my own ears, so I imagined it sounded worse to them. The quintessential patronizing adult trying to talk to pre-teens, clueless about what was going on in their world. Was I really that old? Only thirty-one and already a chasm between me and two kids ready to step into their teens?

Neither of them even bothered to look at me this time.

They spoke more, talking in quiet, rapid tones. The words were so impossible to decipher I wondered for half a second if they were speaking another language. Maybe both of them were studying French or Spanish. But it didn't sound like another language. It sounded like a code. Whispered half-words that meant something only to the other.

They were clearly talking about me.

Was it only my stupid questions about the puzzle that had them murmuring to each other, or was it something else? Bryce and I had been gone for several hours. Had Ember told them about the sitting and how antsy I was? Or maybe something else was going on.

The intensity of the murmuring increased. They moved their heads closer together over the table, their voices like a hum that sounded like an infestation of yellow jackets. I had the irrational urge to duck under the overhang of the bar, taking cover before I was covered with welts from their stingers.

I grabbed the edge of the counter to keep myself from acting out the scene playing in my mind, making myself look like a lunatic because I felt as if they were watching every move I made, even though they hadn't looked at me since the girl first stared at me, then deliberately looked away as if she couldn't be bothered. Or, as if I wasn't even there.

21

NOW: MORGAN

I gulped down the water, refilled my glass, and left the room without looking again in the direction of Avery and his friend. I wandered into the living room and stared out at the patio. I wanted to go for a swim, but it seemed like too much effort. I was famished. Why wasn't anyone making dinner? I felt utterly helpless and captive to their schedule and whims.

Bryce had urged us to help ourselves to whatever food or drinks we wanted at any hour of the day or night. We were to consider this our home for the ten days we were their guests. I wondered how Avery felt about that.

It was my impression that Ember was always working on someone's portrait, which meant the family had a revolving door of guests. Having a constant flow of strangers staying in the room across the hall from his bedroom, swimming in his pool, hanging out in the living room, and eating every meal with his family must be a strange, highly invasive experience for an almost teenager. It was possible the girl I'd seen was the only friend he felt comfortable inviting to his house. Maybe he didn't want the subjects of his mother's artwork talking to him, as if they'd emerged from their paintings and were trying to become part of his world.

I opened the door and stepped out of the chilly house into the warm early evening air. It was comforting after the climate inside. I walked to the pool, kicked off my flip-flops, and sat down. I lowered my feet into the water. It was cool and soothing. I moved my feet slowly around, watching the ripples and feeling the pool water tickle my ankles.

After a while, I returned to the house.

The aroma of chicken roasting in the oven wafted into the living room. I followed it and found Colin in the kitchen. He was making pulled chicken for tacos. Avery and his friend were gone, as was the puzzle. It seemed a shame they'd cleaned it up after putting effort into it. I'd had the impression it was large and complex. It wasn't possible they'd finished it in the short time I'd been outside.

"Is there anything I can do to help?" I asked.

"You're our guest. Just relax." He gave me a warm smile.

If one more person told me to relax, I might punch them.

His grin broadened. "You seem tense. Would you like a glass of wine? Or a beer?"

"A glass of wine would be nice."

He opened the fridge and pulled out a bottle of white wine. He unscrewed the cap and filled two of the glasses that were already on the counter. He handed one to me. "Cheers."

"I love tacos," I said.

"Good. Most people do."

I grimaced, straining for something else to say. I wished he would let me help. I was honestly tired of relaxing and I wanted to be busy. I felt as if all I did was drift around this beautiful house, gaze at the landscape, and sit like a bug pinned to a board in that chair. It had only been three days. It felt like three weeks.

"Avery and his girlfriend were working on a puzzle, but they broke it apart," I said. "That's too bad."

"She's not his girlfriend."

"Oh."

The silence stretched between us.

"Is it hard for him, living such a distance from his friends and his school?"

"No. Kids stay connected digitally. They spend most of their time communicating on social media anyway. Even when they're in the same room, right?" He laughed softly.

"Is it hard for him, having all these guests?"

"Don't feel like you're intruding. We love having you."

"But for a boy his age, it must be … he seems a little hostile, to be honest. I just wondered if he feels overshadowed by his mother's success. Her career is so … huge, so all-consuming."

Colin put his glass down on the granite with such force I thought it might break. "Avery is doing great. I don't appreciate the criticism."

"I didn't mean to criticize him. I was being sympathetic."

"You're not a parent, so there's nothing you can offer sympathy about."

"Okay. I—"

"Avery totally *gets* his mother's passion. He *absolutely gets* it. And he does not feel at all overshadowed. He has a full life of his own. He's taking several AP classes. He's won science fair awards. He's a smart, competent kid. And he's doing great. If you found him hostile, as you put it, maybe you're projecting."

"I don't think I am. I …" I didn't want to tell him they'd been whispering about me. He would think I was paranoid. It sounded paranoid when I thought about it.

I'd clearly upset him. I hadn't meant to criticize his son. I didn't have a lot of experience talking to parents about their children, but my friends with small children could be very defensive at even the slightest comment that was perceived as criticism. I'd thought I was expressing support, but just as I had with Avery's friend, I'd managed to hit the wrong note. "It's great that he has a female friend."

"I agree."

"I didn't mean to sound critical."

"You don't need to worry about Avery or anyone in our family. We're living the life we want. Avery and I respect Ember's genius and we love making space in our lives for her work and for the subjects of her portraits. It's an honor. Avery is incredibly proud of his mom."

"I'm sure he is."

"Actually, I could use your help. Do you mind putting these wine glasses on the table?"

"Sure." I moved my glass to the side and picked up two of the clean ones. Walking out of the room, I felt his eyes on my back.

In the dining room, I allowed myself to relax. I walked back and forth between the two rooms, carrying first the wine glasses, then the water glasses Colin had placed on the counter. I didn't speak, and neither did he. I enjoyed the rhythm of moving and having something useful to do.

I decided I was going to set my alarm to get up at sunrise the following day to go for a long walk in the desert. I would walk every morning and swim laps every afternoon. I needed some structure and a schedule. I needed to find a way to make my time here the calming getaway I'd expected.

I wondered if I could figure out a way to spend more time with Jade. For such a large house, in such an open landscape, I felt I was being slowly smothered.

22

NOW: MORGAN

*D*inner was enjoyable because the food was delicious, and because I indulged in all the wine Colin wanted to pour into my glass. I was tired of thinking, and the food and wine helped me to avoid too much of that. Of course, I knew the downside was that the thoughts I held at bay for now would come in with reinforcements once the buzz of the wine faded. But for now, it felt nice.

Avery was sullen. I wondered if, despite Colin's protests of how well-adjusted and marvelously happy Avery was, I'd been correct in my earlier impression. It had to be hard on a pre-teen to face a parade of strangers through his house, constantly witnessing his mother center stage. What was it like to hear people calling your mom a genius, to feel them tiptoeing around her as if she were a goddess deserving of adulation, bordering on worship?

As much as I felt a deep hole in my life from the loss of my mother, I could see that his experience had its own kind of pain.

When the meal was over, I began clearing the dishes. Colin insisted I leave it to the family, but I ignored him. Setting out the glasses before dinner had gone a long way toward putting me back on solid footing. I refused to let them behave as if I were staying at a resort and their sole function was to wait on me. It was awkward and slightly ridiculous.

I continued stacking plates to carry into the kitchen. Colin shrugged his shoulders at Ember. She pushed her chair away from the table and both of them left the room. Jade followed, and a few minutes later, I saw them sitting on the patio, gazing up at the darkening sky. Jade was pointing up, appearing to identify constellations for them.

Olivia and I were alone in the kitchen. She refilled her wineglass. "Care for a bit more?" She held up the bottle.

"Sure."

She poured some into my glass. I took a sip and began placing glasses in the dishwasher.

"It's nice of you to help out," she said. "Most don't."

"I don't like feeling useless."

She pressed her hip against the counter, watching me rearrange the contents of the dishwasher. She took a sip of wine. "You had your fair share of wine tonight."

I felt my skin grow warm. I hadn't realized she'd been counting my glasses of wine. "I'm having a hard time getting Derek out of my head."

She took another sip of wine. "Knowing what he did has that effect on people. Maybe that was his plan."

I shivered. "Do you think so?"

She shrugged. "Sometimes I think people who kill themselves are on a power trip. It's so cruel. The worst fuck-you in the world to everyone left behind. His fiancée was a mess. As far as I know, she still is."

"I read some of her social media stuff," I said.

"You can't let it get inside your head. It might be hard to sit for your portrait if you're thinking about that all the time."

"Not all the time." I laughed. "But it bothers me. I keep thinking I've put it out of my mind, and then it reappears."

"Like a ghost." She giggled.

"His fiancée was sure he was ..." I gulped my wine. "That someone killed him. But I guess the police decided that wasn't it." I put my glass on the counter.

"Because there wasn't any evidence. And because of the note."

I closed the dishwasher door. "Who found the note?"

"She did."

"Ember?"

"Yes. She found his body. The note was painted over his half-finished portrait."

I gasped softly. "Oh. That's ..." I took another sip of wine. Somehow, when I'd read about a note, I'd pictured an actual note. This felt like a personal attack on Ember ... that he would vandalize his portrait with a suicide note. And ensure she felt her studio had been poisoned by his corpse. He must have hated her.

It seemed as if Olivia was reading something in my eyes, because she nodded slowly, keeping her gaze locked on mine, even as she sipped her wine. "Aren't you going to ask?"

I placed my glass on the counter again, sharply aware that I'd tipped over the edge into far too much wine.

"What it said?" she prompted.

"What?"

"Don't you want to know what it said?"

I nodded slowly.

"He painted it in thin red brush strokes on the neck: *I can't do it.*"

"That's ... awful."

She sipped her wine. "Why do you think it's awful?"

"It could mean so many things."

"Right?"

"Ember told the police he had a lot of doubts about getting married and maybe it referred to that. So you can see why Zoe flipped out."

"But it could mean anything."

Olivia nodded. She took a long swallow of wine. "Zoe didn't think he wrote it."

I folded my arms across my waist, trying to fight the chill that seemed deeper and more intense than the usual cold air of the house.

"Are you okay?" Olivia asked.

I nodded.

"So that's what Zoe thought. And she fought like a wildcat. She came here to the house. Twice. The first time she acted semi-normal, for a while. She came inside and tried to talk to Ember, then she started screaming and throwing things. She broke a three-hundred-dollar glass vase in the entryway—smashed it all over the tile. We were picking up slivers of blue glass for weeks after."

"She must have been—"

"She was hysterical. In an absolute rage. She said she would shout the truth all over social media. And she did. But it backfired. People were fascinated."

I shivered. *That.* Again.

"The second time she came, Colin wouldn't let her inside. They had to call the police. And then they got a restraining order. We haven't seen her since. When she saw how it was giving lots of attention to Ember's career, she stopped posting rants about it. She kind of disappeared."

"It's all so sad." I picked up my wineglass and despite the uneasy feeling in my stomach, the spinning inside my head, and the ache behind my eyes, I took a sip, then another.

"Anyway. Who knows what was really in his head. The note sure didn't say much. Ember was kind of a mess. Colin was furious. Avery was ... well, he was Avery. So cool on the surface, but who knows what he's thinking? Kids that age act like they aren't thinking much, but it's a jungle inside their skulls. We all remember what it was like, but we think we were unique or something." She laughed.

It didn't seem all that funny, but maybe she was a little drunk too.

As if to prove me right, she opened the fridge, took out the bottle of wine, and splashed more into her glass. "Want some?"

I shook my head.

"But it doesn't really make sense if you think about it for half a second. Would someone narcissistic enough to pay thirty-five-grand for a portrait, when a selfie would do just as well, suddenly decide he couldn't do *IT* anymore, no matter what *IT* meant?"

I could feel my mouth opening in shock, reacting on its own to what she'd said. Was she calling me a narcissist? Was she also comparing her sister's highly acclaimed portraits to selfies? Or was she just drunk and rambling? Her words were crisp and clear. Nothing about her suggested she was drunk, beyond her inappropriate laughter and the outrageous things she'd just said.

23

NOW: MORGAN

When Olivia wandered out of the kitchen, Jade was still sitting on the patio with Ember and Colin. I rushed to finish washing pans and storing leftovers in the fridge. I went into our room and popped open my laptop. I returned to Zoe's Instagram account and scrolled back to the timeframe when Derek had died. I began reading every post and all the comments.

It was a heartbreaking read. Pain dripped from every word. The hurt and outrage, the confusion and unanswerable questions moved me without the assistance of colorful emojis telling me how I should feel. Just simple blocks of text illustrating a woman's life coming apart.

Next, I checked a few press releases on Ember's gallery website, noticing the timeframe when her career began to take off and how the posts from Zoe died down shortly after. Olivia had been right about that. I wondered if Zoe regretted trying to get someone, anyone, to pay attention to what she was saying.

Closing my laptop, I leaned back against the headboard. I was so tired. I needed to sleep, but my mind wouldn't stop. Zoe was dead certain Derek had been murdered. Olivia had hinted around that she agreed. Hadn't she?

His suicide note, if you could call it that, looked to me like an attack on Ember. He'd defaced her painting, clogging his virtual throat with words that said he couldn't *do it*. If his experience was anything like mine had been so far, that was one way to read his words—that he couldn't sit any longer, that the pressure of her demands was too much. Had he been told to control his blinking, to sit without moving, almost afraid to breathe? Told to relax when he was already relaxed, over and over, until his mind was filled with an endless, silent scream?

I wondered how many sittings he'd had. She hadn't even begun using a paintbrush for my portrait. Maybe by the time my painting was that close to completion, I would lose my mind and want to leave my body absolutely motionless for her. Without blinking, utterly relaxed to the point of death.

The thought was so awful, I started crying. I pushed my laptop to the side and brought my knees up close to my chest. I pressed my hands over my face and felt the tears spreading across my cheeks and down my chin.

If Derek felt so tormented that he killed himself … and no one had heard from Grace in over a year, was it possible that she … ? I shivered. It was too awful. Lots of others had stayed at the estate. They sat for their portraits without killing themselves, or taking off without saying goodbye to their families, leaving unfinished paintings behind. Was I making a big deal out of two people who had reacted so badly? If that was even it?

My brain was twisted into impossible knots.

I must have dozed because I woke to Jade standing at the foot of my bed, hugging my laptop to her chest. "Oh. You're awake. I didn't mean to disturb you."

"I need to wash my face." I got off the bed and held out my hand for the laptop.

"The nights are so beautiful out here. I hated to come inside," she said.

I nodded.

"You should sit outside with us tomorrow night."

"Sure."

I let her use the bathroom first. When I was finished washing up and changing into my nightshirt, I sat on my bed and took a sip of water with some ibuprofen. "I was talking to Olivia."

"Mmm," Jade said.

"Derek, the guy who killed himself, left a really strange suicide note."

"Please. Can we not talk about that?"

"Has Ember said anything about him?"

"I really think it's best if we keep all that in the past now. It's too sad."

"Olivia doesn't mind talking about him. I wonder if she talked about him to Grace. I wonder if—"

"Morgan, please."

"I just wonder if you should be more ... concerned." I told her about the note scrawled on his portrait. "Maybe Grace left suddenly because she was upset. What if she was ..." I couldn't say the words. It was too awful. But Jade seemed to be almost in denial, simply assuming her daughter was fine. She should at least make more of an effort to get in touch. To confirm she was okay.

"She certainly wasn't suicidal, if that's what you're trying to say." Her voice was sharp. A reprimand. "You don't know Grace. If you'd met her, even for five minutes, you'd understand. She's a hothead. I'm sorry to say that about my own daughter, but it's the truth. I thought being engaged would calm her, but apparently not. She's impulsive, and she does what she wants, when she wants. Without thinking about anyone else. I will not go chasing after her, physically or virtually, just to be told I'm interfering in her life or that I'm a compulsive worrier."

"Is that what she said?"

"Yes. So, can we go to sleep now?"

"I imagine her fiancé was pretty upset that she broke up with him so suddenly."

"He was. But he's moved on."

"Do you still talk to him?"

"Not anymore."

"It didn't bother him that she took off without saying goodbye?"

She let out a long, deep sigh. "I really, really do not want to talk about this. I invited you here to have a lovely, memorable engagement portrait done. I thought we would enjoy the desert and some superb food and wine. Are you not having a good time? You seem awfully tense."

"I'm a little tense. But mostly it's really nice." I forced a smile. "The desert is so beautiful. It has its own kind of peacefulness. I really appreciate—"

"So why don't we enjoy it and stop thinking about death and worrying about my daughter? She's always been this way. I'm sure she's having the time of her life. Colin told me she was fine when she left. She hurt Michael terribly, and she was extremely rude to Ember and Colin. I don't like thinking about it, and I really don't like talking about it."

"I just wasn't sure if you should be a little concerned. Based on what Derek's note said."

"That man's note has nothing whatsoever to do with Grace. Or you, for that matter. Now, can we *please* talk about something else? Or better yet, get some sleep?" She turned off her bedside lamp, flopped down, plumping the pillows around her head, and turned her back to me.

So much for getting closer to my future mother-in-law. Now it seemed as if she thought I was going out of my way to upset her, stirring up unnecessary fear about why she hadn't heard from her daughter. I'd probably shoved a hot stick into a wound that she'd worked hard to heal.

I felt tears pooling in my eyes again. I turned off my light and slithered down onto my side. In a few hours, I would be back in Ember's studio, trying not to blink, trying to relax, and trying not to picture a man's body hanging from the rafters.

24

NOW: MORGAN

*T*he aroma of coffee filled the kitchen, but no one was there when Jade and I walked into the room. Two places were set at the bar. Between the placemats was a bud vase containing a white rose. Propped against it was a thick white envelope. I opened it and removed the card.

It read: *Sitting at three o'clock this afternoon.*

I'd assumed my sitting would be in the morning. Now I would have to spend all day battling my conflicting, constantly changing thoughts.

I took the mug of coffee Jade handed to me. She and I sat at the places laid out. We ate yogurt with fruit and buttered whole grain toast. There was also a plate of waffles on the warming tray, but my stomach was still wavering from all the wine I'd consumed.

Jade talked as if our conversation the previous night hadn't taken place. She was warm and friendly. She launched immediately into an eager discussion of our wedding plans, asking if I was willing to share my thoughts about my dress or if I wanted to keep that top secret. I was thrilled that she was interested. I brought up my Pinterest account and showed her some of the wedding gowns I liked.

We both had a second cup of coffee, talking about dresses and flowers and colors.

Later, we changed into our swimsuits and went out to the pool. The weather was slightly cooler after an overnight thunderstorm. The cloud-filled sky made for an even more dramatic landscape, as well as a pleasant atmosphere for lying beside the pool. Only one day in, I'd already broken my vow to get up early for a long walk, but at least I could make up for it with some vigorous swimming. I needed to burn all the nervous energy I could before three that afternoon.

After a while, Jade returned to the house to make some phone calls for a silent auction she was in charge of at the end of June. The auction was an annual fundraiser for Alzheimers, which both her parents had suffered from before they died.

I jumped into the pool and swam without counting my laps. I moved back and forth through the water as fast as my arms and legs would take me, kicking furiously now that I didn't have to worry about splashing water all over Jade. I swam until my legs felt wobbly. I glided to the shallow end, stood, and walked up the steps. Olivia was now reclining on the lounge chair left vacant by Jade.

I went to my chair, grabbed my towel, and began drying off.

"Did you exorcise all the demons?" Olivia's laugh was shrill, almost maniacal. The eery sound of it was given a more ominous quality by the black clouds splitting the blue sky, causing the rays of the sun to shoot down like lasers.

"It felt good to get some exercise."

"Are you anxious because your sitting was postponed to the afternoon?"

How did she know every detail of what was going on? Was there some master schedule they were all privy to? Or was she closer to her sister than I'd realized, discussing every aspect of her day and her work? Maybe she had so much time on her hands, all she did was keep track of what others were up to. She didn't appear to do anything but hang around watching TV and fiddling on her phone.

"It doesn't matter when it is." I laughed and settled into my chair. "I don't have any other plans."

"I suppose not."

She was quiet for several minutes. "Are you feeling better this morning?"

"Better?"

"You seemed anxious last night. I hope you're not worried about your own state of mind, now that you know what Derek's note said. And how he wrote it. Maybe you're worried he lost touch with reality and you might do the same."

"I'm not worried about my mental health at all. But thanks for asking." The question irritated me. It also unsettled me. Maybe I was lying to myself. Maybe I was very worried about it and this was the reason I couldn't stop thinking about him, couldn't stop asking about him, searching out his former fiancé online. Maybe that's why I was so concerned about Grace.

I also didn't like the question because my gut was whispering that maybe she wanted me to be unsettled. She seemed like she could be the type of person who liked to stir up trouble. The night before, she'd suggested she believed Derek might have been murdered. Maybe she wanted me to feel uneasy. I had no idea why, but it was a thought that once it wormed its way into my mind, it refused to go away.

"Don't be defensive," she said.

"I'm not." I stretched my feet a few times, then crossed my ankles. I closed my eyes, even though she couldn't see them behind my dark glasses, so she didn't know I was calmly shutting her out.

It was quiet for so long, I wondered if she'd left. Finally, I opened my eyes. She was still there, sitting up and staring out across the desert.

"Have other clients of Ember's been upset by Derek's suicide?"

"Most are intrigued. They wouldn't come if they weren't."

"But some might commission a portrait not knowing about it."

"Like your future sister-in-law?"

"Did you spend much time with her?"

"We talked some. She's …"

"She's what?"

"How well do you know her?"

"Not at all. I've never even met her. Tyler and I have only been together eleven months. She's been traveling, I guess. She hasn't been in touch."

"Colin said she was a little frantic about needing to get her head together. Then she was off—the proverbial bat out of hell."

I wondered if, in Grace's situation, leaving Ember's studio had felt like fleeing hell.

"She's a bit like you," Olivia said.

"In what way?"

"A very sensitive, intuitive person. Wanted all her questions answered."

"About Derek?"

"She thought …" Olivia picked up the water bottle that she'd placed on the ground beside her chair. She sipped her water, leaving me waiting for her to say more, wondering if she *would* say more. The swimming pool water glittered under the rays of light still shooting through the clouds.

Finally, Olivia spoke. "She thinks my sister is a control freak."

"Is she?"

"She's full of herself."

"Was Grace upset about Derek?"

"She didn't like being lied to. She really didn't like that her mother hadn't told her about it."

"What else did she say?"

"That's all I know."

"Do you think it's strange that she left before her portrait was finished?"

"Strange compared to what? Her mother has a lot of money, maybe she doesn't think it's any big deal to walk away from a project that costs that much without getting what you paid for. Or maybe it was worth it to her."

I closed my eyes again. Feeling deceived would definitely explain why Grace wouldn't be in touch with her mother. Did it explain why she was also shutting her brother out of her life? Tyler said they hadn't done a great job of staying in touch once they'd become adults. He blamed himself because he was slow to respond to her messages. He didn't do social media. Neither did she anymore, apparently. Since she'd zipped off to find herself.

I couldn't imagine letting a member of my family slip through my fingers like that. What kind of family was I marrying into? Did they not pay attention to each other? But Tyler wasn't like that— aloof, distant, shutting me out for periods of time. Everything about him ticked all the boxes on the mental list I hadn't realized I'd been compiling over the years.

Tyler and his mom were closely connected to each other. He went to her house for dinner once a month and they met for lunch on a regular basis. He spoke to her on the phone every week and texted her on and off in between. It was casual and easy. No pressure and demands from her, no guilt or obligation.

It was only where Grace was concerned that there seemed to be a fracture in their family.

25

NOW: MORGAN

*T*wenty more laps in the pool, that I counted this time— obviously—left my body feeling loose and flexible. Olivia had left me alone when her phone began buzzing with a call she *absolutely needed to take.*

After showering, blowing my hair dry, and putting on light makeup for my afternoon sitting, I stepped into the hallway outside the guest room.

The sound of Avery's voice came from his bedroom directly across the hallway from ours. I'd thought he was at school. I hesitated, surprised that I could hear him so clearly through the closed door. He must have been sitting on the floor with his back against the door because it sounded as if he were right beside me.

"It's fucking creepy. No one can disagree with that," he said.

I glanced down the hallway, not wanting to be caught eavesdropping, but I desperately wanted to know what he was talking about.

"I know I've said it before. But now I have to put on the clothes and put on the smile and put on the bullshit for this reception. I'm gonna puke. I'm telling you, it's—"

I pulled out my phone, holding it so it looked as if I'd just received a text, in case someone rounded the corner at the end of the hallway. I rested my shoulder against the wall, waiting for Avery to say more.

"Every single painting makes them look like they're fucking insane." He laughed. "Maybe they are." He continued laughing, changing his voice so he sounded like a character in a monster movie from the 1950s, cackling wildly. "Mad, I tell you. They're all maaaad!" He laughed again in his normal tone. "Yeah. Yeah."

Several moments of silence passed.

"I don't know why I have to be one of her pimps." He groaned. "Yes, I am. You know I am."

I wondered if he was talking to the girl I'd seen or to someone else. I wondered why he wasn't in school. I wondered why he was so unconcerned about being overheard. Maybe he assumed he was alone in this wing of the house, or didn't realize how leaning against the door amplified his voice.

"Stop telling me that. I hear that every day." His tone changed to one that mimicked condescension. "You'll see her genius when you're older. You need to show her the respect she deserves. People need to know you *respect* her work, that the whole family is behind her. A hundred percent."

There was a long silence. I wondered if I should leave. Any minute, someone might pass by and look down the hallway. Olivia might come out of her room, just a few yards beyond Avery's. As the silence stretched on, Avery himself might decide to stand up and suddenly open his door.

I moved away from the wall where I'd been leaning.

Avery laughed, followed by another silence.

I held my breath, waiting for him to say more. I wasn't sure what I was expecting. So what if Colin foolishly believed his son was being polite and respectful when that was clearly not the case? It wasn't any different from pre-teens all over the world. For all I knew, half of what Avery had been saying to the person on the other end of the phone call was also a lie. Maybe he wanted to make himself look independent from his parents, so he was posturing to look like he had opinions of his own.

The silence continued. Was he still listening to someone talk, or had the phone call ended?

Against my better judgment, I pressed my ear against his door, thinking I might hear another voice leaking from the earphones, or the sound of Avery's breathing, telling me if he was listening to something that was getting him wound up. I might hear him moving around his room.

There was nothing.

I stepped back and knocked on the door. I waited a few seconds, then knocked again.

"Yeah? Who is it?"

"Morgan."

"What do you want?"

"I wanted to talk to you for a minute."

"Why?"

"Why did you stay home from school?"

"None of your business. Go away."

"I just … it's a little lonely here, and there's nothing to do while I'm waiting for my next sitting, so I thought—"

The door swung open, and he was facing me. His hair was unruly, obviously not washed. He was holding his cell phone, wearing sweatpants and no shirt. His feet were bare. "You thought we could be friends or something? You're a little old for me to hang out with. Sorry to disappoint you." He started to close the door.

"This sitting for a portrait thing is really weird. It's messing with my head and I just wanted someone to talk to."

He laughed. "Then why are you doing it?"

"It's complicated, I guess."

"You *guess*? Aren't you like forty years old? Shouldn't you *know* what you think by your age?"

"I'm thirty-one. And this might surprise you, but life can be just as confusing when you're an adult. Hasn't anyone mentioned that?"

"Nope."

"You must have noticed that adults make mistakes."

He laughed.

"Obviously, adults get confused and aren't always sure about things."

"Well, I have a migraine. That's why I'm not at school. And I'm not really in a talky mood. So ..."

I looked past him into his bedroom. It was as elegantly decorated as the rest of the house. The only features that made it look like it belonged to a pre-teen boy were the clothes tossed on the floor, the laptop sitting open on the unmade bed, and the three empty soda cans on the nightstand. Other than that, the beautifully framed artwork on the walls, a sleek modern desk with a silver lamp shaped like a man's arm, the light hidden in his palm, and a small sofa with decorative pillows, made it look like Avery was staying in a hotel room.

"Do you mind if I ask you about Derek? The guy who—"

"I fuckin' know who Derek is. Was."

"You didn't like him?"

"I didn't have an opinion."

"You sound angry."

"I don't appreciate someone offing himself where I live."

"Do you feel sad about—"

"I feel like he should have kept his problems away from me. And my parents."

"It didn't have anything to do with you. Or do you think it did?"

"It had to do with me because I *live* here. And he brought cops to my house. And he brought reporters to my house. And he brought his freaked-out fiancée to my house. And I have to ... never mind. I have a migraine from hell. So what's your question and then I'm going back to bed?"

"Using your laptop when you have a migraine probably doesn't help."

"Are you a doctor?"

"No, but—"

"Then ask your question and hit the road."

"I didn't mean to listen in, but I … you were talking loudly when I came out of my room, so I heard you. I …"

"Spit it out."

"Your mom's paintings disturb you?"

"People see what they want."

"What do you mean?"

"They're just weird. That's all. Haven't you noticed that the eyes all kind of look … similar?"

"Not really."

He scowled. "The eyes are kind of alike. Not the same, but they all look a little like the person is in their own world. A different reality or something. Like they're insane."

"I haven't noticed that."

"Look harder."

"I will." I felt a blast of cold air on the back of my neck that traveled down my spine, as if someone had turned up the air conditioning. "And about Derek, I guess I wondered how it made you feel, and now I know."

"Yup. Now you know."

"Was it upsetting for your mom? And your dad?"

He shrugged and looked at his phone. "Ask *them*."

"Did they talk to you about it?"

"You have a lot of questions. If it's bugging you, if you don't want to sit in the room where he did it, maybe you should get out of here."

"Is that what you would do?"

"Counting the months." He closed the door slowly, but firmly, forcing me to step away to avoid being hit in the face.

I was pretty sure my guess that he could have been posturing for his friend was wrong. Colin had lied about Avery's respect for his mother, lied that he was fine with all the people staying in their home.

Was Colin simply protecting the family's reputation? Or did he feel the need to reassure himself that Avery was well-adjusted, repeating some kind of mantra to himself that everything was okay? Was he trying to numb the fear that his son might *not* be okay?

26

NOW: MORGAN

I stood in the hallway, no longer worried about being seen. I placed my hand on the closed door, as if I might somehow will it to open again. But what else would I ask him? I wasn't even sure why I'd knocked. I wasn't sure about anything. Clearly Derek's suicide had disturbed me deeply, and the others' strange reactions to it were making me even more uncomfortable. I wished I wasn't there. But I didn't see a way out that wouldn't damage my fragile, slowly blossoming relationship with Jade.

More than anything else that I wanted in my life right now, aside from Tyler, I wanted to be close to Jade. I needed her. Starting to plan our wedding had made me realize afresh one more thing I'd been robbed of when my mother died. Most of the time, I accepted her absence. I lived my life feeling grateful for my extended family and all my friends, knowing I was fortunate to have caring grandparents, and that my dad had done the best he could.

But there were times when that vast, empty space in my life was so overwhelming I thought it might suck me in and I would disappear into the depths of the earth.

Planning my wedding was one of those times.

When you think about wedding arrangements, you don't think

about mothers. You think about couples and love and romance. You think about bachelorette parties and cake and champagne. You think about flowers and dresses and friends. You think about creating a beautiful event and a spectacular party with your future husband.

But in the background, taking care of a thousand details, other girls had their moms. When I went to bridal shows, everyone was visiting the displays with their moms and sisters. Sometimes there were groups of friends, but mostly, moms. When I checked out a few bridal gown shops just to feel the thrill of trying on a few amazing dresses before I started looking seriously, it seemed as if every single bride-to-be was there with her mom.

I wanted to cry.

It wasn't as if I thought Jade was going to replace my mom. That was insulting and stupid and not possible. But she would feel mom-like. She was Tyler's mom, and she was my new family.

There was no way I could tell her I didn't want my portrait painted. That I was too upset by a man I didn't even know killing himself in a room that was really quite peaceful and beautiful. I couldn't reject her gift that was so generous it was embarrassing.

I thought about calling Tyler, but he was at work, which I would be too if I weren't out in the desert, drifting around inside a freezing cold house, waiting for appointments in a room where I sat in torturous discomfort trying not to think about a dead man.

Tyler and I often called each other during the workday. One or the other of us would send a text asking if it was a good time for a phone call, but what would I say if we did talk? If he knew how upset I was, he would tell me to leave. He would tell me his mom would understand. And maybe she would. Probably she would. But there would be this rough spot between us, and that wasn't how I'd imagined things.

I moved away from Avery's door, suddenly aware I'd been standing there for quite a few minutes, as if I wanted him to come out and tell me what I should do. I wasn't used to being indecisive.

I'd always made decisions quickly. My mom instilled that in me when I was little, and it stayed with me after she died. Often, I felt as if she were patting me on the back when I made a decision and moved forward confidently. And I had made a decision. I was going to stay, obviously. I just didn't feel great about the decision. And I did want the portrait.

Maybe Avery thought the subjects of the portraits were slightly creepy, or strange, but I loved them. I found them intriguing and mesmerizing in a way that didn't allow you to easily take your eyes off them. I wanted a portrait like that.

I'd even allowed myself to wonder if I might see my mother in my face.

My mother had been my age when she gave birth to me. There was a photograph of her, just a year younger than I was now, tucked into my journal where I sometimes made notes for ideas that came to me for upcoming catering events. It was a three-by-six print that I'd had in a frame. I removed it before I left, wanting to have it with me when I saw the completed portrait.

When Jade had shown me her portrait, she'd said she saw something of her mother *and* her daughter in her face. That was one of the things she loved about it, one of the aspects of Ember's talent that she admired so deeply. The ability to paint beyond mere bone structure and the suggestion of a person's likeness. Ember seemed to be able to capture pieces of their DNA itself, and thereby reveal family and generational resemblances.

I didn't know if Jade imagined all of that, if she truly saw it or only saw it because she wanted to, but she'd managed to convince me it was there, and I desperately hoped for the same. Maybe it was wishful thinking based on the cost of the painting. She needed it to be valuable. Still, I hoped all the same.

My conflicting, anxious thoughts made me long for Tyler even more. It had only been four days since we'd said goodbye, but it felt like fourteen. I couldn't recall how it felt to hold him or lie beside him or even the smell of him. He was starting to feel like words in a text box on my phone screen, an image in my photo app that I could look at when I was craving him.

I sent a text asking if he had five minutes to talk. There was no reply, but I went into the guest room, hoping that any minute, I'd feel the comforting vibration of my phone. I opened one of the windows to let in some of the warm outdoor air to reduce the air-conditioned chill. I smiled at the absurdity of doing the opposite of what most people did when opening windows. I tilted the shutters slightly to keep the bright light that was shining directly into the courtyard from blinding me. I settled into one of the armchairs and checked my phone.

There was a text from Tyler saying it wasn't a good time. I was overcome by disappointment beyond reason. I sent him a string of hearts and kissing emojis, followed by a miss you text.

He replied with the same, and that was it.

As I started to get out of the chair, I heard voices in the court-yard. Colin. His voice was much deeper than Bryce's and he only had to speak a word or two for me to recognize it was him.

"This isn't good."

"Don't be so jumpy. She's in her studio."

Olivia was with him.

I stood and went to the window. I looked out through the slats of the shutters, standing back far enough to be sure they weren't aware of any movement inside our room. I wondered at myself that I'd taken to listening in on other people's conversations. What was wrong with me? It was either sheer boredom, or the generally strange and secretive atmosphere of the West family that made me want to do it. I wasn't sure why I felt they were secretive. The fact that I hadn't known Grace came here for a portrait, or about Derek's suicide, was a result of Jade's secrecy, not the people who lived here. But I still felt that part of the reason Jade kept those things to herself, especially Derek's suicide, was due to the secrecy that seemed to envelop Ember and Colin.

"What do you want?" Colin asked

Olivia's voice was too low for me to hear her answer. But what I saw was more startling than anything she might have said. Colin put his hand on her face and moved her hair to the side. He ran his fingers down the side of her cheek and then along her neck. She tipped her head back. I half expected her to let out a soft moan, but the only sound now was the splash of water in the fountain.

His hand was still on her throat. Both of them were frozen, hardly seeming to breathe.

A moment later, he let his hand fall away. He shook his head, shoved his hands into his pockets, and turned toward the front door. He walked quickly away and disappeared into the house. Olivia moved toward the front of the courtyard and out of my line of sight.

I stepped away from the window and settled into the chair again, leaning my head against the back. I closed my eyes. My thoughts spun around Avery and the scene I'd just witnessed. I thought about Derek and wondered if his death had silently blown apart Ember's family. I thought about Colin's obvious lie about his son. And now, this—touching his sister-in-law in a way that shouted they had shared more than dinnertime conversation.

Who was this guy? Maybe he'd made a pass at Grace and that's why she'd taken off.

Or maybe it was because she'd felt lied to by Jade, or at least victimized by a lie of omission.

I massaged the tight muscles at the base of my skull, then picked up my phone. I needed to have a real conversation with someone who wasn't giving me sharp, cryptic answers or shrugging off my questions. I knew I should talk to Ember, but Bryce acted as if I would sabotage my portrait if I did anything to upset her.

I went to Zoe's Instagram account, followed her, then sent her a private message. I wasn't sure what I wanted to find out from her, but I needed to know if Derek had told her anything about these people. All I had was Jade's gushing love and admiration for them, and it wasn't fitting very well with my own experience.

27

NOW: BRYCE

*M*organ was due at the studio at three. I'd arrived early to organize Ember's brushes and paints the way she liked them, even though I knew she wasn't planning to start painting today. She'd only done a few charcoal sketches, and she liked to work with at least six or seven charcoal sketches to be sure she'd captured a range of expressions. At the same time, she also liked all her brushes and paints at her fingertips. She felt lost without them. She'd never said this, but I felt it. Her hands occasionally fluttered helplessly when they weren't within reach.

I also wanted to make sure the room was a pleasant temperature since Morgan kept complaining she was cold. I'd brought a small wood block that she could rest her feet on to help her relax her posture. It would help when she needed to focus her gaze and keep from blinking. They all hated that aspect, but they all forgot their complaints and so-called torture once they saw their finished portraits.

Suffering for art.

That saying is meant to refer to the artist, but those who want to collect and appreciate art, and experience it as an integral part of their lives, need to contribute a little suffering as well. That's what I'd been told.

I was startled, but shouldn't have been surprised when Morgan walked through the doorway a full twenty minutes before she was supposed to be there.

I was realizing that Morgan was not like Ember's other subjects. Possibly because she hadn't been drawn to Ember and paid for the painting herself. She wasn't caught up in Ember's spell. She was fighting the rigors of sitting for a portrait more than the others did. For one thing, she was obsessing over Derek. I wished I could wipe that image out of her mind. I was worried it was going to make it difficult for Ember to paint something truly magnificent. I felt like I had to be constantly selling the value of Ember's work. It was exhausting.

Part of me wanted to suggest Morgan should simply leave. If she couldn't accept the process with her entire heart and soul, it was only going to get more difficult. I should tell her to leave while she had the chance. Once Ember was deep into her work, she wouldn't react well if Morgan walked out.

I could feel that Ember recognized Morgan needed to do this to please her mother-in-law. Her longing to make the older woman happy, to form a bond with her surrogate mother, was palpable. Everyone was trying to please someone. Morgan wanted to please Jade. Jade wanted to please Colin. Everyone wanted to please Ember.

"You're early," I said.

"I wanted to talk to you."

"It's not the best time. I need to get the room set up. You'll be sitting for three hours, it would be good to get some exercise. I know it's hot, but why don't you go for a walk?"

"Are Colin and Olivia having an affair?"

I wanted to laugh, although I wasn't quite sure why. Possibly because it was the furthest thing from my mind. I'd expected more questions about Derek, concerns about Grace, questions about why

Ember was taking so long with the sketches, why Morgan wasn't allowed to see the work in progress. Most of the questions I'd heard before, from Morgan, and others.

"Why is that any of your business?"

"Because I feel like I'm in the middle of a dysfunctional family. I thought it would be relaxing here. But the atmosphere is really tense and … I don't know, heavy or secretive. Something I can't put my finger on."

"You're imagining it."

"I don't think I am."

"You're tense about the painting and about how difficult it is to sit still. I promise you'll get used to it." I took the notebook off my chair and placed it in the rack beside it with the other notebooks. I repositioned the chair, then went to the doorway where Morgan was standing. "Please go for a walk. You need to get some exercise before you sit. Trust me."

"You haven't answered my question."

"Is it really any of your business?" I shoved my hands into the pockets of my shorts and studied my toes, trying to think about how to answer her. I probably already had. If they weren't, I would have said so, and she knew it.

"So they are," she said.

I looked at her dark brown eyes boring into mine as if she wanted to drill holes through my skull. "They had a thing for a few weeks. But it's long over."

"How do you know? Did Colin tell you?"

"You asked, and I answered. Why does that matter?"

"It feels uncomfortable. I saw him touching her."

"Then why did you ask?"

"It's confusing. Avery seems really unhappy. Ember walks around like she hardly notices anyone else is even in the house, but at the same time, everyone seems to revolve around her. It's … I feel like we're intruding."

I took her upper arm and guided her through the doorway. "Let's

119

go outside."

"Is she here? Are you afraid she'll hear us?"

"She's not here and if she was, I wouldn't be afraid. Do you always overthink every situation?"

"I'm not overthinking. It feels uncomfortable."

"Maybe you're just really tense."

She let me steer her across the patio and into the cactus garden. It was hot. Too hot to walk much, but I started along the pathway through the garden anyway. "I knew they slept together a few times because when you all live together, you notice things."

She paused in front of a bench. "It's too hot." She collapsed onto the bench, then stood immediately. "And too hot to sit." Her laugh was shrill. "Can we go back inside?"

I sighed. She would regret it later, but she wasn't going to take my advice.

"How can he sleep with her *sister*? Does Ember know? Why does she let Olivia stay here? She must know, because they weren't very subtle about it, so I'm sure she's seen them."

"I have no idea if she knows. It's over and Colin regrets it."

"He told you?"

"He knows how Ember is and he accepts that, but it's not easy for him. He knows her work is different. Colin's work is what he does. Ember's work is who she *is*. She's never separate from it. Not for a moment. For Ember, her painting is her lover. Colin understands that intellectually, but he's still a man. It's hard to be second in her life, to live with that every day. She's his world. But Ember's painting is her world."

"How do you know all that?"

"Isn't it obvious? When you see how Ember is?"

She nodded.

It was obvious. It made for a painful atmosphere in their gorgeous, sprawling desert home. It wasn't surprising that Morgan felt the discomfort of Ember's family as they lived in her shadow, as they loved her desperately, fully aware that she often hardly noticed them at all.

28

NOW: MORGAN

*I*t was a relief to step inside the studio from the raging heat. Even in the shade, I felt like I was breathing in the hot flames of an open fire. There was no balance in temperature here. It was either a blast of heat that felt like my skin was blistering or a chill that penetrated to my bones. The only time I felt truly comfortable was submerged in the swimming pool or fast asleep, wrapped in soft sheets and blankets.

Ember was already standing behind her easel. Her hair was piled on top of her head, held in place with a large silver barrette. She wore long silver earrings that were a series of flat sticks, moving like shimmering streaks of rain every time she turned her head. Her feet were bare, and she had on a black knit tank dress that hung to mid-calf. It looked like the perfect outfit for being outside in the heat, but I felt cold looking at her. Maybe the effort of sketching kept her warm enough.

I took my place in the chair and rested my feet on the box Bryce had placed there as a makeshift footstool. "Will you be painting today?" I asked.

"More sketches," Ember said.

Already I could hear the charcoal scratching across the paper, small quick strokes, then longer scraping sounds, suggesting she was drawing the outline of me. The not-knowing what it looked like was as tormenting as it was to try to hold myself still. Did she see me as cheerful and interested, or was she making me appear dark and troubled? Some of her paintings had that air, and when I'd viewed them at her main gallery, I'd assumed that was the mood of the subjects. Now, I wasn't entirely sure. Especially after Avery's comment that all the eyes of her subjects had a tinge of madness. I'd meant to look at her small gallery again when I arrived, but I'd been so consumed with thoughts of Colin and Olivia conducting an affair in the home they shared with Ember, I'd forgotten.

Ember stepped out from behind the easel and walked toward me. She touched my temple, moving my hair away from the side of my face. She leaned closer and gazed into my eyes. I blinked. She continued staring at me. I blinked again. She stepped back and studied me.

A moment later, she touched my temple again, as if to move my hair. It surely hadn't fallen across my brow, and I wasn't sure why it needed to be moved.

She returned to her easel.

I sat for a few minutes, trying to steady my breathing, trying not to blink excessively.

Ember hummed softly to herself. The humming stopped, and she walked toward me again. She stopped and touched my face, tucking my hair behind my ear. Her fingers were cool. There was nothing sexual about the way she looked at me or touched me, yet I felt invaded. I felt as if I had no choice but to sit there and be touched, and I didn't want to be touched. There was no reason I could identify. I just didn't like it. I wanted her to stop.

She ran her index finger along the arch of my eyebrow.

Everything I knew about myself and the way I'd been in the world, my autonomy and power, screamed at me that she had no right to touch me. I had no obligation to sit there and allow it. But I couldn't seem to open my mouth and ask her—to *tell* her—to stop.

My breathing was shallow. I wondered if she heard the change, the tiny gasps for air, and then the increase in my pulse as my heart rate accelerated.

She ran her finger over my other brow. She touched the delicate skin under my eyes, causing me to blink furiously, bringing tears to my eyes that blinded me. She stepped back, stared at me until the tears evaporated, then returned to her easel. Always, she was hiding behind her easel so I couldn't see her face or read her expression.

Bryce wasn't looking at us. He was busy writing in his notebook.

For three hours, she sketched, taking frequent breaks to touch my face, my lips, my neck, my ears. My skin crawled, and I wanted to scream, but the longer I said nothing, the more impossible it became to say anything.

She stepped out from behind the easel. She looked at her blackened fingertips, then wiped them on her dress. "That went really well. I think there are enough sketches now." She left, walking down the short hallway that led to her workroom. I heard the door close.

I couldn't say anything to Bryce because I was afraid that if I spoke, I might start crying. I'd never been so exhausted in my life. And ashamed. I was ashamed of myself for saying nothing, and even with that, still uncertain about whether I could have said anything without preventing her from doing what she needed to do to complete my portrait.

"You did a great job." Bryce was standing in front of me, holding out his hand for me to take as if I needed help getting out of the chair. Maybe I did. My legs felt weak. I wasn't sure if propping my feet on the box had somehow slowed circulation to my legs, or if it was my whole body reacting to the assault of Ember's fingers trailing across my skin.

I refused to take his hand. I didn't care if I collapsed at his feet. I wasn't going to be treated like an invalid who couldn't sit in a chair for a portrait for three hours without falling apart. I was a strong person. I was confident and knew what I wanted in life. I wouldn't allow them to turn me into a quivering, questioning victim. Although what I was a victim of, I wasn't sure.

"Are you doing okay?" Bryce asked.

"I'm fine." I shoved myself out of the chair. I ran my fingers through my hair, tugging it gently to feel the power of my own hands touching my head. I twisted my hair into a coil and tucked the end up into a loose bun. It immediately flopped down to my neck, but it felt good to do something to take control of my body.

"Are you sure you're okay? You don't look okay."

"I said, I'm fine." I started toward the door.

"I'll walk back with you."

I opened the door and stepped outside. The air was more pleasant, but only slightly cooler than earlier. I started walking, taking long strides along the pathway.

"You seem really upset," Bryce said.

I stopped and faced him. "I didn't like being touched and I didn't like the unspoken implication that I was supposed to simply take it."

He reached out as if to pat my arm, then seemed to think better of it. With his hand still raised, he nodded. He shoved his hand into his pocket. "I know she can be strange. But she needs to feel your bone structure. And she wants to really see your eyes. I should have warned you. I'm sorry."

"Her subjects need warnings? That sounds a little ominous."

He laughed.

His laughter sounded as if he were trying to appear calm. "My bad. Not a warning. A heads up." He laughed again. "It's good you could remain stoic."

I shrugged. I felt anything but stoic.

"I know Ember can be a little unusual. But it's obvious you're a strong person, that you know who you are. You aren't subject to manipulation."

I appreciated his effort to make me feel better, but I had been manipulated. So I didn't feel stoic or strong. I felt as if she had some kind of control over me and I didn't like it. I'd given it to her. And only because I wanted to make Jade happy. I wondered if Jade had experienced the same things when she'd had her portrait done. I wasn't sure I wanted to ask. It would certainly be a way to get to know her better, but I didn't yet know her well enough to tell her how I'd felt with Ember's hands on my face, as if she owned me. As if she had a right. As if I were part of her art.

We were close to the back patio. I looked at the swimming pool, the water darker as the sun moved closer to the horizon and the house cast its shadow over the pool.

"I hope you'll start enjoying the experience more," Bryce said. "I really want you to have fun with it."

"She's so intense. It doesn't seem like there's anything fun in this at all."

"Again. Wrong word. I guess I mean relish the experience. Drink in every bit of it."

"She's very intimidating and kind of—"

"I know it's uncomfortable having her touch the bones around your eyes. But if you can understand ... I think if people knew the effort she puts into capturing the essence of life that's in the eyes. That spark of life. The passion and sweat and even the agony she pours into her work ... on getting the eyes to come to life ... you'd be ..."

He didn't finish his thought. I didn't really care. I wanted a swim. I wanted to wash the memory of Ember's fingers off my skin.

29

NOW: MORGAN

*I*n my room, I checked my phone. There were several messages from Tyler. I messaged back that I was tired, and it was dinnertime, I'd get in touch later. There was also a message from Zoe Ellis.

Before I could click on it, the door opened.

"How was your sitting?" Jade asked.

I gave her a what I hoped was a confident smile. "Interesting. She's done sketching, so that's exciting."

Jade clapped her hands. "Your portrait will be fabulous. I know you'll love it. So will Tyler." She gave me a hug."

I decided to leave Zoe's message until I was by myself.

After a swim and a shower, I felt mostly normal again and ready to join the others for dinner.

Avery wasn't at the dinner table, so I assumed he was still suffering from his migraine, if that had been the truth. I no longer thought he was a quiet, easy-going kid. He seemed ready to blow at any minute. He clearly did not appreciate his mother's work, and he did feel neglected and was possibly withering in the shadow of her career, no matter what his father believed, or pretended to believe.

The meal was a pork tenderloin dish with wild rice. It was absolutely delicious, and I ate two servings of everything, surprised by my hunger. I also drank three glasses of wine, which helped me look Ember in the eye and smile.

She returned my gaze as if groping my face without my permission that afternoon had been completely normal. She smiled and was more talkative than usual, asking if I swam regularly or was only doing it here because the pool was available. When I told her it was the latter, and that I'd missed swimming once I was out of college and no longer had easy access to a swimming pool, she beamed as if she'd given me the greatest gift imaginable.

Dinner was long and leisurely, followed by a decadent chocolate dessert and coffee. When it was over, Ember announced she would clean up. Colin and Jade went off to play pool, and I darted down the hall to our bedroom.

I grabbed my phone, ignored the messages from Tyler and my best friend. I opened Instagram.

Zoe: *Derek was murdered. No one believed me, so I'm done. Good luck.*

I messaged her back, telling her I needed to know more. I placed my phone beside me on the bed and turned on the sound. I laid on my back and stared at the ceiling, waiting for the phone to ping.

Thirty-five minutes passed before it chimed.

Zoe: *There's nothing to know.*

Morgan: *Would you be willing to talk on the phone?*

Zoe: *Why are you so interested?*

Morgan: *I explained.*

Zoe: *Are you afraid someone might kill you?*

I hadn't been until that moment. I still wasn't even really sure I believed her. That's why I wanted to talk to her. She seemed so certain. But the police had also been certain.

Morgan: *I don't know. It's unsettling here.*

Zoe: *You should leave.*

Morgan: *It's complicated.*

Zoe: *Is it?*

Morgan: *Do you mind giving me your number so I can call you?*

Zoe: *I don't see the point.*

Morgan: *Please?*

Zoe: *What's your number? I'll call you.*

I gave her my number, jumped off the bed, and went into the hallway. Carrying my flip-flops, I hurried down the hall, through the entryway, and out to the courtyard. As I stepped into my flip-flops, my phone rang. I hurried out of the courtyard toward the front of the property. I couldn't go too far or I'd lose the signal that came from a booster device in their house. I stopped near where Jade's car was parked under a covering.

I answered the call from a blocked number.

"Zoe?"

"Yes."

"Thanks. I think I just really need to talk to someone. The portrait is a gift from my mother-in-law and I'm just getting to know her. I don't feel comfortable rejecting her gift and leaving. Besides, she's close with Ember's husband—he's her godson. And there's no way she would leave, so ..."

"Well ... maybe you're safe. Maybe one murder to skyrocket Ember's career was enough."

"Do you really think that's what happened? It sounds horrible. Demented."

"I don't know if that's why," Zoe said. "But that's absolutely what ended up happening, right?"

"That's what everyone says."

"I don't know ..." Her voice caught in her throat. "I don't know why she killed him. I assume it was her. Maybe some weird psychological drama ... She wasn't famous, and she blamed the people in the portraits or something." Zoe laughed bitterly. "When someone you love dies, you get all kinds of ideas going through your head. That's just one of my thoughts. I've had thousands."

"Why are you so sure ... that she ... that someone killed him?"

"Because I *knew* him! We loved each other. We were getting married. He told me everything. I know that sounds like a cliché. Everyone believes that about the person they love, and you don't really know, you *can't* know if someone tells you everything. But I know. The police pretty much laughed in my face. Like how dare I think I know the man I'm marrying. Well, I did. And that's why I wouldn't back down. But I still lost."

"They didn't find any evidence ... I don't know. The note ...?"

"That was another thing. It was crazy. Why would he do that? They said it showed hostility toward Ember. Which was their whole agenda. That he hung himself in her studio because he was angry at her. She fed that story to them. He was so traumatized, so sensitive, some people can't handle the pressure, weak personality ... blah blah, that he interpreted her questions as existential threats. All kinds of bullshit."

"But you're sure he was murdered?"

"I'm not going to talk to you if you're going to argue with me. I *knew* him. Inside and out. The words on that painting were not his words. He wouldn't write those words, wouldn't say that. Wouldn't kill himself. He was full of life. We had plans. He was totally centered. He had a strong sense of himself and knew what he wanted. There is no way in *hell* he killed himself."

"I ... that's terrifying."

"Yeah. So you should leave."

"I'll definitely talk to Jade. It's so difficult because Colin is her godson. Even telling her about this is going to upset her. I'm not sure she'll listen."

"Then maybe you need to take care of yourself."

I sighed. "Thanks for talking to me."

"No worries." She hung up without saying anything more.

I slid my phone into my pocket. I stared down the long driveway that led from Ember and Colin's home to the main road. Finally, the air was a comfortable temperature. The sunset over the desert was quietly spectacular. There wasn't a sound for miles now that I'd stopped chattering on my phone.

The stillness and the orange glow across the inky blue sky should have made me feel peaceful and calm, but instead, it felt threatening. Too quiet. Too isolated.

30

NOW: MORGAN

o escape the desolate feeling creeping over me as the sun slipped lower in the sky, I pulled my phone back out of my pocket and called Tyler. He answered on the half ring.

"Hi, Babe. Finally. For someone relaxing all day, you sure seem busy."

I laughed, but my voice sounded weak and tired.

"Are you okay?"

"I think so. It's ... it's not what I expected. Sitting for a portrait is exhausting." What was also exhausting was the thought of telling him how miserable that day's session had been. I didn't have it in me to describe Ember's fingers creeping around my skin with enough detail to fully communicate my disgust.

"Sitting in a comfy chair for a few hours?"

"With no phone. You could never do it."

He laughed. "You got me. I couldn't."

"And no napping allowed."

"Maybe it is harder than it sounds."

"And someone is staring at you, inspecting every inch of your face, staring at you ... anyway. That's not all that's bothering me."

I told him about my conversation with Zoe.

"Why are you talking to her?"

"Because she was his fiancée."

"Exactly. She's gutted. So she's lashing out. She wants an explanation for something that has no explanation."

"But she knew him better than anyone."

"You don't know that," he said.

"If someone tried to tell me you had killed yourself, I would know without a doubt it wasn't true. So I think—"

"That's morbid," he said.

"I'm just saying—"

"You can't know how well someone knew another person."

"She said …"

He was quiet. I wasn't sure if he was waiting for me to finish, or if he was thinking about what I'd said and realizing I was right. Or maybe he wanted me to stop and think about what he'd said and realize he was right.

"You don't know her. My mom knows Colin. She knows Ember. Are you saying one of them, or someone who lives with them, is a murderer? Because that's what this Zoe is saying."

I closed my eyes, trying to stop my mind from spinning. As much as I believed Zoe knew her fiancé inside and out, I couldn't believe that anyone I knew, even casually, was capable of committing murder. I hated admitting that I wasn't thinking clearly. Maybe the self-conscious discomfort of sitting for the portrait, of having too much free time, and the dysfunctional relationships in Ember's family had twisted my thoughts.

Although Zoe's certainty about Derek's personality and state of mind sounded genuine, her accusation was still outside the realm of anything I could imagine touching my life. Ember was aloof and strange and oppressive, but that was such a long way from what Zoe was suggesting. The same went for the rest of them.

Still, my mind felt like it was splintering. I couldn't quite disbelieve either explanation. I began walking toward the courtyard. "What's going on with you?" I asked.

While he talked about his work, I approached the courtyard door that I'd left open. I stepped inside and closed it behind me. It was dark now. The small lights wrapped around the tree branches and strung overhead filled the courtyard with a magical feeling. I sat on the edge of the fountain and slipped off my flip-flops, pressing my feet onto the terra-cotta tile. It was surprisingly cool.

I realized Tyler had been quiet for several seconds. "Are you really that worried?" he asked. "Do you feel unsafe or something?"

"I'm not sure."

"What does my mom think?"

"I didn't tell her about talking to Zoe. She would never … she adores Colin. You know that. When I tried to talk to her the other day, she didn't want to discuss Derek. She thought it was too upsetting and best left in the …"

I heard the front door close. I turned sharply. I hadn't heard it open. I hadn't been aware of anyone in the courtyard, any feeling of movement behind me. Until now, it had seemed as if the splash of the fountain was quite loud, but the click of the door had been distinct.

I stood.

"In the past?" Tyler prompted.

"That was it. That it was the past, and it had upset them terribly and they wanted to forget all about it."

"Then you should too."

But I couldn't. I just couldn't. It wasn't only because of Zoe. It was the way Hendrix had seemed almost … happy about Derek's death. I didn't get a clear impression that anyone was truly sickened by the fact that his death had dramatically enhanced her recognition, accelerated her career, and made her a much wealthier woman.

"I should go," I whispered.

"Why are you whispering?"

"I didn't mean to."

Tyler laughed gently. "Okay."

There was no one else in the courtyard. The person who had

closed the front door, who had obviously listened in on at least part of what I'd said to Tyler, was no longer there. But it still seemed prudent to whisper. Maybe I was losing my grip.

"You're sure you're okay? If you don't want to do this, you don't have to. Just talk to my mom. She's easy. You know that."

I nodded, forgetting we weren't having a video chat, wishing we had. "I will."

We talked for a few more minutes, whispering now because we were saying goodnight as if our heads were side-by-side on our pillows, murmuring that we loved each other, that we missed each other.

After I hung up, I sat by the fountain for a long time, hoping that when I finally went inside, I would be able to walk directly to the guest room without seeing anyone.

31

NOW: MORGAN

When I finally went inside, I was startled to find Jade sitting alone in the living room. The entryway and the other rooms opening onto it were dark, but a single lamp glowed on the table beside her. She was gazing out the window, appearing to be focused on nothing. All that I could see from where I stood were the strings of lights on the patio that mirrored those in the courtyard. Everything else was covered by darkness.

"What are you doing?" I asked.

"Enjoying the quiet." She continued staring out the window. "You can join me if you'd like. I've probably had enough quiet."

"Do you want something to drink? Tea?"

"You know what would be nice?" she asked.

"What?"

She turned, smiling. "A shot of that really good tequila Colin keeps in the dining room." Noticing my hesitation, she said, "He invited me to help myself."

"Okay."

I went into the dining room and got the bottle. I carried it to the kitchen, took a shot glass and two nice drinking glasses with weighted bottoms out of the cabinet, and poured a careful shot into each glass. I left the bottle on the counter. If Colin was being generous, maybe we would want a second drink.

When I was settled across from Jade, she raised her glass. "To great art."

It was a tired toast because she'd already made it with our wine every night at dinner. I'd thought it was to flatter Ember. Now, I realized it might be coming from her heart.

"To great art," I said.

As I looked at her face, perfectly composed into a friendly smile that looked eager to have a meaningful conversation, I knew I couldn't say anything that was meaningful to me. At least nothing that was meaningful right now. I couldn't tell her how the wife of her beloved godson, the artist she revered, had made me feel assaulted and degraded as she ran her fingers over my face. Not about Zoe or the things Tyler and I had talked about. I couldn't tell her I was conflicted about whether or not one of her close friends was a murderer.

She didn't want to hear it, and she wasn't going to believe any of it. At the end of the day, she and I hardly knew each other. Sure, we'd shared some holidays and quite a few dinners. Jade, Tyler, and I had even spent a weekend together in Carmel. But we weren't close. Our relationship was more superficial than I'd realized. It was fragile enough that I could fracture it with a single word. She was one hundred percent Tyler's mother, Colin's godmother, and I was the outsider. She had deeper feelings for Ember than she did for me at this point.

Jade sipped her tequila. "It gives you such a warm feeling, doesn't it?"

"Yes."

She placed her glass on a coaster and moved forward until she was perched on the edge of the sofa. "Should we sit outside? I know it's still warm, but it feels pleasant in the dark. And there's a bit of breeze. It might feel nice."

I agreed I wouldn't mind escaping the icebox atmosphere. I

wanted to breathe fresh air and look up at the stars. It might clarify my thoughts.

We went to the fire pit and sat on the cushioned wood chairs surrounding it.

"I would love to have a fire just to watch the flames," Jade said. "But we'd burn up." She laughed and took a sip of her drink. "We should have brought the bottle with us."

I assured her it was easy enough to go back for it.

I liked sitting in the near-darkness with nothing but the small lightbulbs strung overhead and the stars twinkling far above them. It felt safer in some ways. Out here, no one could eavesdrop on our conversation without us being aware of their presence. Although I supposed our voices might carry farther than I realized, so it was possible someone was concealed by darkness beyond the edge of the patio and I would never know it.

"I'm so glad I came with you," Jade said. "I worried that I was intruding on something that should belong only to you."

"Not at—"

"But we've hardly seen each other, so I don't feel like the clingy, invasive mother-in-law I was afraid of being. And it's so good to see Colin after all this time. I've missed him so much. I can't tell you what he's meant to me over the years. Being around him for days at a time is not something I've had the honor of enjoying very often. You've given me an incredible gift, and I want to thank you for that."

I cringed. "You're welcome."

"His mother and I were like sisters. When she gave birth to Colin, it seemed like such a miracle to me. She was the first of my girlfriends to have a child and he absolutely took my breath away. The entire process was so miraculous. To see that tiny baby emerge into the world and to know that she, and all the people that knew her, and now him, had a chance to shape his life. What a privilege."

I felt slightly ill, knowing with even greater certainty I couldn't tell her anything that Tyler and I had discussed.

"When I see what an amazing man he's turned out to be, I feel some credit. I shouldn't, but I do. Not a lot. But I was there for his mom, and I spent hours playing with him, talking to him, and so I know I helped create who he is. I'm not delusional—it's so tiny, hardly noticeable, but deep inside him, there are slivers of me, small as they are."

I sipped my tequila. It seemed to be going quickly to my head because her voice sounded as if it were moving away from me.

"Let me get the bottle," she said. "Your glass is empty."

"I shouldn't—"

"We didn't have much. Just a little more."

She disappeared into the house without seeming to even get up from her chair. A moment later, she was back. Without using a shot glass, she refilled both our glasses. "Not too much. But it's nice for a mother and daughter ... in-law ..." she laughed, "Daughter-in-*law* to share a drink."

"Yes."

Her face was distorted, half in shadow, a sharp slice of bright light cutting across the other half.

"What was I saying? Oh. Colin. It's almost as if he's one of mine. Tyler, Grace, Colin. I'm inside all of them. I poured myself into my children because they were all I had. Until Thomas came into my life, of course. I'm a woman with a heart filled with love. I need a lot of love in my life. We all do, but not everyone can admit that."

"Maybe not." I took a tiny sip of my drink.

"I hope you can love me, Morgan."

"I do."

"Over time. You hardly know me now. But you will. And I'll come to know you ... over the years. You need a mother. Because you lost yours. It's such a terrible thing to lose your mother when you're young. The same thing happened to Colin. He wasn't as young as you were, but he was young. And it leaves a scar."

I sipped my drink.

"If your mother were here, I wonder what she would say to you.

About the portrait. About what's coming in your life. Marriage. It's a big step."

I watched her lips moving. I heard the words. Her voice sounded strange in my ears. She didn't sound like herself. Was it the tequila? Had it changed her voice, made her speak differently than she normally did? Or maybe the tequila was affecting me, making me moody and unfocused. Maybe it was the widening gap between her adoration of Colin and my fear of Ember and her family.

It almost seemed as if she could be my mother, as if my mother might be talking to me through her. I did wonder what my mother would say. I wondered what she would think of Tyler. Of course, I assumed she would love him, but how did I know? I hardly remembered her now. I assumed everything about her. But she'd faded into nothing but a memory and sometimes I wondered if she was less than a memory—dissolved into a figment of my imagination.

Jade was real.

"You're a gracious, intelligent young woman, Morgan. You're so successful with your catering business—I admire what you've accomplished. And you're very beautiful. The portrait will capture that, and you'll have it forever."

I swallowed the rest of the tequila all at once, consumed with a shocking, irrational thought that my mother *was* speaking to me through Jade.

My mother had said she loved me, of course. She knew she was dying. I knew too, but I never really believed it. Even though she was so thin and so frail and so weak. I knew, but I didn't know. And then she was gone, and it was too late and I felt as if I forgot all the things she'd said. I thought she'd said she was proud of me. I thought she'd said I would be okay, but had she really?

I looked at Jade's eyes. I couldn't see their color in the darkness and they seemed as if they were my mother's eyes.

3 2

BEFORE: BRYCE

*a*dam had always been smart. I knew that about my big brother when I was a little kid. But lately, my brother sounded both smart and crazy stupid at the same time. For one thing, he was convinced an asteroid was headed straight toward us, and we might as well all be dancing on the deck of the Titanic while its bow was pointed up at the moon for all the concern we were showing about the certainty of our sudden death.

"There are a million of them headed right toward us."

"I don't think we—"

"Stop telling me not to worry!" His voice was so loud, I put my hands over my ears. "Take your hands off your ears! Do you know how condescending you sound? You're too young to know this stuff. If you read more instead of trying to talk to girls all the time, you would have a brain in your head."

My brother was three years older, and he spent a lot of time reading. He had to because he didn't have any friends. He used to have friends. Now, all his friends were online. He spent all his time in his bedroom. It worried my parents, but he told them to get off his back. He said they were ignorant when he talked to them. He only came out of his room for dinner. The past few weeks, he hadn't even eaten with us. He put food on his plate and took it back to his room and ate while he sat in front of his computer. Reading.

"Ninety-eight-point-nine percent of the asteroids near the earth are still undiscovered."

"Then how do you know about them?"

He glared at me. His eyes were almost black, his pupils so large I could hardly see the dark brown of the iris.

"It's an estimate from the European Space Agency."

"But haven't there always been asteroids? You said they have telescopes watching—"

He rolled his eyes. "You would think. There was one they missed completely. It came right at us from the sun. Their super telescopes didn't even catch sight of it until after it passed by and was headed *away* from the earth. So yeah. We might not be around much longer." He rubbed his eyes.

"We can't do anything. So I guess we can't worry about it."

"People who don't worry are ignorant."

"I don't think I'm—"

He rubbed my hair. Then he smacked the top of my head. Really hard. "It's okay little brother. I'll worry for you. For now. And I'll keep you informed."

I wasn't sure if I should be worried about *him*. He seemed a little … not normal. Sometimes he stared at me like he wasn't sure who I was. Other times, it looked like he thought he could read my mind. He was big into people reading minds lately.

He opened his bedroom door when I walked by, whispering my name. "Bryce."

When I asked what he wanted, he told me to shush. He grabbed my arm and pulled me into his room.

"I think they know what I'm thinking when I'm on my computer."

I pressed my teeth into each other, trying to bite down hard. How could he be so clueless sometimes? He was on the computer all the time. He read about technology. I was only fifteen, and I knew how it worked. "No one knows what you're thinking, Adam. They track what you search for and show you ads."

"I didn't search for anything. I was reading about asteroids and I keep getting ads in my email for telescopes!" He grabbed my shoulder. "Let me show you. They must know I was thinking about telescopes. Why would I get that? I never shopped for a telescope."

"But you clicked on articles about—"

"But I didn't shop for a telescope. I only thought about them. How do they know?"

I couldn't make him understand.

My father got irritated. Then he got angry. He told Adam to stop being willfully ignorant. He told him to quit spending so much time on the internet, it wasn't healthy.

But my dad was also willfully ignorant.

It was another eight months before my parents even considered that maybe my brother should see a doctor. And then it took three more months before they could actually get him to *go* to a psychiatrist.

During that time, things got worse. Adam yelled about earthquakes and how unprepared we were. He screamed at my dad that if he didn't get his act together, we would all starve if we didn't die of dehydration first. He put together a list of what was needed for a home earthquake kit and what should be in the trunk of every single car to prepare for the big one. Living in California, we always knew the big one was out there. It was mentioned every few years on the news, but we lived our lives in willful ignorance of that, too. All except Adam. He wanted to be prepared. Maybe he was right about that one.

He took things from my room. Small things. Things that made me think I was the one whose brain was slightly fractured. I would leave a can of soda on my dresser and return to my room five minutes later. The soda would be gone. Thinking I must have left it in the kitchen, I retraced my steps. The kitchen was spotless without a stray, open soda can anywhere in sight. I would walk back to my bedroom and find the soda on my nightstand.

Two days later, I couldn't find the key to my bike lock. I tore my room apart, knowing I'd left it in the wood box on my dresser like I always did. I told my mom I couldn't find it and she complained I wasn't careful with my things. She told me I needed to keep my room cleaner. She told me to look again.

I ended up walking to school. For three days.

On the fourth day, the key was in the wood box where I'd left it.

Adam said he hadn't taken it. My mom said I must have misplaced it. I told her he kept taking things from my room and she told me to stop making wild accusations about my brother. She told me to keep better track of my things and to clean my room.

My parents closed their eyes and pretended Adam was a-okay.

But when he grabbed my arms in the hallway and pushed his face close to mine, staring into my eyes as if he thought he could look right inside my head, I was scared. When I wasn't scared, I was angry at what was happening to him. To all of us.

When he stared at me like that, I wondered if he was begging me to look inside his head and tell him what was going on in there. To explain why he was afraid and why he couldn't stop thinking about things he didn't really want to be thinking about. He wanted to know why he thought about asteroids every single day and the rest of us never gave them a thought. He wanted to know why he believed the people across the street were parking their motorhome at the curb so they could set up surveillance equipment to listen to our conversations and read our email and tap our cell phones. Part of him knew this probably wasn't happening, but another part of him was very, *very* concerned about it.

I just wanted to be a normal fifteen-year-old kid with a normal older brother. I wanted him to move out of our house.

I wanted to run away.

Both of us were trapped. I was trapped by my age, and he was trapped inside his own head.

33

NOW: MORGAN

hen I woke on Thursday morning after drinking tequila shots with Jade, I expected a raging headache. The tequila had seemed to go to my head with far more intensity than I would have expected from just a little over two shots. I'd sipped them slowly, for the most part, but I still felt absolutely ripped when I fell into bed.

Instead of a headache and a queasy stomach, I felt refreshed and full of energy. I decided to go for the early morning walk that I'd vowed to start, but hadn't yet managed. Gray light was seeping into the room, so I guessed it was about six.

I slid out of bed and took my phone off the dresser. Six-ten. I dressed in running shorts and a sports bra, although I had no intention of running. When I'd last checked the weather, it had forecast some cooling, but the temperature was already in the high seventies.

As I started to open the bedroom door, I saw a white card lying on the floor. I picked it up, expecting a reminder for my sitting time that afternoon. The card announced that today was Colin's forty-eighth birthday. A catered brunch would be served in the dining room at eleven that morning. In the afternoon there would be swimming, with mist machines to keep us cool when we weren't in the water. This would be followed by a pool tournament, then a steak dinner that evening.

I propped up the card on Jade's dresser.

All the energy I'd felt when I'd opened my eyes seeped out of my body. Celebrating with their family felt like crashing a private party. I hardly knew them. Why did it have to be the entire day and into the evening? Two extended meals and so much togetherness in between?

I took a deep breath and went out for my walk, trying to shake off the surreal experience of the night before as well as the dread I felt at spending the morning drinking champagne and the afternoon waiting my turn in a pool tournament.

When I returned to our room, Jade was already dressed in a floor-length flowered dress with red high-heeled sandals, eager for brunch and a day-long party.

The dining room had been decorated as if they were expecting fifty guests. There were white and red helium-filled balloons tied to every chair. The sideboard contained a lavish bouquet of red and white roses, and the table was covered with a white tablecloth, set with red plates, red napkins, and champagne flutes with red satin ribbons tied around the stems. The room smelled of roses and something like fresh-cut grass, which was slightly disorienting in the desert setting where I hadn't seen a blade of grass the entire time I'd been there.

No one else had arrived, so Jade and I stood at the entrance, admiring the display and wondering if we were supposed to be seated or wait for the guest of honor.

A woman wearing black slacks and a long-sleeved white shirt walked up behind us and into the room. She went to another side table that had been set up for the occasion. There was a large tub with several bottles of champagne on ice, and more glasses with red ribbons. She filled two glasses and handed them to us. Again, I wasn't sure what was expected. Were we supposed to take a sip? Start drinking without the man we were here to toast?

Jade sipped her champagne. "This is excellent."

"Shouldn't we wait?"

She took another sip. "We don't want it to get warm, or flat."

I raised the glass to my lips. The ends of the ribbon trailed across the back of my hand, making me want to place the glass on the table and rub my hand vigorously to stop it from itching. I took a sip.

Within a few minutes, the others arrived, including Avery, who eagerly accepted his own glass of champagne. Obviously his migraine headache was gone, drinking was allowed, and he wasn't going to school today, either. The longer I was around them, the less I understood this family.

After a while, Ember went to the head of the table and raised her voice above the others. "Happy Birthday to the man who loves me. To the man who has become my muse." She raised her glass. "Cheers!"

I looked at Colin. He seemed to bask in her praise. I didn't think I'd ever heard a birthday toast that was more about the person making the toast than it was about the person being celebrated. I wondered if the glowing look on his face reflected his true feelings. I couldn't imagine feeling good about being called someone's muse, my entire existence buried under another's career and interests. It seemed as if he existed only in her orbit.

As the glow on his face became more pronounced, I realized maybe it wasn't a glow from her toast at all, but the effect of the champagne. The caterer had refilled his glass and before the foam had subsided, he'd already swallowed half the contents.

While we made small talk, the caterers passed platters of bruschetta and grilled baby octopus tentacles. They also served crispy baked phyllo filled with cheese and skewers of the tiniest cherry tomatoes and scallions I'd ever seen. All the while, the champagne flowed. I felt myself getting slightly tipsy. I vowed I wouldn't allow my glass to be refilled, but each time one of the staff passed by, the champagne splashed into my flute before I could move it away.

Jade was laughing and talking to Ember as if they were the best of friends. Bryce had pulled two chairs away from the table. He and Avery were seated knee-to-knee, their heads close together, deep in conversation. Olivia stood near the bifold doors, gazing out at the patio. Her glass was full, and she didn't appear to be taking any of the appetizers that were offered to her or taking any sips from her glass.

I found myself standing beside Colin.

"Happy Birthday." My face felt warm as I spoke, hearing how pedestrian the words sounded, as if I were the most uninteresting conversationalist in the world.

"Thank you."

"Was this a last-minute surprise?" I asked.

"Yes. I had no idea." He gulped his champagne and held out his glass. It was filled within seconds.

"It's a lot to pull together at the last minute."

He shrugged. "Ember has resources. She can usually get what she wants. And she wanted to surprise me."

"I guess she succeeded."

He nodded. "She likes to include the subjects of her art in our family life. She sees all of her life as one big integrated piece of art, so ..."

"It must have been so awful to have one of her subjects die. In her studio."

He took a long swallow of champagne. "I don't like to think about it. No one does."

"Hendrix sure was ... he didn't seem that upset about it."

Colin scowled. He took several sips of champagne. "Hendrix cares about publicity. And revenue."

"You must be thrilled with her success."

"Absolutely."

"Are all her subjects okay with it—Derek's suicide? Do they all know about it? I guess some of them are attracted by it?" I shuddered.

He shrugged. "I don't question them."

"I suppose that might be why Grace left so suddenly. She must not have known, and when she found out … I know how I felt. It's made me feel really uncomfortable. I imagine it might have upset her. Maybe she felt lied to or—"

"I don't want to talk about that tragic …" He turned away abruptly. He took several steps toward the champagne table, pulled a bottle out of the ice, and refilled his glass, taking a long swallow while he still held the bottle in his other hand.

I moved closer to his side. "Tragic? Why is it tragic?"

He took a step back, bumping his elbow on the edge of the ice tub. Champagne splashed out of his glass. Bubbles fizzed across the back of his hand, clinging to his skin before popping. The ribbon was soaked and now hung like a bloody rag from the base of the glass. "Because … because she, uh … she broke off her engagement. She was an emotional mess, so …" He drank his champagne, looking around the room. "I think they'll be serving lunch soon. I'm famished. Champagne makes me hungry."

"Why did you say her situation was tragic?"

"I didn't say anything about her situation."

"It sounded like you were starting to. You said something was tragic. Lots of people break engagements. It's not tragic."

"Poor choice of words. I misspoke."

"I don't know why you would say *tragic*. What else did you mean to say?"

He glowered at me. "Will you let it go? I said I misspoke. This is my birthday and I don't know why you're obsessing about something that's really none of your business. Why do you persist in sticking your nose into other people's lives?" He walked away without waiting for my response.

A moment later, I saw him speaking to the caterer, and a few minutes after that, we were asked to take our seats. Clearly, everyone had had at least one too many glasses of champagne. The

conversation over lunch was loud and disjointed, filled with bois-
terous laughter, and even more champagne.

I could hardly eat. A sick feeling had settled into my stomach.

Zoe had been absolutely certain that Derek was murdered. No
matter how difficult it was to imagine how that might have taken
place, there was no doubt in her mind.

From the moment I'd learned Grace had disappeared and hadn't
contacted her mom or her brother, I hadn't been able to get my
head around it. And now, I found it impossible to believe that Colin
had said something about her was *tragic,* but had used that word
without meaning to.

Was it possible ...? I gulped my champagne, knowing more
champagne would only make things worse. Was it possible Grace
had also been murdered in Ember's studio? The thought was so
chilling I couldn't eat more than a few bites of lunch. After that, I
didn't take another sip of champagne.

34

NOW: MORGAN

*T*he rest of the day-long party fizzled into nothing.
It's possible everyone went to bed with a champagne-induced headache like I had. After lunch, I'd returned to our bedroom, taken off my dress, and slid between the cool sheets. I fell into a deep sleep that lasted until three-thirty in the afternoon.

When I woke, I got up, dressed in jeans and a tank top, and quietly opened the bedroom door. The house was silent. I closed the door, grabbed my phone, and propped my pillows against the head-board. I sat on the bed and called Tyler. Despite my deep sleep and the lack of dreams or any time spent considering my conversation with Colin, I was more certain than when I'd gone to sleep that something had happened to Grace.

At one point a few months earlier, Tyler had casually mentioned that she no longer used social media. But what about her job? I wasn't even sure where she'd been working. I realized I knew almost nothing about her, despite having heard numerous family stories about her during the time Tyler and I had been together. They talked about her as if they were in touch and she was an inte-gral part of their lives. But she hadn't been. Not for the past year.

Tyler answered just as I thought the call might go to voice mail. "Hey. How's the desert?"

"Strange."

"It's a strange place. I guess that's why people see mirages there."

"Maybe. Did you ever report Grace's disappearance to the police?"

"What brought that up again?"

"Did you?"

"I told you, she didn't disappear."

"It seems like she did. No one has heard from her that I'm aware of. It's not normal to take off and not communicate with your family for over a year. It's just not."

He laughed. "You have it all wrong. This is so on-brand for her. I wish you could meet her."

"Well, if she hadn't disappeared, I could."

"She hasn't *disappeared*. I'm pretty sure she's been in touch with my mom."

"She hasn't."

"Hm. Well, like I said, on-brand. When she was fifteen, she disappeared for two months."

"Two months isn't an entire year."

"But she was fifteen. My mom was a mess. I was worried all the time. We did everything we could to try to find her. And yes, we reported it to the police. Immediately. They investigated, searched for her. Checked with all her friends. Everything the cops do when a teenager goes missing."

"What happened?"

"She'd gone to stay with our father. The guy who we hadn't talked to in nine years."

"And your dad didn't tell your mom?"

"That's the kind of guy he is."

"How come the police didn't find her for two months?"

"He was in New York. They called him, asked him if he'd seen his daughter, and that piece of work lied. Because Grace begged him not to tell anyone she was there. Then she got tired of that lifestyle and came back home. Like it was no big deal that she put my mom through all of that."

"And nothing happened to your father? It seems like—"

"My mom would have had to accuse him of kidnapping or something. She was just glad to have Grace back. And she wasn't up for an ugly legal battle."

I tried to remember myself at fifteen. My mom was gone already. I was living with my grandparents. It wasn't perfect. They didn't really know what to do with a teenager, but they knew where I was. Always. They made sure I went to school and did my homework. They drove me where I wanted to go. I couldn't imagine what they would have done if I'd disappeared for two months. I couldn't imagine doing that to them. Of course, my father wouldn't have invited me to go to another state with him and then lied about it. The whole thing was so far outside my experience, it seemed like something that happened in a film.

"Now do you get it?" Tyler asked.

I didn't get it. Not at all. "You're not worried?"

"I'm not. I'm more annoyed than anything. She does what she wants. She's always been like that. There's nothing I can do about it."

"What if she's dead?"

"I don't think she's dead."

"Why not?"

"We would know."

"How?"

"I think we would have a feeling."

"What about her job? Did she quit? Or take a leave? Where was she working?"

"She's an elementary school teacher. She's between jobs. That's why it was easy for her to take the time to get her portrait done. She didn't like the politics at the school where she was teaching and when she got engaged, she decided to take a year off. She would do the portrait, plan her wedding, get married, and then regroup."

"And you don't think it's strange under those circumstances that she broke off her engagement? When her whole life was designed around her marriage plans?"

"Why are you so upset about this? If she was dead, we would *know*. I feel like you're trying to scare my mom, or upset her or something. What's going on with you?"

I let my head sink into the pillows and closed my eyes. My hand ached from holding the phone to my ear and I wished I'd put in my ear buds before calling him. I couldn't think. I had a bad feeling that was growing worse, and I couldn't seem to find the words that would make Tyler feel the same way.

"My mom said Ember was asking Grace a lot of questions about what she wanted in life. That got her thinking she was tying herself down too soon. She's only thirty-two. She decided to travel. To think about what she wanted out of life."

"How do you know that?"

"I guess Colin or Ember must have told her."

"What else?"

"That's all I know. But I wish you would relax about it. It seems as if this place, or the painting, or someone there is making you a little crazy."

"No. And I don't like it that you're calling me crazy for thinking it's really strange for someone to take off like your sister did and no one has heard from her. For over a year!"

He was quiet for so long, I wondered if I'd lost the signal. I moved the phone away from my ear. There was no problem with the signal.

"For most people, maybe it would seem strange. I can see that. But knowing Grace, it's one hundred percent on- brand, like I said. I'm honestly not worried about her. Okay?"

"You don't think you should be?"

"No. The things people do only seem unusual in the context of each person. And for Grace, this doesn't feel unusual. You know how my mom is with me. She's absolutely devoted. Don't you think she'd be concerned if there was something to worry about? Her maternal instinct would tell her if something was wrong."

Jade was a really sweet and caring person. It didn't make sense for her to be so unconcerned about her daughter. I'd just wondered if she was somehow blinded to thinking clearly because she was so devoted to Colin. Because she seemed to think he couldn't do anything wrong. The same went for Ember.

Trying to figure it out made my head hurt. Part of me was screaming that it seemed very likely that two people had been murdered in Jade's studio. Another part of me was wondering why I was thinking about murder and why I was questioning everything people said. Especially Tyler. I loved him. He'd never spoken a single word that made me question his view of reality.

But the one solid feeling inside me was that Colin had said Grace's life was tragic. That was the word that had slid easily off his tongue, the word he'd tried so hard to reel back in. That word had sounded like the most honest thing he'd spoken to me since the moment I'd met him.

35

NOW: MORGAN

*A*fter my phone call with Tyler, I'd found Jade watching TV in the living room. As I'd suspected, the others were all napping off the champagne. Dinner that evening was leftover pasta salad from the lunch. No one mentioned the steak. Everyone ate on their own schedule, sitting at the bar in the kitchen or on the patio after sunset, when it was cool enough to enjoy.

Jade and I both went to bed early without discussing the party. I didn't tell her what Colin had said about Grace. I wanted to, but I knew she would argue even more forcefully than Tyler had that all was normal and fine, to-be-expected and *on-brand*.

The next morning, Colin took Avery to school. Olivia left shortly after to go shopping, and Ember and Bryce went out to the studio, telling me my sitting would be that afternoon.

With Jade lying beside the pool and the house to myself, I decided I would indulge my near certainty that Grace had not simply wandered off to figure out and readjust the rest of her life.

Hoping there were no hidden security cameras, I boldly opened the door to the wing that I'd been told housed Ember and Colin's bedroom, a sitting room, and Colin's home office. I did not know what I hoped to find, and no idea why I thought I would find anything at all, but I was more than a little curious about why that section of the house was closed off. It made sense they wanted some privacy with a constant parade of strangers through their home. But they didn't offer that privacy to their son. So what was different about this wing of the house?

Directly across from me was Colin's spacious home office. To my right was a short hallway. I turned and walked into a massive bedroom with a walk-in closet and a palatial bathroom that included his and hers showers, a jacuzzi tub, and a small steam room. None of the artwork in their bedroom was Ember's. There were tapestries, carved wood pieces, and several photographs of the Grand Canyon, Monument Valley, and other landmarks from the southwest.

I walked back past the sitting room to Colin's office and went inside.

My immediate impression was that it belonged to someone meticulous and analytical. A man who did not consider himself an artist. The walls were decorated with the framed floor plans of houses Colin's company had built. The desk was completely empty except for a black notebook and an expensive-looking pen. One wall was consumed by a huge bookcase filled with books on home design, construction, landscaping, and history. Like the master bedroom, there was a large picture window offering a spectacular view of the desert.

Behind the desk was a matching oak credenza. I went to that first. It was locked. I turned to the desk and opened the center drawer, hoping to find a key. The drawer was as neatly organized as the rest of the room, containing mechanical pencils, drafting notebooks, and other office supplies. I found the same anonymous contents in the drawers at the side of the desk.

Obviously, I hadn't expected to find frayed rope left from hanging Derek or some other horrific object that would tell me Colin was murdering his wife's subjects to bring scandalous attention to her career. Maybe I had it wrong. Maybe, despite the animosity I felt toward him, he was the incredible man Jade believed him to be. His bothersome conversation might have been the result of having been turned into a muse against his will.

I closed the drawer and stepped away from the desk. I turned slowly, taking in the room, thinking about Colin and his blatant desire for me to believe he and his son were wholehearted supporters of Ember's art, while Avery hunkered down in his room, whispering about how her paintings gave him the creeps.

I still couldn't get that word out of my mind. *Tragic.*

I moved back to the desk and opened the drawer again, lifting out the notebooks to see if there might be a key underneath. There wasn't.

I couldn't spend much more time. Usually Colin stayed in Palm Springs until Avery was out of school, but I had no idea how long Olivia would be out of the house, or how much time Jade would spend by the pool. Bryce or Ember might return and catch me stepping into the entryway. Closing the door to the hallway had been a mistake. Now I had no way of knowing what I would face when I opened it.

Everything was so neat, so perfect. Even the books on the shelves had their spines lined up in perfect order. The untouched nature of his possessions, the lack of any suggestion that Colin worked or spent time in this room, made me feel as if there had to be something. Even if there was nothing to tell me about why he considered Grace's life tragic, there had to be a clue to what kind of man he was, something that would help me understand what was going on in this house, this family.

I wasn't sure why I'd fixated on him. Everything revolved around Ember. Why were my thoughts centered on Colin? Possibly because he was the one who captured Jade's devotion. He was the one who would prevent her from leaving, and as long as she didn't sense any danger, I couldn't very well leave her here on her own. Maybe my thoughts focused on him because I felt that he'd lied to me. Ember was cool and standoffish, but she seemed honest about who she was. Colin had cheated on his wife, and was still inappropriately affectionate toward his sister-in-law, despite claiming he'd ended their relationship. The picture I had of him and the awe Jade felt for him were miles apart.

I crossed the room and stood in front of the bookcase. I ran my finger along the almost silky wood of the shelf in front of me. Several shelves contained other decorative objects—small glass vases with swirls of color, a few picture frames with candid shots of Ember, Avery, and other friends and relatives.

Taking a step back, I looked at the shelf just above eye level. A dark brown pottery bowl partially blocked another framed photograph. I stood on my tiptoes and pulled it out. It was a photograph of Jade when she was about fifty. Standing beside her with their arms around her waist were a teenaged Tyler and Grace.

It seemed strange to find it behind the bowl, almost as if the bowl had been deliberately placed in front of it. There was nothing in the photograph that suggested it was a picture he no longer wanted to look at. And if there was, why not just put it in a drawer? Why not get rid of it?

I turned it over. Taped to the back was a small key.

My heart thudded against my bones as I peeled the key off the back of the frame. I crossed the room, shoved the key into the credenza lock, and felt it click into place. I turned it and pulled open the top drawer. The only thing inside was a shoebox. I took it out and removed the lid.

Inside the shoebox was a lacy, pale gray bra. On the upper edge of the right cup was a dark, reddish brown stain. I knew, without pausing to think, it was blood.

It could be anything. It could be rust. It could be paint. But my first unfiltered thought was blood. And once the thought was there, I couldn't see anything else.

I shoved it into the waist of my jeans, put the lid on the shoebox, returned it to the credenza, and locked the drawer. I took a fresh piece of tape from the dispenser in Colin's desk and taped the key to the back of the picture frame, placing it on the shelf with the bowl in front of it.

My hands were damp and trembling slightly as I closed his office door and stepped into the hallway. I stood by the door leading to the entryway, afraid to open it. I had no idea who might be on the other side. I'd been so fixated on my search, and what I'd found, I'd been oblivious to any sounds coming from other parts of the house. It felt as if all I'd heard for the past twenty minutes was the sound of my own breath, the thud of my heart beating too hard.

If anyone was out there, I could say I was overcome by curiosity about the other wing of the house. No one could argue with that. They might be angry or consider me rude, but no one would know what I'd found. The only people I might meet would be Jade, Bryce. or Olivia. There was no chance Colin had returned in the middle of the day.

I pulled open the door and felt my body relax as I looked across the deserted entryway, turned, and saw the darkened kitchen and dining room, the empty living room.

I stepped into the entryway, closed the door behind me, and nearly ran to the guest room. I went into the bathroom and closed the door. I pulled the bra out of my waistband and tucked it into my cosmetic bag. I had no idea what I was going to do with it.

36

NOW: BRYCE

*M*organ hadn't shown up for lunch. Ember was concerned because sitting for a portrait on an empty stomach leads to fainting. It happens every time. She told me to cut short my own meal and find out where she'd gone, to make sure she had something solid to eat.

Repeated knocking on the guest room door got me nowhere. She wasn't in the poolroom and we'd already seen from the dining room that she wasn't anywhere on the patio or in the living room. I went out to the courtyard. It was quiet and peaceful in the midday heat, the splash of the fountain the only sound.

I returned to the house and walked through to the patio. I shielded my eyes from the sun and looked toward the cactus garden. It was possible she'd gone to the studio, but her sitting wasn't for several hours. I began walking along the path. I peered around the garden wall. The iron table and chairs were empty. I walked through the walled area to the other side.

I went to the studio and opened the door. The room was quiet and cool when I stepped inside. "Morgan?"

There was no answer, but I heard the soft tap of canvases being moved coming from the storage room. I hurried down the hall.

Morgan stood with her back to the doorway. She was looking through Ember's unfinished and discarded paintings, experimental works and other pieces that hadn't yet been framed for hanging in the gallery.

"What are you doing?"

She answered without turning to look at me, continuing to move the canvases. "I'm looking for Grace's portrait."

"Why do you want to see it?"

"I need to refresh my memory of what she looks like now."

"Why?"

"Because I want to see it."

I walked into the room and put my hand on the edge of the painting she was moving. "Please stop touching the paintings."

"I'm not hurting anything."

"I told you, Grace's portrait was never finished."

"I don't care. I want to see it."

"Please stop. This is Ember's space." I took her forearm and pulled her gently away.

"Let go of me."

"Please come out."

"No. I …"

"What's going on? You look upset."

"I think Grace is …"

"What?"

She shook her head. "I don't know. I just want to see her portrait. I don't understand what happened to her and I'm—"

"Why are you so concerned about Ember's other subjects? You should be focused on your own portrait."

"Because it feels like people die or disappear here."

"Why didn't you eat lunch?"

"Because I need to see that painting. Let me look at the rest of these."

"Ember doesn't like people to see her unfinished work."

She looked like she was going to start crying. Or screaming. I wasn't sure which. I tried touching her arm, stroking it gently to calm her.

"Stop touching me!"

"I just ... are you okay?"

"No. I'm not okay. I told you—"

"You've let one upsetting, very sad situation get to you and it's making you imagine all kinds of things."

"I'm not imagining anything. I found something that I think belongs to Grace, or maybe I should say, it did belong to Grace. Because I think she's dead."

I swallowed. It wasn't surprising she'd come to that conclusion, since it was clear no one had heard from Grace in over a year. At the same time, there was no evidence to suggest she was, starting with the fact that no one had found her body. It seemed as if Grace had evaporated into the desert as quickly and completely as a few drops of water disappear from the surface of a rock when the temperature rises to over a hundred degrees.

"Why do you think she's dead?"

"Because of what I found."

I stared at her horror-filled eyes. I wondered if she'd stumbled across a makeshift grave, or had she simply found something Grace left in the guest room.

"It's too awful. And I can't really say where. But ..."

She paused, looking at me as if she wanted to pry open my skull and look around inside my head, trying to figure out whether or not she could trust me. She looked so scared, I felt sorry for her. At the same time, after living with my brother, I'd grown a thick skin around people who were consumed by fear. Looking at Morgan, I knew how she felt. For not being on the earth very many years, I had a lot of reasons not to trust people. I couldn't think of very many who hadn't disappointed me in one way or another.

"I found a bra. With blood on it. I wanted to see her portrait because I wanted to get an idea of what her body is like ... was like, if that's what this is. To see if it might be her size. I mean ... it's definitely not Olivia's or Ember's. I've seen photographs of her, but it's been a while and … I don't know." She closed her eyes and tilted her head back.

"Where did you find it?"

"I can't say." She lowered her chin and opened her eyes. "I just can't. Not right now."

"Okay. And why do you think there's blood on it?"

"It's blood. It's obvious."

I nodded slowly, trying to decide what I should say. But first, I needed to get her out of Ember's supply room because Ember would not be happy at the intrusion into a place she considered extremely private. "Let's go into the studio where we can talk."

She followed me willingly, the first willing thing she'd done in a while.

I took the chair she usually occupied for her sittings and gestured toward the wicker chair I usually sat in, thinking it would make her feel more at ease. She needed to calm down. A change of roles might help.

Apparently, it did, because she started talking so fast, I didn't have time to think.

"Okay. I'll tell you. I went into Colin's office. I know I shouldn't have, I know. It was wrong, but I don't trust him and I … I'm not even sure why, or what I thought I was going to find. But now, I think he tried to seduce her. I think she rejected him and they struggled. She tried to fight him off, and he hurt her … he killed her. Maybe it was an accident. But I think she's dead." She started crying.

I gripped the armrests, trying to figure out what to say. My job was to keep her calm and focused on sitting for a portrait. Ember hired me to help organize her subjects and her supplies, to take notes when she had flashes of inspiration she wanted to capture, even to make occasional sketches to jog her memory. But since her career had exploded, the majority of my time had been spent on the first part—keeping her subjects focused and calm, helping them reflect on their lives and be responsive to Ember so she could draw out their feelings through their facial expressions and body language.

Every time I saw Morgan, she was more upset, less focused. Truthfully, she *was* focused, but on the wrong things. She seemed to feel a connection of some kind to her predecessors.

"It's hard to imagine Colin killing someone," I said carefully.

"Situations get out of control."

"True. But there's not anything to suggest she's dead."

"It's her bra! With blood on it."

"You don't know for sure ... what are you planning to do?"

"I don't know. I should call the police. But Jade ... I probably shouldn't have taken it. I should put it back, but then how would the police find it? Now, no one would believe I found it in his office. And if I put it back ..." She put her hands over her face. "I should have thought this through. I was so shocked and upset, I just took it."

"It's a terrible thing to accuse someone of murder," I said. "And there's no body. You don't really know what happened. It could be a lot of things. If he killed her, why would he keep it? You should be sure before you say something you'll regret."

She stared at me for several seconds.

"Why don't you come back to the house and have something to eat," I said. "You need to think, and you have your sitting. All of this talking about death is making you so upset. Try to put it out of your head just for a while. Enjoy sitting for your portrait and give some thought to it later. When you're not so upset."

She continued to stare at me. Finally, she nodded slowly.

She stood and started toward the door. I followed her out. We walked back to the house in silence, but I didn't think she was any calmer.

37

NOW: MORGAN

I sat in the chair, knowing that what was happening inside me did not match what was showing on my face or in my posture. I knew my shoulders were relaxed because Bryce had massaged them slightly until I felt the muscles ease under the pressure of his fingertips. I knew I had a pleasant expression on my face because I'd plastered it there. I knew I was staring, blinking infrequently, because my mind was racing at such a furious pace, it felt disconnected from the rest of my body, which was left feeling as if it were suspended in a jar of oil, hardly moving.

Now that Ember had finished her sketching, I no longer heard the scrape of charcoal. The brush on the canvas was silent. I imagined the liquid flowing across the white, the colors that captured my skin tone and hair, the blue top I was wearing, the shadows on the sides of my face and neck, the light in my eyes.

"Tell me why you fell in love with Tyler," Ember said. "Just one thing. What's the one thing that makes you love him?"

I froze. I wasn't sure I could answer the question. My mind was suddenly empty. Love seemed impossible to define. How could anyone list the attributes that caused them to love another human being? Doing so turned their loved one into a cardboard figure. Choosing only one thing made it feel like a test. If I mentioned something superficial, did I truly love him? If I named an attribute that turned out to be selfish because it was tied to something he did for me, or a way he made me feel, like the fact that he listened to me, did that mean I didn't love him at all?

Was this what she'd done to the others? Asked questions that sounded mundane on the surface, but because you were being watched and scrutinized, caused you to overthink everything? Had questions like these caused Grace to feel weak and therefore vulnerable to Colin?

"Your eyes aren't reflecting a woman who's deeply in love," Ember said.

"I love Tyler with all my heart." My voice sounded weak and pleading. There wasn't anything in my tone that suggested my words were true. "The one thing that makes me love him is his kindness."

"How has he shown that?" She fired back so fast, her question felt like a slap across my face. Before I could think of a way to respond, she continued talking. "Your eyes are angry and confused. Is that how you want to be reflected for the rest of your life and beyond? Oil paintings can last for hundreds of years. The purpose of this is to capture your essence and help you live on. The eyes of a young woman at the prime of her life, on the verge of marriage, should be saying something else. Are you afraid you don't really love your fiancé?"

"You don't know what I'm thinking."

As she'd been speaking, I could see the end of her paintbrush moving. Bryce sat motionless in his chair, his attention on what Ember was doing.

"There's a reason it became a cliché that the eyes are the windows to the soul. The eyes of my subjects make my work stand out. The eyes in my paintings have made me famous. Without the life in the eyes, a painting doesn't look like a human being. It can look as if the subject is dead. Did you see the example in my private gallery?"

I nodded, afraid that if I spoke, my voice would tremble.

"Our eyes reveal who we are. Think about Tyler. Think about when you first met. Don't try to answer my questions. Just think about him. Think about your feelings. Relax into them. Can you do that for me?"

I nodded. I felt like a child, sent to her room for being disobedient. Had my mother ever done that? I couldn't remember. The tiny, daily memories of living with my mother had been blurred beyond recognition when she got sick. When I did have memories, I could never be sure if they were real or if they were things I wanted to have happened, things I'd wished had happened. Or things that I saw in other families and assumed had been the same in ours. Because it was so hard to remember my mother as a living, vibrant person.

I started crying.

Immediately Bryce was out of his chair and standing beside me. "What's wrong?"

"She wasn't thinking about Tyler, that's for sure." Ember placed her brush in a jar, the brush thick with dark brown paint. "Let's take a break." She walked out of the room.

"Why are you crying, Morgan? Did you and Tyler have a fight?"

"No. I was thinking about something else."

"You shouldn't do that."

I laughed. "I can't always control the direction my thoughts take. Is that part of the sitting too? I can't blink, must only think pre-selected thoughts, must have a perfectly straight yet relaxed posture? Anything else?"

"I know it's hard," he said.

I laughed. He kept assuring me he knew how difficult this was. Did he really? Had he ever done it? I knew he was on my side, even so, a little recognition that I wasn't a professional model would be nice. If Ember was really that great, maybe she should be able to paint without torturing her subjects into unnatural positions. Maybe she should be able to work with a normal, casual pose in an armchair.

"Don't be angry," Bryce said.

"I'm not."

Ember returned. She stood a few feet away and looked down at me. "Feeling better?"

I gave her a tight smile.

She moved closer. Her skirt brushed against the bare skin of my knee. I pushed it away.

She stepped to the side and placed her hand on my head, lacing her fingers through my hair. "I didn't mean to upset you, Morgan. I need to connect with my subjects. We need to be intimate with each other. I need to feel what you're feeling so I can capture the essence of who you are. Do you understand that?"

"I ..."

She took her hand away from my head and moved to the front of the chair, facing me. She took my chin and lifted my head until I was forced to look directly at her.

"My subjects need to yield themselves to me. It can be uncomfortable for some people. But I need to feel your heartbeat and your breath. I need to see in your eyes what's going on inside. I need to know ..." She pressed her other fists against her chest. "...I need to *know* that what I see in your eyes is the same thing I'm hearing in your words."

Her grip on my chin tightened.

I twisted my head, but her fingers were strong.

"Let go. You're hurting me."

"I will. But I need you to understand. My art can't breathe without its subjects. And you wanted to be one. I hope you see the honor in that. I'm pouring my soul into making you come to life on the canvas. Everything I am. While I'm painting you, nothing else and no one else exists."

Her grip on my jaw loosened, but I found myself unable to turn my head, as if her eyes held mine locked into hers.

"Only you," she said. "My heart and every ounce of passion I have belong to you, my subject. A unique creature in this universe."

Slowly, her hand fell away from my face, but I continued looking at her.

She did love her work more than her family. I should understand why her husband and her sister had an affair. I could see how it must be for him. For Avery. Even for Olivia. No one else existed for Ember but the people she was painting.

She called us her subjects as if she were our queen.

38

NOW: MORGAN

As soon as Ember told me we were finished, I'd rushed out the door as if running for my life. Again. Maybe I was. Bryce called after me, but I ignored him and kept moving—out the door, across the patio, and along the pathway back to the house. I went to our room and changed into a comfortable dress. I put my hair up in a messy bun, slipped into flip-flops, and grabbed my phone. I stopped by the kitchen for a bottle of sparkling water and went out to the courtyard.

I'd come to love sitting out there. Even though it was hot, sitting beside the fountain felt refreshing as the mist of the water drifted across my skin. The stillness of the air and the sound of the falling water calmed me.

I tapped Tyler's number and waited for him to answer. It was just past five, and he didn't normally have meetings after that time, so I could count on him being at his desk. Alone.

When he answered, I talked over him as he tried to tell me he missed me and loved me.

"I found a woman's bra with blood on it locked in a credenza and I'm almost positive it belonged to Grace. I feel terrible saying this to you, but I'm scared that she's ... I think she's dead."

"What?"

"I know how awful that sounds. But why haven't you heard from her in so long? Not a single message. Nothing. No posts on social media. Something is really wrong. I think in your gut you must know that."

"I don't. I've already explained—"

"No one cuts off all communication with their family for no reason. If you'd told me you had a massive fight, I might believe it. If she had a falling out with your mom and she was cutting you out of her life too, I might believe it. But not this."

"But she took all her stuff. Her cell phone still receives messages because I sent a few, so she's paying the bill. And—"

"Maybe her bills are on autopay. And if she had enough savings—"

"Colin told my mom she … have you talked to my mom about this?"

"No."

"Why not?"

"Because I don't—"

"That's right. Because she wouldn't believe it for a minute. Because she knows Colin and Ember. They're part of our family. I don't get what's happening to you there. I feel like … the point is, she's not dead. It's not possible. Where's her body? You found a bra? How do you even know it's hers? And stashed where? How would she be dead? She was staying in a house full of people. Just like you are."

I took a slow, deep breath. I wanted to keep my voice calm. I didn't want to sound hysterical. I knew what I was saying sounded a little out there. "I think maybe you're in denial. I'm not saying you're deficient or something. It's part of grief."

"I know that."

"I really think you're in denial. It's so obvious that something is wrong and you can't deal with the horror of it, so your brain is categorizing it as part of her normal behavior. But it's not. Going to stay with your biological father when she was a teenager without telling you is not at all the same as completely disappearing for this length of time."

"I think the intensity of sitting for this portrait is getting to you. I'll admit, Grace's lack of communication is weird. And from what you've said, I'm starting to get worried. My mom is probably more worried than she's saying. But to jump from that to being dead? It's so … where did you find this bra? It could belong to anyone. Ember. Her sister. A hundred other guests."

"It was hidden in a box in a locked credenza."

"How did that happen … that you were opening a locked credenza? Where?"

I sighed. "In Colin's office. He was obviously hiding it. He went to a lot of trouble to hide it." I told him about the shoebox and explained where I'd found the key.

"Why were you snooping through his office? Why were you even in his office?"

"Because something doesn't feel right. A man died here. Remember?"

"Yes, I remember. Because you keep telling me about it."

"Why are you acting like none of this matters?"

He was quiet for a few seconds. He cleared his throat. "I don't like it that you're so upset. And I'm not sure what to do. I agree there are some disturbing things, but I have to come back to the fact that Colin is part of our family. My mom has known him all her life. She adores him."

I laughed sharply. "So I've noticed."

"Okay, yes, she's infatuated with him. With both of them. I get that. But he's a good guy. He's not a killer, for crying out loud. If that's what you're implying."

"He might not have done it on purpose."

"God, Morgan. Listen to what you're saying."

Even though his voice was getting louder, I kept mine soft. I was alone in the courtyard. All the windows facing the courtyard were closed, but after the last time, I needed to be careful. I was seated so that the front door was squarely in my view, but still. "Maybe he came on to her and she said no and he wouldn't listen. Ember acts like her subjects are almost her lovers and—"

He laughed. "Are *you?*"

"Of course not. In her mind, I think she feels that way. I'm not sure if she realizes that or not, but she talks like they are. Maybe he was jealous and he … I don't know. If he assaulted her and it got out of control and he killed her."

"First, that bra could belong to anyone. And without a forensic test, you don't even know if it's blood. Maybe it's a keepsake from his past. Who knows? It could be anything. You didn't belong in his office, and you sure shouldn't have been looking for a key to a locked cabinet."

"But why did he tape it to the back of a picture frame? And one that includes Grace?"

"I have no idea. But that doesn't make him a killer." He cleared his throat again. "Do you want me to come stay there with you?"

I wasn't sure if I felt love in his offer or something else. "I don't need rescuing."

"I'm worried about you."

"You should be worried about your sister."

"If you think someone in that house is a killer, then I should be worried about you. And my mom."

"Like I said, maybe it was a situation that got out of control. But something happened to your sister and I'm going to find out what, but I don't need someone holding my hand."

"I don't want you to feel unsafe."

I put my hand under the water. It was cool on my wrists. The fountain and flowering trees had a way of making the courtyard feel like the most pleasant, temperate part of the estate.

I changed the subject to his work. I told him nothing about the sitting and the details of what Ember had said to me. Maybe I needed to stick to text messages for a day or so. I was making him upset, but there wasn't really anything he could do. He was definitely in denial, although not as deeply as his mother.

I didn't feel unsafe. But I didn't feel particularly safe either. By the time our call ended, I wasn't sure what I was feeling.

39

BEFORE: GRACE

*M*y mother was obsessed with me sitting for this portrait. She promised I would love the experience, but since I didn't believe her, she'd promised that if I did it, I could have the destination wedding I wanted. It made me feel like her decorative little doll.

Mostly what she wanted was to make her virtual son happy. I shouldn't have called Colin her virtual son, but that's how she treated him. Even though we didn't see him a lot when we were growing up, we heard about him all the time. His amazing mother. Her best friend. Her brilliant, talented, underrated friend. The most amazing woman she'd ever known. Her beloved friend who was killed in a car accident, so my mother became Colin's surrogate mother. Except Colin was like twenty when his mom died. I don't think he really needed a mom anymore.

It wasn't as if I resented him or was jealous of him. I was just a little tired of hearing how awesome he was. It didn't bother Tyler at all. It should have bothered him more since she acted like she had two sons. I was her only daughter. Why did I feel squeezed for space?

I didn't, really. I just got tired of hearing about him. That was all.

It was boring. Colin and his brilliant wife. Maybe I was equally tired of that. And now I had to sit all day and listen to his supposedly brilliant wife complain about *how* I was sitting, asking me questions that made me doubt every decision I'd ever made.

Well, just one, really.

My decision to get married.

Her *Muse*, Bryce, or whatever he was supposed to be, was carrying on a whispered conversation with Ember the entire time she was painting. It was driving me mental. He was talking to her in a low tone, just loud enough that I could hear her voice and the whisper of his responses, but not loud enough for me to pick out a single word either of them spoke. It was right on the edge of my hearing. So close that I kept thinking I'd deciphered a word, and then realized I hadn't after all. So I kept straining, forcing myself to listen. Their voices were loud enough that I couldn't ignore them either.

I wanted to scream at them to stop. They were clearly talking about me. First of all, because I could feel it in the way they looked at me, feel it in the way they paused, and the glances they exchanged with each other. But also because he would whisper, she would reply, they would repeat this, and then a few seconds later, he would ask me a question.

Why did I love Michael?

What single trait made me fall for him?

Why had I decided to get married?

How did I know he was the one?

Did I believe there was only one true mate for each person on the planet?

Then there would be more whispering, some silence, and another question.

What did I want most out of life?

Would I leave my future husband if he cheated on me?

What if he cheated on me before marriage?

Would I ever cheat on him?

How did I feel knowing I would never experience another man again, that I would go to my grave not knowing what it was like to be with any other man after Michael?

How did I deal with the uncertainty of not knowing what might happen in my life, while locking every piece of my future into an assumed certainty?

The questions wore me out. Some of them were unanswerable. Some of them fell into the category of overthinking things, and getting married was not something I wanted to overthink.

Now, it was about to get a whole lot worse.

"Will you look out the window, please?"

It wasn't a request. I turned my head slightly.

"Don't turn your head so much."

I moved it back.

"That's right. Widen your eyes."

I widened them as best I could. I felt them burn with the effort. I blinked away the resulting tears.

"Please don't blink."

"Sorry."

"You blinked again."

"I didn't."

"You did," Ember said. She stood and came toward me. She placed her fingertips on the tops of my cheekbones, pressing gently. "That's right," she said. "No blinking."

"I have to blink once in a while."

"I need to see your eyes. I need to look deep inside you. The constant blinking is a distraction."

I glared at her, widening my eyes, hoping they bulged out, even though I knew that was impossible. I wasn't an animated character.

"Perfect," Ember said.

"Why are you making this so hard?" I asked.

"Calm down," she said. "I didn't mean to upset you." She stroked the side of my face. A chill ran down my neck. I shivered. My body trembled, and another chill followed the first.

"Are you okay?" she asked.

"What's going on?" Bryce asked.

"She's upset."

"Do we need a break?"

"I'd rather push through," I said.

"Then you need to relax. And stop batting your eyes." Ember returned to her easel.

Bryce laughed gently. "Why are you so nervous?"

"I'm not."

"Should I rub your shoulders?"

"No." I tipped my head to the side and pulled gently, stretching my neck. I did the same on the other side.

"Let's try again," Ember said.

I stood suddenly. "Is it always like this? Thousands of people have their portraits painted. I've never heard of it being a form of torture. Why can't you just paint and pay attention to my eyes in the moments when I'm not blinking? You're making me feel like I'm in a straitjacket."

"Please calm down," Bryce said. "You're the one making this more difficult than it needs to be."

"I don't understand all the questions and all the contortions. Maybe I should just get some professional photographs and call it a day."

I heard a tiny intake of air from behind the easel.

I felt a rush of pleasure that I'd offended or insulted Ember. Maybe both. The idea of an oil painting was cool. And there was something mesmerizing about her portraits. I loved looking at the one of my mother. It was part of the reason she'd finally talked me into this. But it truly was torture, and I wanted it to be over.

"Maybe you're not cut out for this." I heard the tap of Ember's brush stick as she placed it in the jar. She stepped out from behind the easel. "I'm going to take a break. If you can get her calmed down, Bryce, that will be great. But right now, we're wasting time."

She walked over to the chair where I was sitting. "The eyes are

179

everything, Grace. Don't you know that? Even in a photograph, the eyes are what draw people into the image. The eyes are what make people feel a connection with the person they're looking at. You can either participate in this work of art or not. Your choice."

She walked out of the room.

I stared after her. Who the hell did this woman think she was? Michelangelo? The room was utterly silent. I could feel Bryce looking at me. Feel the closeness of him, almost touching me, studying my face.

I realized I hadn't blinked for several very long moments.

I wanted to laugh.

40

NOW: MORGAN

*J*ade and I emerged from our room the following morning expecting breakfast in the dining room as we'd had most days. Instead, we found the room table pushed against the wall, set up with warming trays and platters awaiting food, stacks of paper plates and fans of turquoise paper napkins. The table and ice tub used for Colin's birthday had made another appearance. The tub was filled with twelve bottles of champagne.

The artwork had been removed, and two portraits by Ember were hung on the wall facing the table. Small lights were attached to the frames that gave an eery glow to the paintings, even in the morning light that filtered through the bifold doors.

As we stood in the entryway, I glanced toward the living room. It had also been rearranged. Some of the furniture had been removed and small groupings of wood folding chairs had been set up. There were also three tall cocktail tables.

Bryce walked out of the kitchen and saw us standing in numb confusion. "Did you have breakfast?"

"Another party?" Jade asked.

"Ember's reception. It's the five-year anniversary of her opening at Hendrix's gallery. Didn't she tell you?"

"How exciting!" Jade rushed toward the dining room. "Are these the first portraits that she had displayed there?"

"I don't know," Bryce said. "You'll have to ask Hendrix. He's around somewhere."

It was only seven-twenty in the morning. I couldn't believe all this decorating and setting up had happened without us hearing furniture being moved or voices as chairs were carried through the courtyard.

We grabbed mugs of coffee, cups of yogurt, and berries from the kitchen and retreated to our bedroom to eat.

Cars began arriving for the reception in the late afternoon. The gong of the doorbell echoed constantly as past buyers and potential future buyers flowed through the courtyard and up to the majestic front door. It seemed like a lot of activity, but in the end there were only about thirty or forty people. The house and patio were large enough to accommodate them easily. The hum of conversation and quiet background music of harps was soothing and pleasant.

Once again, caterers had taken over the task of pouring champagne and serving appetizers, leaving Ember and her family free to mingle with collectors, some of whom appeared to be friends.

The moment I saw Colin, I felt a wave of uneasiness pass through me. I placed my champagne flute on the table behind me. I pressed my hand on my breastbone and swallowed, tasting bile. I thought about the blood-stained bra. I thought about the sister-in-law I was now certain I would never meet.

I felt another surge of nausea as I tried to imagine what had happened to her body. She must be somewhere on the estate. Or out in the endless dry landscape that stretched around us without a sign of human life in any direction. Maybe her bones were bleaching in the sun just beyond the point we could see from the back patio. I gripped the edge of the table and took a few steps toward a chair, sitting down heavily. I rested my head in my hands.

I felt someone touch the back of my shoulder.

"Are you okay?" Bryce asked.

I nodded carefully, not wanting to upset the delicate balance inside my body.

"Too much to drink?"

I gave him another single nod of my head.

"I'll get you some water."

"Thanks." My voice was a hoarse, faint whisper. I lifted my head slowly and watched him walk quickly toward the kitchen.

After drinking half a glass of water, I felt better.

"Something to eat?" Bryce stood in front of me, his face creased with worry.

"I'm fine. I just needed water. Thanks." I took a few more sips to enhance my lie. There was nothing wrong with my body. It was all inside my mind. But the pictures I was painting inside my head seemed more real than anything I saw around me. They were certainly more believable than anything I'd been told by the people who lived and worked in this gorgeous, but blood-chillingly cold house.

I made small talk with Bryce until the creases faded from his face and he wandered off to mingle with other guests.

Now that my stomach had stabilized, I was determined to upset the status quo. I refused to be the only one feeling sickened by the situation. They all acted as if a man's death and a woman's disappearance were mildly unfortunate accidents that were easily forgotten.

Talking to Avery seemed like the best way to poke around and stir things up. Listening to his grievances the day he'd stayed home claiming a migraine, I'd realized he was somewhat short-tempered. He argued easily, saying exactly what he thought, once he was enticed into speaking his mind.

He was standing in the corner of the living room, looking trapped. I stood, finished the water, picked up my champagne flute, and approached him, not caring if it looked as if I had an agenda.

I raised my glass toward his. "Cheers."

He gave me a sour look and took a sip of champagne.

"Your parents are pretty cool for letting you drink alcohol."

"Everyone's parents let them drink alcohol. It's supposed to help kids know they can be safe at home. It keeps us from getting drunk in dangerous situations."

"Is that right?"

"That's the theory."

"All your friends do it?"

"Yup." He took another sip.

"No limits?"

He didn't respond.

"I'm surprised you're not in your room, since you're not a fan of your mom's work. Aren't they worried you'll say something rude?"

He shrugged.

"Or they don't know how you really feel about her work?"

"Why are you asking me all these questions?"

"You looked lonely, so I thought you might want someone to talk to."

"Think again."

"I guess the lure of drinking alcohol was bigger than having to deal with your mom's fans. Having to pretend you're one of them."

"I'm not pretending shit."

"Showing up implies you're a supporter."

"Does it?"

We sipped our drinks in silence. I turned to face the room. What I really wanted was to poke the hornet's nest that was Avery's hormones and barely concealed rage, with his father as a witness. What I really wanted was to force Colin into exposing the truth about himself. It wasn't that I believed he would confess to killing Grace in front of Ember's collectors and fans and admirers. In front of anyone. That he would ever confess, but I thought maybe I could put him on the spot. That I could get something more concrete than what was happening in my imagination so that I could go to the police.

Tyler was right. I didn't know that the bra belonged to Grace, and I wasn't sure how that could be proven. I wasn't even sure how I could get the police to search Colin's office. He wouldn't allow it, and I doubted admitting that I was looking around in someone's private things was going to bring them into the house with a search warrant and cadaver-sniffing dogs.

Colin was just outside the living room, where Avery and I were huddled in the corner. He was talking to a young couple. The woman was gripping his forearm and looking up at him with a pleading expression on her face. I wondered if she was begging him to find a way to let her jump the line to get a sitting with Ember.

I took a few steps away from Avery, trying to figure out how I could draw him closer to where his father stood.

"No need to think of a polite escape," Avery said. "I wasn't lonely before and I'm absolutely good with standing here by myself watching all the sycophants."

As if he sensed my attention on him, Colin looked over the head of the woman who was clinging to his arm, meeting my gaze. I widened my eyes and took a sudden step away from Avery, as if shocked by something he'd said, perhaps startled by an inappropriate touch from him.

A moment later, Colin was lifting the woman's fingers off his arm and backing away from the couple. He crossed the room with a welcoming smile on his face.

"Morgan. How are you doing? I hear your portrait is making fabulous progress."

"I wouldn't know. I haven't seen it."

He laughed, his voice too loud, even in the large room. "Of course you haven't. And neither have I. The finished masterpiece is what matters."

I nodded. "That's what I've heard."

Avery took a long swallow of his champagne. His glass was

nearly empty. I wondered if he would rush off for a refill under his father's watchful eye. Despite his insistence that his parents were happy to let him drink freely, I had to believe there was some kind of limit.

"I was surprised to find out that Avery doesn't think his mother's works are masterpieces. You said—"

"Art is all personal taste. And sometimes our taste needs time to mature. Isn't that right?" It wasn't clear if Colin was directing the question to me or to Avery. Possibly neither one of us. Maybe he was trying to strike a balance between the obvious lie he'd told me about how his son admired and respected his mother's work and his realization that I knew the truth.

"Your son seems very mature for his age," I said. "He's a deep thinker."

Avery rolled his eyes. He gulped down the rest of his champagne. As they were trained to do, one of the servers was immediately at his side. Avery shoved his glass toward the server and champagne flowed into it.

I held out my glass as well. I'd already passed my limit. I could tell by the reckless feeling that made me want to see Colin squirm. I knew because I could feel a willingness to say whatever was necessary to unsettle him and make him say something useful.

"Slow down, son," Colin said.

"No worries, Dad." Avery took a sip and grinned, foam clinging to his upper lip.

"To be honest, Avery has made me a little nervous about my portrait," I said.

"No need to be nervous. Ember is a genius." Colin swept his arm around the room. "This is a fraction of the people who collect her work. Only the serious buyers were invited today. Trust me."

"Trust you?" Avery let out a loud burst of laughter.

"Don't you want to know why I'm nervous?" I asked.

Colin looked nervous himself. "You shouldn't be."

"Avery tells me the eyes of all Ember's subjects are slightly ... what word did you use, Avery?"

Avery gulped his champagne and stared at me.

I waited.

Avery took a few more sips of champagne. He and his father were staring at each other. It was clear that Colin was warning his son not to say any more. To stop drinking if he couldn't hold his tongue.

"Insane!" Avery laughed so loudly most of the conversation in the room stopped.

"They all look insane!" His voice was commanding. Everyone looked at him.

"Calm down," Colin murmured.

A moment later, Hendrix was standing with us. He spoke in a low, almost threatening tone. "This is a critical event for Ember. Let's not fuck it up, okay?" He tried to take the champagne glass out of Avery's hand.

"Get away from me," Avery said.

All four of us took a step back from each other. I felt my hand tremble slightly, wondering if I'd started more than I'd planned, more than I'd wanted. I glanced over my shoulder. Jade was looking at me. She appeared ready to cry.

"They look insane." Avery was no longer shouting, but his voice was still clear. He gulped the rest of his champagne. "Did you want this?" He shoved the glass at Hendrix, then strode out of the room.

Colin looked at me and laughed softly. "Teenagers. Right? He'll be one before I know it. Can I get you a refill?"

I shook my head.

I'd certainly changed the status quo, but I wasn't sure what I'd changed it to.

41

NOW: MORGAN

*E*ager to escape from Colin and Hendrix and all the champagne, I walked out of the living room. I went to the kitchen and filled a glass with water since the one I'd abandoned had been cleaned up by the caterers. I drank the entire glass, taking deep breaths in between, trying to figure out whether I'd accomplished anything at all. Colin hadn't admitted he'd lied about his son's support for his mother. He'd managed to slither out of it with a platitude and then written it all off to typical pre-teen behavior. And now that behavior was exacerbated by alcohol.

The way Colin managed to mold the conversation to fit his view of the world made me even more certain there was something manipulative and untrustworthy about him.

The hum of voices had resumed, drifting into the kitchen from the rest of the house. It sounded like a swarm of bees had congregated. I couldn't pick up any conversational threads. The sound made me feel as if the champagne bubbles were pulsing through my brain, dulling my nerves.

I refilled the glass and took another sip of water. I closed my eyes, leaning hard into the granite edge of the counter, grateful for its solid, almost painful, but reassuring presence against my hipbone.

The sound of footsteps and a gasp made me open my eyes.

Olivia stood a few feet from me. "Oh. Were you having a moment?"

I nodded.

"You weren't expecting this, were you?"

"No. It's unnerving. Waking up to find parties are planned. They seem to materialize out of thin air."

She laughed. "When you have this kind of money, you can make magic happen whenever you want."

"But this must have taken planning. Inviting the guests."

"Not really. With social media, and when you have thousands of devoted fans ... the word goes out, and it doesn't take much to get a modest crowd like this."

"But Colin said these people are a select group."

She shrugged. "Whatever."

Instead of going to the fridge for a glass of water as I'd expected, she turned toward the cabinet where they kept the liquor. She opened it and pulled out a bottle of whiskey. She poured a liberal shot into a glass and swallowed it in its entirety. "Ahh. That felt good." She poured another shot.

"Did you and Colin have an affair?" I asked. "Are you having an affair?"

She stared at me for half a second, then burst out laughing. She held up the bottle. "Want some?"

I shook my head.

She returned the bottle to the cabinet and closed the door. "What brought that up?"

"Did you? Are you?"

"I don't think I'd call it an affair. That implies feelings for each other. And a relationship. And longevity. We didn't have any of that."

"But you—"

"Yes. We did the thing. Three times." She laughed. "What made you think we had?"

"I saw him touch you."

She sipped her drink. She seemed to be waiting for more, as if she were trying to recall when he might have touched her and if that was enough to suggest what I'd guessed. I wasn't going to tell her what Bryce had said. It didn't seem necessary, and I didn't need to weave the threads of gossip more tightly than they were already. Even though it probably appeared as if I were the one doing most of the gossiping. Maybe I was.

Maybe Tyler was right. The intensity of the situation was creeping under my skin. Maybe that's why the eyes of all Ember's subjects looked slightly insane. You reached a certain level of mental instability by the time you were finished sitting in that chair for hours at a time, day after day, being scrutinized and questioned. "Why did it … I don't mean to pry. Do you feel guilty for doing that to your sister? And living here, still being around him … it seems incredibly awkward. Does she know?"

"She's oblivious. She's in love with her work. Which is probably why it happened. Colin knows he'll never have her whole heart. He's kind of lost."

"He doesn't seem lost. Just the opposite. He seems very sure of himself."

"On the surface."

"Don't you feel guilty?"

"No. It was a mistake. Mistakes happen. Artists know that." She laughed. "Art is full of mistakes. You don't create a masterpiece without a lot of mistakes."

"It's not the same."

"Well, he seduced me and I was in a vulnerable place after my divorce. And it happened. So what can I say?" She took another sip of her drink.

"It's all his fault?"

"I didn't say that. But he did seduce *me*." She gave me a coy smile.

"Seduced, or coerced?"

"Don't be vicious," she said.

"I'm not. Just asking."

"Why would you think that?"

"I just think it would be a huge thing to do that to your sister."

"Do you have any sisters?"

"No."

She nodded. "It can be a complicated relationship."

"I think sleeping with your sister's husband is pretty rare. Even in the most complicated relationships."

She shrugged. "You're probably right. I don't really know."

"Did he coerce you?"

"Why are you so fixated on that? Did he try something with you?"

"Why would you think that?"

"Because you keep asking me that question!"

"No."

She glared at me, clutching her glass, holding it close to her mouth. She licked the edge of the glass, then placed it on the counter. "What's going on?"

"Nothing."

"It sounds like something's bothering you, like you have something on your mind and you're afraid to ask the real question."

She was absolutely right. I was afraid to ask the real question. Once I asked that question, everything would blow up. And I couldn't do that to Jade. Not yet. I had to find out something that would make Jade believe the truth—that something bad had happened to her daughter. But I didn't know how to get there.

"You're not going to tell me?"

"I just wondered. I think it would be uncomfortable to have sex with your brother-in-law and then stay in their house."

"Why?"

"Because it's … are you still attracted to him?"

"I said, he seduced—"

"I know. And you make it sound like you weren't really into it. So you just did it to punish her, or something like that? Or did he force you into it?"

"He didn't force me. And I didn't do it to punish her. It just happened. We're two adults. A man whose wife pours all her passion into her artwork and a woman who got dumped by her husband and had her career cut out from under her and has a sister rubbing her success in her face all the time—a gorgeous husband she hardly notices, a great kid she ignores, a stunning house she barely appreciates, and a fabulous career that doesn't seem to make her all that happy."

"So you were punishing her? For having everything you want and don't have?"

"You are vicious."

I was. I couldn't believe those words had come out of my mouth. It was easy to blame the champagne. But it was probably something deeper. My gut was telling me to be afraid of these people, while my logical mind was insisting they were one step away from being my virtual family.

Even though she'd called me vicious, she didn't look particularly upset over my accusation. She stared at me, sipped her drink, and waited for me to say more.

"I guess that means, yes, you were punishing her," I said.

She put her glass on the counter. "It's not that complicated. Sure, I'm jealous. It's really annoying that she doesn't appreciate what she has. But there's nothing so deeply Freudian or whatever you want to call it that I'm *punishing* her."

"And Colin?"

"You think he's punishing her?"

"Is he?"

"Sometimes sex is just sex. Animal desire. Two hungry people." She picked up her glass and looked inside at the minuscule amount of liquid remaining. She laughed. "Stress relief. Burning off the rage."

"Are you angry?"

"When life doesn't go your way, people can get angry. Sure."

"Is Colin angry?"

She laughed.

"Why is that funny?" I asked.

"You can feel the rage in this house. In every room." She tipped her glass back and drank the rest. "I'm sure you've noticed." She put it on the counter, turned, and walked out of the kitchen.

I hadn't felt anger in the atmosphere of their home. It didn't feel warm or inviting, that was for sure. But rage? Not until I'd spoken to Avery, that is. And now that she mentioned it, as I thought about it, maybe Colin's aggressive need to tell me how Avery adored his mother's art felt a little bit angry. Having an affair with his wife's sister could absolutely be viewed that way. Two hungry people, burning off the rage. Maybe they hadn't burned it off at all.

42

NOW: MORGAN

*A*ll the guests were gone. The caterers were finishing the cleanup and moving the furniture back to where it belonged. As Hendrix darted around giving instructions, his black hair slicked back, dressed in a black T-shirt, pink jeans, and black sport coat, all I could think of was a beetle scurrying across the tiled floors.

Now, he and Jade stood in front of the two paintings that had been lit and put on display in the dining room.

I lingered in the entryway, wanting to retreat to the guest room, but also wanting to listen to every conversation I could, searching for a way to crack the shell surrounding these people so I could prove to someone—Tyler? The police? Jade? My self? That not only had Derek been murdered, Grace was also dead.

As I watched, Colin came in through the patio door and joined them. The three stood gazing at the paintings. The paintings were a pair—two women who were engaged to be married. They'd attended the reception that afternoon and posed in front of their portraits for several photographs that would appear in the local newspaper and be shared all over social media to promote Ember's work.

The portraits were stunning. It looked as if the women were gazing at each other from their respective frames. I couldn't imagine how she'd accomplished that effect, because their pupils weren't oriented in that direction, but still, that was the feeling you got. Everyone had commented on it.

I crossed the entryway into the dining room and stood a few feet behind the others.

After a few seconds, I spoke, raising my voice slightly. "It's too bad Grace's portrait was never finished," I said. "Since these two women have blonde hair, it would have made an interesting triptych to include Grace with her striking dark hair."

Hendrix turned to look at me as if I were the most stupid person he'd ever encountered. As if I'd suggested the Mona Lisa should have a second figure added to enhance the painting. "Are you an art collector?" he asked.

"I just like odd numbers," I said. "Aren't uneven numbers supposed to be more artistically satisfying?"

"There's a purpose to what we're doing here and you don't understand the strategy at all." He gave me a condescending smile. "In case you haven't noticed, these two are a couple. And the effect Ember has accomplished with the eyes is absolute, unparalleled genius."

I looked at Jade, hoping with all my heart this wouldn't damage our relationship, but the opportunity, with Colin looking slightly ill, was too good to pass up. "Do you have Grace's unfinished portrait?"

Jade shook her head and turned her attention back to the paintings in front of us.

"I'd love to see it," I said.

"Ember doesn't show unfinished work." Hendrix reached over and flicked off the light switch under the first painting. He stepped around Jade and did the same to the second. "It was a fabulous reception. Thanks so much for your support, Jade." He took her hand, lifted it to his lips, and kissed her fingers.

Jade smiled serenely.

He let go of her hand and walked out of the room. A moment later, I heard the front door close sharply. Almost with a bang.

"I'm tired." Jade laughed. "Champagne tired. Too much." She kissed my cheek. "I'm going to take a late nap. If I don't wake up for dinner, don't worry about it." She drifted out of the room and down the hallway as if she were already half asleep.

I looked at Colin. "Have you seen Grace's portrait?"

"You heard what Hendrix said."

"You're her husband."

"Ember's art belongs to her. She shows it to whomever she chooses. When she's ready. Sometimes that's never. I understand what she needs and I respect that. And her. Maybe you don't understand that kind of respect in a relationship."

"Sounds like a threesome. A love triangle." I smirked.

"Don't be absurd. Why are you trying to stir up trouble?"

"I'm not the one that stirred things up. I didn't know someone died here and I'm still a little disturbed since finding out everyone went out of their way to hide that fact."

"No one hid anything. It's public knowledge."

"My future sister-in-law went missing from your home and you seem completely unconcerned about it."

"She didn't *go missing*. She left. You know that and—"

"No one has heard from her for a year. All they know is what you told them."

"I don't like what you're implying."

"What am I implying?"

His skin flushed slightly. He must have felt it because he turned away from me, staring at the paintings as if for the first time. "Ember is a genius."

"So I've heard. It must be hard living in her shadow. Competing with her art, her subjects. All these people in your home having such intimate relationships with her."

"I really don't like your tone."

"I'm wondering if Grace is dead too. I think she might be. Not a word to anyone for all this time?"

"You sound drunk, Morgan. You need to go sleep it off like your future mother-in-law. I'll forget everything you said. I'll take some responsibility—we should have been more careful in pouring the champagne. We trusted our guests to be responsible drinkers." He took a few steps away from me.

"I'm not drunk."

"You look … messy."

I ran my fingers through my hair. It was tangled, grabbing at my fingers and preventing them from sliding all the way through to the ends.

He squeezed my shoulder. I jerked away from him.

He laughed. "Settle down. You've gotten yourself all worked up over nothing. Go sleep it off." He walked out of the room.

He'd given me a decidedly creepy feeling. More than creepy. Sinister. I didn't like being called messy and I didn't like him grabbing my shoulder. If I closed my eyes, I could see him putting his hands on Grace, refusing to back off. I could imagine him lying to Jade, and everyone else, about Grace's sudden *departure*.

I moved closer to the paintings and studied the eyes. Did both women look slightly demented as they gazed at each other? I wasn't sure. Demented or insane wasn't the right way to describe it. They looked … lost, maybe. As if they weren't sure what was going on. But did all of Ember's portraits look that way? Would mine?

43

NOW: MORGAN

I was awake half the night, staring into the darkness. At times, I thought I saw shadows moving across the ceiling. Each time, I blinked, realizing they were tricks played by my tired eyes. But tired as they were, aching to close, dried out from straining to see, even when it was impossible, I couldn't keep them closed.

My thoughts turned more restlessly than my body did on the mattress, twisting this way and that.

It was surreal to think that someone I knew, someone that my fiancé considered part of his family, had committed murder, but I couldn't stop thinking about that. I'd tried to think of another explanation for Grace's sudden disappearance, but nothing came to me. No one ends their engagement and cuts off all communication, no matter how much they want to devote themselves to introspection. It's not rational. It's just not.

I could understand how Tyler and his mother were able to find so many reasons to dismiss what I found impossible to explain. The last thing they wanted was to consider that their beloved daughter and sister could be dead. And they definitely wouldn't want to think she'd died while she was visiting Colin and Ember. That she'd died, and no one told them. Worst of all, that this man they revered had killed her.

But I was an outsider. To me, it was easy to see.

Jade saw a charming and admirable man she'd cherished since the day he was born. I saw a man who was ignored by his wife and had sex with his sister-in-law right under his wife's nose. An unfeeling stranger who casually accepted a man hanging dead in his wife's art studio and went on living his life as if it hardly meant a thing. A gruesome opportunist, along with the others, who relished watching his wife's career take off in the aftermath of that death.

It made my skin crawl.

It had crossed my mind that maybe Hendrix had murdered Grace to deliberately create a dark, mysterious persona for his most important client, but that idea didn't stick. Hendrix wasn't the one keeping a blood-stained bra locked in his office.

I thought about waking Jade to tell her what I was thinking. But as I imagined her reaction, I turned my back toward the bed where she slept. She would hate me for saying something so ugly about her beloved godson.

I tried closing my eyes. I tried taking a few slow breaths, tried removing Grace's disappearance from my thoughts, but the moment I exhaled, the memory of her bra, locked in his drawer, came rushing back. When I took another breath, drawing it deep into my lungs, I could almost hear Colin's patronizing voice, weaving an elaborate story for Jade about Grace's impetuous departure.

He knew what Grace was like. He would have heard the story from Jade herself of Grace going missing when she was fifteen. He would have known all about her habits and her relationship with her mother. It would be so easy to make it sound as if Grace had behaved no differently than she'd behaved as a rebellious teenager.

I flopped back onto my other side and tried to make out Jade's form in the darkness. Her breathing had grown quieter. Was she awake? Maybe my constant movements had disturbed her, and she was lying there wondering what was bothering me. Maybe she wanted me to speak.

I coughed quietly. I whispered into the darkness. "Excuse me."

There was no response.

I sighed.

How would I convince her to believe me? She had to know that Colin wasn't the good, decent human being she thought she'd known all her life. How much contact did they actually have? Based on the reminiscing they'd done that first night, they sometimes went several years without seeing each other.

Besides that, she only knew what he wanted her to know. That went double for Ember. It seemed to me that whatever relationship Jade thought she had with Ember, it was probably an illusion. Ember drifted through the rooms of her home as if she hardly saw any of the people who lived there. I couldn't imagine she gave more than a passing thought to the people who were old friends of her husband, who visited less than once a year.

I rolled onto my back. I forced my eyelids closed. I couldn't look tired for my portrait. I needed to get some rest, so my head was clear for talking to Jade in the morning.

The other thing keeping my mind whirling and my eyes open was the tiny prick of fear that my life might be in danger. I thought I was safe sleeping in the same room as Jade. But was I safe walking around the property alone? Especially before sunrise. Had I made Colin uncomfortable enough that he thought he needed to silence me? If Grace had died accidentally and he'd buried her body on their property, he might be afraid I could shatter his world.

A chill ran through me. I clutched the edge of the blankets and pulled them tightly around me, making a cocoon that didn't feel any safer and did nothing to stop the chill.

In the morning, despite feeling as if I'd been awake all night, I realized I must have slept at some point because I was aware that the room was suddenly light enough to see the shapes of furniture and the outline of Jade's peacefully sleeping body. My mouth was dry, and I recalled fragments of a terrifying dream, but I couldn't remember any of the details.

44

NOW: MORGAN

I sat up and slid my legs over the side of the bed. I ran my fingers through my hair. I decided to shower and dress, not caring if I woke Jade, not caring if it was still quite early. There was no chance I would get any more sleep.

When I stepped out of the bathroom, it was just after six-thirty.

Jade was sitting up in bed, looking at her phone. "You're up early."

"I didn't sleep much." I went to the armchairs on her side of the room and settled in the one farthest from her bed. I wouldn't be able to relax until I told her. She would be upset, angry, disbelieving. She would be a hundred different things. But I had to tell her. I couldn't figure out what I should do next until I told her.

The small bit of sleep I'd managed had clarified one thing. I would tell her about the bra. It was the clearest proof that something bad had happened to her daughter. It couldn't be argued with, except for my disrespect of Colin's privacy.

I rushed through the story, ignoring the shocked, then angry expressions passing across her face. I'd also decided not to pull my punches. It was difficult to speak the words, but I kept talking, letting them fall out of my mouth without censoring them. "It's obvious that something happened to Grace. It's painful … it hurts so badly to say this, and I'm so, *so* sorry, but I think she's …" I leaned forward, placing my hand on her ankle. "I'm scared she's dead. I think maybe Colin … came onto her. Grace fought back and something … happened."

She jerked her leg to the side, dislodging my hand. "Stop," she said. "Stop talking."

"It was probably an accident or something. But I think he killed her."

Jade laughed. "I shouldn't laugh, because what you're saying is so awful. It's despicable." She laughed sharply. "But it's so absolutely impossibly wrong, there's nothing I can do but laugh. Have you lost your mind?"

"No. The bra—"

"Why on earth would you assume it belongs to Grace?"

"It's too small to belong to Ember or Olivia."

"So what?" She threw off the covers and got out of bed. "I will not listen to this, Morgan. I hope you haven't said anything like this to Tyler. Or anyone else. It's embarrassing and upsetting that you would even *entertain* these thoughts, much less speak them out loud. I don't understand, but I'm not going to try. I want to forget everything you've said."

"It might even be worse than that."

"Stop. I want you to stop. Right now." She started toward the bathroom.

"Derek was probably murdered too."

"Probably? That's—"

"If he killed Derek, and Grace found out, he would have killed her to stop her from going to the police. So maybe not an accident, but—"

"Stop!" She turned, putting her hands on her hips. She appeared confident and so in control. I felt like a child begging her to listen to my silly story. But it wasn't silly. I knew I was right. There wasn't a single doubt in my mind that two people who sat for portraits with Ember had been murdered. Maybe more.

"Stop saying such ugly things. I don't know where you're getting these ideas, but you need to stop. Right now. Colin is a wonderful man. I love him as much as I love my own children and I won't listen to this."

I moved to the edge of the chair, leaning forward, desperate to make her see that she had to listen to me. As if somehow I could make the horror I had inside of me seep out of my body like some kind of vapor that would fill the room. She would breathe it in and her thoughts would be transformed. She had to understand, she had to realize how blinded she was. She was clinging to unbelievable stories fed to her by Colin and Ember.

I knew denial was so powerful it could twist your mind into something unrecognizable. I knew that from when my mother got sick and they took me to a counselor who told me all about it. Denial was a force that could make your brain believe something that was completely untrue. There had to be a way to get Jade to realize that was happening to her.

"I'm scared," I said. "Two people, at least, who sat for portraits here are gone."

"One killed himself," she said. "One is traveling."

"I think we should leave." I felt myself buckle under the intensity of her anger. "It might not be safe," I whispered.

"Absolutely not."

"But I—"

"If you don't want the portrait, that's fine. I won't hold a grudge. But I'm not leaving. No one's been *murdered*." She grabbed her robe off the bench at the foot of the bed, shoved her arms into the sleeves, leaving it untied as she opened the door and walked out of the room.

I closed my eyes. It hadn't gone at all the way I'd hoped. I shouldn't have been surprised. Now I was trapped. I couldn't leave her here. No matter what I believed Colin might be thinking, I had to stay, for now. After what happened with my mother, I wasn't about to abandon my mother-in-law.

The day my mother died, I was at a sleepover. She made me go. She told my father I had to go. She said it would be fine. She was feeling good. She still had time left. There was still time for lots of hugs and talks. It was okay. I was almost a teenager and I needed to have fun with my friends, to live my life.

And then she died.

My dad didn't come get me because ... he could never really explain why he didn't come get me in time. I guess it happened fast, or something. He was vague about the details. Over the years, I came to realize he wasn't in the room with her, and that's why he was so unclear when he tried to explain what he'd done, or rather, what he failed to do. He hadn't even known she was gone.

She died all alone in that white room with no one to hold her hand.

I abandoned her. He abandoned her to get a cup of coffee, or whatever he thought was so terribly important. She had to leave the earth all by herself.

I would not abandon Jade with these people. Even if I felt more anxious every moment I was there, I would stay. Even if I felt more unsafe every day, I couldn't leave. Of course, it wasn't the same thing. Not even close. But I couldn't leave.

45

BEFORE: BRYCE

*B*y the time Adam was twenty-three, I had become my brother's keeper. Not financially. But mentally and emotionally. And before long, I would be his keeper financially as well.

I was the one who worried about him. I was the one who tried to keep track of him. I was the one reminding him to take his medications. Usually, when I showed up at his scummy studio apartment where he was burning through the little bit of money my mom gave him every month after my dad decided he couldn't take it anymore and dropped dead of a heart attack, Adam refused to listen to my reminders.

For a while, Adam was given antipsychotic medication through injections every few weeks. I drove him to his appointments. But in the end, that didn't work out either. It was Adam's firm belief that needles were how the medical establishment, run by the government, injected disease into the population, making everyone weak and tired. It was also how they made people's brains numb so they would work in desk jobs for the military-industrial complex until they died. Injections of things you couldn't see were how they got you to pay taxes and set you up to do other things you didn't want to do.

His relationship with his medications was erratic, so his stability was non-existent. He drifted in and out of reality. At least in and out of my reality. He had a reality of his own choosing and, honestly, he was pretty happy there.

My mom couldn't deal with Adam. Seeing him broke her heart. Hearing how he was doing was painful, so she didn't want to know. Ignorance was bliss for her. She didn't want to talk about anything related to him. She put her small contribution into his bank account every month and told me I was a saint.

I had no interest in being a saint. I didn't think it was fair that I was my brother's so-called keeper. Besides, I wasn't, really. No one could *keep* Adam anywhere. He thought what he thought and did what the voices in his head told him to do. Fortunately, they mostly told him to do things that didn't bother anyone else.

The problem was, no one else believed that. No one believed he was harmless. And every time the smallest thing went wrong, they wanted to blame Adam. Even I'd done that when we were kids. Before I knew, before I understood. Blame the crazy guy. It must be the *nut case*. Later, it made me want to cry that I'd ever had thoughts like that.

If you didn't know him, maybe he did seem a little scary.

Most people never bothered to really look into his eyes, to really see what was happening there. To listen to what he had to say. Was he really crazy? Everything he said had one or two fine threads running through it that made a little bit of sense. Maybe that's why people were afraid of him.

The problem was, he finally ended up in the wrong place at the wrong time. It's a phrase that gets tossed around all the time. It's a phrase that makes it sound like you're casting blame on other people. Like you're blaming fate. Blaming anyone but yourself. But it really is true. Sometimes, you can be in the wrong place at the wrong time.

Just like you can be in the right place at the right time. When you meet the woman or the man of your dreams, you're in the right place at the right time. Everyone believes that as if it's absolutely true.

Adam was taking a walk at one-thirty in the morning—*the wrong time*—and therefore an activity that immediately raised suspicion. Walking, according to the rules of society, should be done during the day. Early morning or evening is acceptable. Long after midnight is abnormal. And abnormal means you're up to no good.

That was Adam's first problem.

He saw the woman lying in the park behind a bench. He thought she'd hurt herself and he wanted to help. He knelt beside her—*the wrong place*. He touched her leg, shaking her gently, asking if she was okay. When she didn't respond, he shook her more vigorously. Her arm flopped forward and smacked the ground. At the same time, her head rolled back, and he saw that her mouth was open. So were her eyes, but they weren't looking at him.

He was so upset. Even though he knew she was dead, he couldn't stop shaking her. He knew he should stop, but he couldn't believe she was dead and he couldn't stop thinking maybe, somehow, he could get her to wake up.

When he explained that to the police, they looked at him as if he was crazy. Crazy or lying. That's what he told me.

I asked him why he talked to the police at all. Why hadn't he called me? Why hadn't he told them he wanted a lawyer?

"Because I didn't do anything! I was trying to *help* her!" He glared at me as if I were deliberately misunderstanding what had happened. "I thought she needed help!"

Soon, he was shouting at me, which he'd also done with the police. When he shouted, everything got worse.

"This is what's wrong with our fucking society! No one ever tries to help anyone! She had a knife sticking out of her stomach! I pulled it out. I knew it must hurt so bad, and I wanted to help her. So I pulled it out. How was I supposed to know I would get blood all over me?"

When someone in a nearby house who slept with their window open heard Adam screaming, they called the police. They found him holding the knife. His hands were covered with blood. There was blood on his shirt. He said things that sounded crazy. They arrested him. The more they talked to him, the crazier he sounded.

The next thing he knew, he was charged with murder and they weren't looking for any other suspects.

The woman had been jogging. Of course, that wasn't considered normal either. She shouldn't have been out running at that hour of the night. But it was a nice area, a nice park in a nice area. My brother didn't live in that area. He didn't belong there—*the wrong place at the wrong time.*

It's funny how the rules of what was *normal* and expected and what made *sense*, and his diagnosis, and his neighbors telling the police that sometimes he was quiet because he took his medication, but sometimes he didn't take his medication and he said crazy things, but he was never violent, although he scared them because he said a lot of crazy things ... well, it all added up to no one believing that Adam was trying to help. It added up to all the *evidence* suggesting Adam killed that woman who was simply trying to go for a run.

And the wheels of the justice system started turning. Adam was charged with second degree murder and a trial date was set.

46

NOW: MORGAN

As much as I wanted to get out of the confining atmosphere of the house, I was nervous about leaving to walk alone in the desert. But I was equally anxious being inside those walls. It felt like running through a maze as I went out of my way to avoid being alone with Colin.

I was wondering if it was possible that the entire family knew what he'd done. Were all of them covering for him? I wasn't sure I could trust any of them. Being alone with their strong, unpredictable son, or even sitting in a chair in that isolated studio with Ember, might be equally dangerous. Could I really count on Bryce to keep me safe?

There was one person I thought I could trust, even though she was a complete stranger.

I went out to the courtyard. Despite the fact that I was surrounded by windows, observable from Colin and Ember's wing of the house, Bryce's suite of rooms, as well as the entryway, it had become the only place outside of the guest room where I felt somewhat calm and free from the demanding gazes of the artist and her family.

Maybe it was the fountain and the soothing melody of water in the center of miles of dry earth and the expanse of sky with the relentless sun. A sky that was warm even when it turned dark and the stars glittered.

I sat on the bench in the shade facing the fountain and sent a message to Zoe.

Will you meet me for coffee? I really need some perspective on the situation here.

It was nearly forty-five minutes before I received a reply. I almost lost hope, thinking I'd been foolishly self-absorbed to think she would respond to someone she didn't know. She'd already told me she'd moved on with her life. Her fiancé was gone, and no one cared about the disturbing circumstances of his death. I was nothing to her.

Zoe: *Why?*

Morgan: *I don't know if I should be afraid.*

Zoe: *Are you still at the artist's house?*

Morgan: *Yes.*

Zoe: *Why are you afraid?*

Morgan: *I think someone else was murdered here. Besides Derek.*

Zoe: *Who?*

Morgan: *My fiancé's sister also came here for a portrait. His family was told she left before it was finished. But no one has heard from her.*

Zoe: *You should absolutely be afraid.*

Morgan: *Do you think she's dead?*

Zoe: *Why are you asking me? Do you?*

Morgan: *Why are you so sure Derek was murdered but the police aren't? It doesn't make sense.*

Zoe: *Lots of things don't make sense. I know what I know.*

Morgan: *Can we meet?*

Zoe: *I don't see the point.*

Morgan: *Maybe we can go to the police together. I can tell them about Grace.*

Zoe: *I'm done with that. If I were you, I'd get out of there. It's not safe and you know it.*

Morgan: *But they might look at Derek's death differently when they hear about Grace.*

Zoe: *Unless you find her body and she has a bullet hole or a stab wound, they won't believe it.*

Morgan: *We can try.*

Zoe: *I'm done trying. This almost destroyed my life. Please don't message me again.*

I placed my phone on the bench beside me. I thought about asking her if I could message her if I found Grace's body. But how would that happen? It seemed as if Grace had evaporated into the desert air. I could tell her about Grace's bra, but she wouldn't think it was enough.

Resting my elbows on my knees, my chin in my hands, I stared at the fountain. The heat and the sound of the water made me want to go for a swim. At the same time, the stifling air also kept me from moving. There was something about it that made my muscles feel as if they needed to just settle into one spot. If I could keep still, I wouldn't feel it. I could just breathe and let my heart beat and use all my energy simply to keep myself upright.

Jade had made it clear she would not leave with me. And my heart had made it clear I couldn't abandon her. I felt utterly trapped.

I picked up my phone and scrolled through unread messages from friends. I looked at social media for a while. I put my phone down, leaned back, and closed my eyes.

The sound of the water began washing thoughts of murder and bodies buried in the desert out of my mind. I felt my brain relaxing into a calmer state. My muscles seemed to appreciate the heat that required nothing from them. I almost felt as if I were dead myself.

47

BEFORE: GRACE

*I*t seems strange that I need to sit for my portrait at night. It's freaky.

Won't the lighting be wrong? No matter how good the artificial light is in her studio, the darkness outside will change the way it looks inside the room.

Besides, I'm so tired. Two-thirty in the morning? No makeup? I look awful. I wasn't allowed to shower. I got dressed and hurried over here because it was implied that when the Muse strikes, and I do mean *Muse* with an uppercase *M*, because that's how it's treated around here, everyone needs to bow to her. The *Muse* rules everything and everyone. The Muse is treated like an ancient goddess, requiring sacrifices to be fed into the flaming volcano.

Now, I'm sitting in the chair. It's comfortable enough, but I'm so tired. I was in a deep sleep and it feels as if I'm still dreaming. Walking across the patio and along the pathway, through the garden, was like walking in my sleep. The familiar shapes I'm used to seeing in daylight appeared like something else in the darkness. The path was illuminated by lights so close to the ground all I could see were my feet as I walked, as if my lower legs had disappeared.

"Don't close your eyes."

"I'm tired." To prove this, although I don't have to prove anything, I allow my jaws to stretch into a magnificent yawn. Once it starts, I can't stop.

"Grace, please."

I yawn again.

"I need you to not look so tense. You need to make better eye contact. Do you always avoid eye contact like this? I've noticed it even when you're talking at meals."

"I make eye contact."

"You don't. Are you afraid to make eye contact during sex?"

"I—"

"Did your fiancé ever mention it? Did it hurt him that you couldn't look him in the eyes? Did it make him feel as if—"

"I don't want to talk about him anymore. We're—"

"Are you embarrassed to talk about sex? You need to be comfortable with your body. That's one reason you're not ready for marriage, if you feel so much discomfort with who you are."

"I don't."

"Are you ashamed of your body? Is that why you have trouble making eye contact?"

"No. I'm not ashamed of anything."

"Then look at me."

"I am."

"Your eyes keep flicking away."

"I'm tired."

"I don't think you are. Now that we're talking about this, I can sense that you're very wide awake. I can smell your fear."

"That's ridiculous."

"Don't be afraid."

"I'm not." I laugh. I know I sound nervous. Afraid. I am a little. This conversation is so uncomfortable and I don't see the purpose of it. For a portrait.

"I think to help you show some vulnerability for your portrait, which will make it much richer, and to help you feel comfortable in your skin, it would be a good idea to take off your shirt."

"No."

"And your bra."

"No. That's not the kind of portrait I want."

"Your clothing is already captured in the portrait. This isn't about nudity in the portrait. This is to capture the most compelling facial expression."

"I don't need my clothes off for that."

"Do you want an exquisite portrait? Do you want something that will make the man you marry fall in love with you all over again every time he passes by?"

It seems as if my heart is freezing in my chest. It almost stops beating for half a second. The idea that Michael could look at a painting of me and feel those things was part of what made me agree to do this. My mother insisted that's what my stepfather had done when he'd seen her portrait. But now, Michael and I are ... I can't think about him or I might start crying. I told him I wasn't sure I was ready for marriage and he ... that was it. The end. We're finished.

I'm not going to think about him. I'm going to think about this amazing portrait. That's all. A collector's item. No one I know, except my mother, has anything like it. That's the thing I should be thinking about. Capturing myself, preserving myself at the prime of my life in a spectacular work of art.

But take off my top? It's cheap. And tacky. And not what this is supposed to be about. It's degrading and a little bit exploitive. It feels squirmy in the pit of my stomach.

I am not ashamed of my body. Quite the opposite. I'm proud of it. But now? In this room? In the middle of the night? Because it will supposedly cause my eyes to show some poorly defined quality? Vulnerability?

"Most of the time, it comes down to this. Because showing your true self in a portrait means being vulnerable. And being partially naked is when we're the most vulnerable."

"Most of the time?" I ask.

"For most subjects."

"Was it that way for my mother?"

Silence is my answer. Unless I'm being manipulated. It could be the silence is integrity. A refusal to lie overtly. To suggest my mother removed her top, to let me assume she'd done it when she hadn't.

My fingers play with the hem of my T-shirt and I realize I'm thinking about it. I want to do my best. I want to give this experience everything I have. I came into it wanting to do that. And now I have a choice.

It's a choice that really doesn't matter. Who cares if I sit here half naked? It might make me more fully aware of my body's immersion in the experience. Instead of feeling like an object being viewed, I'll feel like a spirit being captured. It might make me feel more grounded, and at the same time, more free. It will make me feel as if I'd given everything, that I have nothing else to give, and nothing to lose.

What do I know about portraying the essence of a person in paint? Spreading colors across the surface of a two-dimensional canvas and creating such magic that the wet, oily colors are transformed into something that look as if the breath of a human being is moving through the brushstrokes?

It is magic.

It's genius.

It's miraculous. Something that makes me feel larger than life when I pause long enough to really think about it. When I looked at Ember's other works, especially her portrait of my mother, and saw how that painting reflected the woman I'd known all my life, the woman I'd called Mommy, then Mom, and now, often, Mother, it was astounding.

I slowly pull my T-shirt over my head.

Without my noticing, the room has grown warmer.

Am I that easy to read? Had it been so obvious I would yield to the demand and remove my clothes that the temperature of the room was set in advance?

I reach behind and unhook my bra. I let it fall to the floor.

Strangely enough, I don't feel exploited. I'm not cold or ashamed or uncomfortable. I feel serene.

48

NOW: MORGAN

*D*iving into the pool didn't feel as invigorating as I'd expected. I felt as if I were being watched. The patio was deserted. No one had been in the living room when I'd passed through on my way outside. As I'd stood by the lounge chair, slipping off my flip-flops, I'd looked into the sitting area adjoining the kitchen and that too was empty. Aside from the dining room, which was closed up, there were no other windows facing the patio. The studio was too far from the house. There was no possible way that anyone could be watching me, yet still I felt someone was.

I swam furiously up and down the length of the pool. It was short enough that I only needed a single breath from one end to the other. After ten laps, I paused. It felt good to be tired in that way, rather than with the lethargy I experienced when all my muscles seemed to be melting like wax in the heat.

It was too hot to lie on the lounge chair, even under an umbrella, so I toweled off and returned to the house, still unable to shake the feeling that someone was watching every step I took, noticing the water dripping from my hair, the drops of moisture on my skin.

In the guest room, I showered and put on a navy jersey dress and sandals. I left my hair wet, weaving it into a single French braid.

I went into the poolroom, picked up a cue, chalked the tip, and took aim without bothering to rack the balls. I was eager to hear the click of the balls and the thunk of one falling into a pocket. I didn't care what ball or what pocket, I just wanted to experience success.

Sinking five balls with only two misses was more satisfying than I would have imagined. I racked the balls, preparing to play a game in which I challenged myself.

The door opened, and Bryce stepped into the room, closing the door behind him. "Do you want some friendly competition?"

"Are you friendly?"

My comment sounded flirty. I hadn't intended it to. Truthfully, I felt more distrustful than flirty. Was he a friend? I couldn't be sure. It had seemed as if he'd been encouraging and helpful since I'd arrived, but right now, I didn't trust anyone, including myself and my mother-in-law.

"Are you doing okay?" He studied me carefully, concern etched across his forehead.

"Not really."

"What's bothering you?"

"I've already told you."

"There are several things—"

"I think Colin murdered Derek. And Grace."

"I know you do. But he's not a killer. I don't know why he had that bra. He—"

"With blood on it!"

"Yes. It's ... he's lonely. He's a lonely man. I think he feels ... I suppose he feels trapped with a woman who loves her work more than her husband, more than any human being, to be honest. And he can't seem to stop loving her. So he's really and truly trapped, and so it's possible he's deeply unhappy. But he wouldn't. He didn't kill anyone."

"How can you be so sure?"

"He's too kind."

"Is he?"

"He doesn't have that … why would he?"

"Because he's jealous of her attention to them?" It made sense to me. That's almost exactly what Bryce had just said to me. Ember loved her work deeply, she spent hours with the people whose portraits she painted. She put all her attention on them. "He feels like she doesn't see him."

He laughed. "Are you an amateur psychologist?"

"It's not funny."

"No. I shouldn't have laughed. Do you really think Grace is dead?"

I nodded.

"But what happened to her … why hasn't anyone found her body? After all this time?"

"I don't know. It's the desert. She could be anywhere."

He gave me a horrified look.

"I don't know. I just know in my heart that someone would have heard something from her after all this time."

He held up the frame to rack the balls. "Do you mind?"

I shook my head, although it felt horribly uncomfortable to be racking balls, setting up a game of pool while we discussed murder. Not the casual conversation of a lurid fascination with true crime involving strangers, but the real and painful death of someone who was part of our lives.

He began scooping balls out of the pockets, rolling them toward the center of the table. When they were all gathered, he swept them into the triangle with a single motion. He straightened the frame, pointed the tip at the center of the table, and carefully lifted the plastic off the group of balls.

"You're probably right. No one shuts off *all* contact."

"I know I am. Tyler and Jade are in denial. And I'm not pretending to be a psychiatrist. Anyone who has been through grief knows what denial feels like. Once you come out the other side and look back."

He stared at me, waiting for me to finish before striking the balls.

"They *need* to believe she's okay," I said. "But running away when she was a teenager is not at all the same as going completely dark, ghosting everyone in her family for no reason when she's an adult."

He positioned the cue ball, pulled back his stick, and broke the balls with a powerful shot. The sound ricocheted through the room as the balls scattered across the table.

"Do you really think Colin killed her, then carried her body all the way out to the middle of the desert?" He walked around the table and eyed his next shot. "It sounds ..."

I shrugged. "I don't know what he did. I just know what I found."

"Maybe he's protecting Ember," Bryce said.

I swallowed, thinking about her cold, singular focus on her work.

"She would do anything for her art," Bryce whispered. "Do you think she would commit murder? Maybe she wants to make some of her subjects truly immortal." His voice caught on the last word. He picked up his cue and hit the ball. He missed. He stepped away from the table and waited for me to take my turn.

"I don't—"

"Hendrix is so crass about how Derek's suicide brought a lot of morbid attention to her work. He laps it up and he really capitalized on that. Do you think ..." he pressed the heel of his hand against his forehead. "Maybe she killed Grace. And Colin buried her body? Is that possible?"

I thought about the painting of the woman with death-like eyes in the small gallery connected to Ember's studio. It was tucked into its own alcove. Hidden, yet given a prominent place that almost called attention to it. I thought about Avery's insistence that all her subjects looked slightly insane. Was her plan for the future to turn to some macabre work for a sick portion of society that wanted death-like portraits of themselves? Is that why she was so fixated on keeping me from blinking?

My mind felt like it was exploding with ridiculous, unimaginable possibilities. Made up stories because I just didn't know. I had no idea what was going on. All I knew was that two people were dead.

We played in silence for several rounds.

I didn't know if Ember would do something like that. I knew nothing about her beyond the fact that she made me more uncomfortable than anyone I'd ever met. So did the rest of her family, but maybe they were all reflections of her.

49

NOW: MORGAN

*O*ur pool game had grown eerily silent, our thoughts oppressed by the reality of murder. The click of balls even felt muffled. The rush of blood through my ears seemed determined to remind me how fragile my life was, blood pumping without my ever noticing, a flow so easily stopped.

I swallowed, not wanting to think how easily a bit of pressure to my throat, a knife in my belly or back, a sharp rock brought down on my head, hands holding me under the water in the swimming pool could stop that flow.

The air struggled to move in and out of my lungs, as if the space was too tight.

Bryce's phone buzzed loudly. The sound was so unexpected, I shot the cue at an angle and it skimmed across the top of the ball, making it skip awkwardly to the side and roll only a few inches.

He glanced at his phone. "I need to go. You win by default." He shoved his phone into his pocket and returned his cue stick to the rack. A moment later, he was gone.

I continued hitting the balls into the pockets, first mine, then his, finishing with the eight ball. I had just broken a fresh arrangement of balls and was studying the table when the door opened. I looked up and saw Colin standing there.

He closed the door and leaned against it. "If you want to accuse me of something, have the courage to tell me to my face."

I stared at him.

"Don't pretend you don't know."

"I—"

"I've known Jade all my life. Did you think she wouldn't tell me what you said? Nice way to make yourself part of the family. I'm not a murderer. And I'm disgusted that you would say something like that behind my back. We've welcomed you into our home. We've offered you everything. We've provided incredible food, all the good wine you can drink, a relaxing and exotic environment. You're here as our guest, and this is how you thank us?"

"I found—"

"Yes. I heard what you *found*. You snuck into our private space and unlocked cabinets and pried into something that was none of your business."

"I probably shouldn't have done that." He was scaring me. He hadn't moved closer, and the pool table was between us, but I had no idea where Bryce had gone. The house had a silent, deserted feeling to it. I wasn't sure if that was my fear making it seem that way, or if it was the truth.

Dusk had fallen. And, as if it felt my fear, or wanted to magnify the endless miles of empty space around us, I heard a coyote howl.

"What you said to Jade is slander."

"It's not. Technically, slander is—"

"Don't be pedantic. You have no right to accuse me of something so heinous. You have no evidence. I've been a gracious and generous host to every single one of my wife's subjects, including Grace. I've devoted my life to Ember's work and her success. And I resent like hell that you would come into my home and say something like that to a woman who respects and cares for me."

"She didn't believe me."

"Of course she didn't. She knows who I am. If it wouldn't damage Ember's project and destroy her vision, I would escort you out of this house right now."

He took several steps toward the pool table. He placed his hands on the edge, leaning over it so that it seemed as if he were bearing down on me, even though the table still stood between us. "Don't you ever speak another word like that to anyone. Do you hear me?"

"Of course I hear you."

"Don't mock me."

"I'm—"

"I don't want you talking to other slanderers. And I don't want you getting it into your head that you're going to call the police and make false accusations based on something you stole from my private office, something you know nothing about. I want it back, by the way."

I glared at him.

"It doesn't belong to you."

"It certainly doesn't belong to you."

He had the decency to blush. He pulled his hands off the table and straightened his back. "You stole it out of my office. I want it returned."

"Did you hurt her?"

"She's my godmother's daughter! I would never—" He made a strange sound, almost as if he were gasping for air. "I want you to return it to my office. You can put it in the drawer."

"I can go get it right now."

He glanced over his shoulder, nervous, even though the door was closed, as if he feared being overheard, feared that I might rush out of the room to get the bra and return, shoving it into his hands while someone else was nearby.

Maybe he hadn't killed her. Maybe Bryce was right about that, but he was not right about Colin being nothing but a heartbroken and caring guy. He looked angry, as if I were in a position to destroy his life.

I didn't think I was. I didn't really know anything. Mostly, I was afraid.

Colin might feel trapped loving a woman who didn't love him with equal depth, if she loved him at all. But he loved her so much, maybe he had helped her. Maybe Bryce was right. Colin had wanted to be sure that whatever gruesome path her art was taking her down, she would be able to follow it with ease. He would remain her protector, even if it meant covering up murder.

"I told you to put it back where you found it. Right now." He turned and flung open the door. He rushed out of the room as if he'd felt more trapped than I had. A moment later, I saw him hurrying across the patio. He took the path that led to Ember's studio and the cactus garden, almost running by the time he disappeared into the darkness.

50

NOW: MORGAN

*C*urious about whether Colin was about to have a confrontation with Ember, I left my pool cue leaning against the table and followed him.

When I reached the path on the opposite side of the patio, I couldn't see him.

I hurried along the pathway. Where the path forked, one section leading to the studio and the other to the walled garden, I saw the studio was completely dark. I heard a man's voice coming from behind the garden wall, so I turned in that direction.

To my left were the concrete benches circling a round concrete table. The tree behind them was backlit against the wall, creating an eerie glow. To my right were several tall cacti that stood like alien creatures, appearing as if they were poised to move closer the moment I turned my back on them. I shivered despite the warm air and walked more quickly toward the opening.

Inside, I passed the reflecting pool and went around the sharp bend. I heard the man's voice again, recognizing Colin's deep, slightly aggressive tone.

Moving more slowly now, I walked deeper into the enclosure. In the daylight, it was filled with sunshine. The walls made it feel protected and private. I'd imagined that during other seasons, when the temperature was more pleasant, it was a beautiful place to enjoy the sunshine and the beautiful stillness of the cacti. It was their lack of response to the wind that was part of their mystique. Now, they made me feel out of place, the only object in motion.

My instinct was urging me to hide from Colin. I realized now he wasn't talking to another person. His was the only voice I'd heard since I'd stepped behind the garden wall.

I couldn't make out the words he was speaking. Then he was silent.

Rooted to my spot on the path, I waited. I slipped off my flip-flops and picked them up. The fine grit of the pathway stuck to my feet, but I didn't want him to hear the slap of my shoes against my bare feet. I moved to the edge of the path and began taking small steps toward the back corner, where the sound of his voice had been coming from a few moments earlier.

In the back corner was another bench, a thick cluster of four of five different types of cacti and a small tree. It had light bark and branches that split from the trunk only a few feet from the ground, growing vertically before they curved gracefully out in long limbs across the surrounding area.

With the help of the lights along the pathway, and some lighting among the cacti, I could make out the shape of Colin's body as he leaned against the tree. He gripped one of the branches that was about five feet off the ground, hanging onto it as if he wanted it to keep him from falling over.

He started talking again, but I still couldn't make out the words. He obviously thought he was alone, assuming I'd followed his command to return the blood-stained bra to his office. But there was no way he was getting that back. He would have to search the guest room himself to get his hands on it. And he would have to do a lot of searching to find where I'd hidden it.

That piece of lingerie was the only thing I had so far, if I could manage to get a police officer to listen to my concerns. I'd taken a steak knife and slit open one of the decorative pillows on my bed. I'd wrapped the bra in a plastic bag and stuffed it inside the pillow. Unless someone used the pillow to rest their head, they would never hear the crunch of the plastic. I'd used the needle and some thread from my travel sewing kit to repair the opening.

As I tried to decide how long I was going to watch Colin, how I was going to judge when he might suddenly decide to start walking in my direction, he began shaking the tree branch he was holding. His murmuring grew louder, and he moaned softly, then muttered something else.

He turned toward the tree and butted the side of his head against a thick, unmoving branch that looked quite painful. Then he let go of the branch he'd been hanging onto and dropped to his knees. He slammed the heels of his hands against the ground and groaned.

"God dammit. God dammit." He slammed his fists into the ground again, then fell forward, almost touching his face to the dirt as if he were praying.

After a few minutes, he sat up. He had dirt in his hands and he wiped them across his shirt, then rubbed his face, not seeming to care that he was scrubbing grit into his skin. He ran his hands across the ground again, as if he thought that might wipe the grit off his palms. Then he began rubbing the ground, moving his hands in ever wider circles, coming closer to the surrounding cacti. If he continued with the angry, vigorous movements, he would end up shoving his hands against the long, sharp needles protruding from the plants.

I watched in horrified fascination. Clearly, our conversation had upset him, but why was he pawing at the ground like a grief-stricken animal?

Without noticing what I was doing, my fascination had drawn me closer so that I was now only a few yards away, I quickly stepped back, letting my bare feet feel their way along the ground until my heels touched the rocks that bordered the path. I stopped, aware that I was also at risk of running into painful needles.

Colin had now gained control of himself. He'd risen to his feet and was once again gripping the lowest branch of the tree that stretched across the cacti and curved back, touching the wall. Nestled against the wall beneath the branch was a small bed of round, pale rocks. He let go of the branch and walked toward it. He bent down and placed his hand on one of the rocks. After a moment or two, he stood and tipped his head back, staring up through the branches at the stars scattered across the sky.

He turned suddenly.

I held my breath and stepped off the path, moving quickly behind a free-standing wall that had a large clay pot almost as tall as me in front of it.

Colin walked out of the garden without looking in my direction.

I remained behind the wall for a long time, unsure whether he was somewhere else in the garden or if he'd returned to the house.

While I stood there, leaning against the wall and thinking about what he'd done, a clear but terrible question came over me. Was Grace's body lying beneath that carefully arranged bed of rocks?

51

NOW: MORGAN

I stayed in the garden for over two hours after Colin's unsettling outbreak of emotion. It felt as if something was holding me and wouldn't let me go. Maybe it was simply my fear of the people inside the house. Or maybe it was my questioning mind, trying to come to grips with the frightening thought that had taken root. It drilled its way into my brain, growing sharper and more painful as the minutes, and then the hours, ticked past.

All I could do was lean against the wall and try not to look at the outline of that tree, still black in the moonlight, still throwing its shadow on the wall behind it. The bed of rocks was no longer visible from where I stood, but I could see it in my mind.

It seemed unbelievably foolish for him to murder someone and bury her body only thirty yards from his wife's studio. It seemed like a terrible risk to bury a woman's body anywhere on their property. Especially when he was surrounded by a desert that offered endless miles of parched earth, space that had very few landmarks, where a grave might go undiscovered for decades.

If you murdered someone, wouldn't you want their body as far away as possible from where you lived? Wouldn't you want that reminder gone from your field of vision? Wouldn't you want all traces removed? Unless it was someone you cared about, whose mother meant the world to you, and you wanted to honor her memory and keep her close.

I opened the guest room door. Jade's breathing was heavy and deep.

I got dressed for bed, slid beneath the covers, and lay awake for a long time. After a brief sleep without dreams, but a sense that I wasn't really sleeping at all, I woke well before the sun was up. I dressed in jeans, a T-shirt, and tennies. I returned to the garden and went directly to the tree that Colin had gripped as if he wanted to wrench the branch from the trunk.

Staring at the bed of rocks, I tried to figure out what I was planning to do. I'd wondered if calling the police was the smart thing to do. I wasn't equipped to start digging up the hard-packed earth, looking for something I didn't want to find. But nothing had changed from when I'd followed Colin out there. The bra was still hidden in the pillow. I could show the police and they could test the blood. I imagined it would take weeks. And what would it tell them? They might not even have a way to match the blood to Grace's. And there was no proof the bra belonged to her.

Would the police come out here and start digging because I gave them a woman's bra and told them a well-respected member of their community had been standing in the garden looking and sounding distraught? The thought made me want to laugh, I knew the reaction it would elicit from them.

At the same time, I didn't have a shovel or pick. I hadn't even thought to bring a large serving spoon. Did I think I was going to dig with my bare hands?

But I couldn't let it rest. I had to know if she was under there. Maybe it wouldn't take much.

I ducked under the branch, knelt down, and began moving the rocks. They weren't heavy. It was tedious, and it made my knees ache as I crawled around, reaching in ever-widening arcs to grab the rocks and move them to the side.

Finally, I had several good-sized piles and a bare area of dirt, the soil loose from where the rocks had pressed into it. I stood and broke a stick off the tree. I began scraping at the dirt, kicking a few remaining rocks out of my way, wondering how long this was going to take, fully aware it was an impossible task.

Was it possible I'd imagined the whole thing, and now someone would find me digging like a lunatic in the garden, scratching and scraping at the dirt, thinking I might burrow six feet into the ground and uncover a woman's decaying flesh hanging onto her bones?

"What are you doing?"

The voice was soft, almost a whisper in the pre-dawn light, but it shocked me like the sound of a gunshot. I fell forward, twisting my wrist as my hand landed on soft dirt where one of the larger rocks had been resting. I felt something squirm beneath the side of my hand. I screamed and yanked it away. I looked down and saw a beetle burrow into the ground.

I gasped for air, half crying at the fright of the voice and the horror of how many other disgusting bugs might be crawling just beneath where I sat.

I straightened and turned.

Bryce stood behind me, his long hair still wet from the shower, combed back from his face, but loose and wavy, not in the ponytail he wore during the midday heat.

"What are you doing, Morgan?"

"I …"

He took a few steps closer. "Are you sleepwalking?"

"No. I'm wide awake."

He bent over me, peering into my eyes as if he didn't believe me and he would be able to tell from how my eyes focused whether or not I was truly awake. "Are you okay?" he asked.

"I'm not sure. Not really."

He squatted beside me. "Why are you up so early?"

"Why are you?"

"I couldn't sleep. I was headed out to the studio to get some work done, and I heard rocks getting kicked around. What are you doing?"

"It sounds … I think Grace might be buried here." I thought he would laugh, but he didn't.

"Why do you think that?"

"Colin was out here. He was crying and acting really strange."

"So you took the giant leap to thinking Grace is buried here? Why?"

I looked down at my hands. They were shaking. I wasn't sure if it was from that monstrous insect or my continued certainty, even though I didn't have a shred of proof and I had nothing to dig with, that I was sitting on the grave of Tyler's sister. "It's just a feeling. But I can't get rid of it, and I won't be able to get rid of it until I check."

"And you're going to dig six feet into the ground with your bare hands?" He took my shaking hand in his. "You're going to tear up those beautiful fingernails?"

I showed him the stick.

He laughed softly. "You seem really sure."

"I was awake most of the night. You didn't see how Colin was acting. Something was wrong. He was really upset."

"If you're right, that would be stupid of him to come to her grave when someone was watching and start crying over her."

"He didn't know I was there. He thought I … he was angry that I'd gone into his office. He told me to put her bra back and I think he thought … I don't know what he was thinking. All I know is that he seemed like he was losing his mind—crying and sort of … praying. So maybe he wasn't really thinking."

Bryce nodded. "Okay. Maybe." He hesitated for several moments. "You're really going to dig?"

"I am." I began stabbing at the dirt with the stick, scraping away chunks of it, then stabbing again to loosen more sections.

Bryce stood and snapped one of the branches, forming his own digging tool. "It's rather primitive."

"It'll work. For now."

"It will take forever." He left, returning a few minutes later with a garden spade and a small hand-held hoe. He gave the spade to me. He knelt a few feet away from me and began carving grooves in the dirt with the hoe. We dug and scraped, neither of us talking.

I wanted to find something. At the same time, I dreaded finding what I was looking for.

52

NOW: MORGAN

The horizon was a strip of bright orange, topped by a strip of cerulean blue, still midnight blue overhead when I heard a cracking sound as my spade struck something brittle.

I sat back on my heels and readjusted my grip on the handle.

Bryce didn't appear to have heard the noise because he continued dragging the hoe through the dirt, digging deep grooves, loosening the soil for me to scoop out. It was slow and tedious and kind of ridiculous that we were trying to dig a hole that, if it contained what we both thought it did, was much too large to dig up with hand tools.

If Ember came out to her studio, it was unlikely she would see us, hidden by the arrangement of the walls that surrounded the garden. But just as Bryce had heard rocks thudding against each other as I kicked them aside, she was likely to catch the sound of metal blades digging into the earth.

I began scooping out a larger hole around the spot where I'd heard the crack, anxious about what I was about to find, concerned about the quickly rising sun and the chance that Ember or someone else might discover us. They wouldn't be as eager to help me as Bryce had been.

I lifted out several shovels full of dirt, piling them beside me in little mounds. Then, I saw what I'd known I would find, but had dreaded throughout the night, and as the sun rose in spectacular silence around me. The unmistakable fingertip of a human hand.

A guttural sound burst out of me, seeming to come from a place so deep I hardly knew it existed. It was half groan, half scream. I dropped the spade and covered my face with my hands. "Oh, God! Oh, God!" I shoved myself away from the spot where I'd been sitting, kicking my feet at the piles of dirt, wanting to get as far away as I could.

Bile shot up through my esophagus, but I gagged and choked it back.

I turned away, digging my nails into my hairline.

"What?" Bryce said. "What? Oh. Oh, I see."

I felt his hand on the back of my shoulder. "It's ... come over here. It's okay."

"It's not okay!"

"I didn't mean ..." He squeezed my shoulder.

I pushed his hand off me and struggled to my feet. "It's too awful. I don't even know what to do. I can't believe this is happening. I knew she was dead, but I didn't ... I didn't really think ..." I was gasping for air. I desperately wanted to talk to Tyler. I wanted him to hold me. I needed to tell Jade, but I didn't want to be the one to tell her. She couldn't see this. How could I tell her? What would I say? I couldn't bring her out here.

My thoughts and stomach spun wildly. I wanted to throw up, but I couldn't even seem to do that. The edges of my vision were turning dark. Everything began to blur as if I might pass out. The sun was moving higher above the horizon, flooding the place where we stood, the temperature rising with it. I was perspiring and shivering at the same time.

"Morgan?" Bryce's voice sounded very far away.

53

NOW: MORGAN

I felt the heat of his fingers gripping my upper arms, pressing into my flesh. He was holding me up. His voice was firm and calm. "Morgan. Are you okay? Do you need to sit down?"

I shook my head.

As I did, my vision cleared slightly. His face, the tree behind him, and the wall surrounding us came into focus. The rising sunlight was so bright, the tree looked black against the pale adobe wall. I squinted, trying to protect my eyes from rays as sharp as knives.

"Are you sure?"

"I'm fine." I tried to take a step back, but his grip on my arms remained strong. I wanted him to let go, but at the same time, it was comforting to feel his hands keeping me steady. Despite my words, I wasn't sure I was fine.

For days, I'd known Grace was dead. I'd known it in the pit of my stomach. Watching Colin twist his hands around that tree and pound his fists into the ground, I'd been equally sure she was buried there. Yet, on some level, I hadn't actually expected to dig up part of her body. I'd scraped at the dirt with a fury and strength I didn't know I possessed. But I hadn't expected to uncover a piece of her. I'd never truly imagined coming face to face with the thoughts that tormented me now—the rest of her arm just inches away, and her body beyond that. Her face covered with dirt, pressing into her mouth and nostrils, her eyelids sealed shut by the weight of the earth.

I started to cry.

"Don't think about it," Bryce said. "Don't think so much. My brother ..."

"What about your brother?"

"Sometimes your imagination can destroy you."

I understood what he meant, but it wasn't as if I could stop the thoughts from rising in my head. They were there before I even noticed them taking shape.

"I need to call the police," I said.

"Let's take a minute to—"

"I'm not digging anymore!" I poked my fingers into my pocket.

As my fingertips touched the edge of my phone, Bryce's hand slid down my arm. He loosened his grip slightly. His wrist pressed against my breast.

I tried to move away from him, but he continued holding my arms.

"Please let go of me."

"I want to be sure you're okay." His hand was still touching my breast, moving ever so slightly as if he wanted to keep it there.

"Let go."

He took a step closer. He let go of my left arm and slid his hand up under the back of my shirt. He began fiddling with the clasp on my bra. As I struggled to shove him away from me, he yanked me so close I could hardly breathe. The hand that had been fiddling with my bra was suddenly around my neck, his thumb stroking my throat. He pressed gently against my throat as he pulled my lips close to his.

I twisted hard, shoving my shoulder against his armpit and grinding my knee into his thigh as best I could. "Get away from me!"

He grunted and let go, stumbling back a few steps. "Oh. Oh, shit. I'm—"

"You're disgusting. We're standing on her grave!"

"I'm sorry." He moved toward me again.

"Don't come near me."

His eyes filled with tears. He blinked, then pressed the heels of his hands into his eye sockets. "God, I'm sorry. I just wanted to make sure you were okay. I thought you might pass out. And then I …" He lowered his hands and took another step toward me.

I moved back.

He held up his hands. "I won't come any closer. I'm sorry. I …" His voice trembled. "I've wanted you since the minute I saw you. I've been falling for you more every day. I just … it was too much, being so close to you."

I stared at him. He'd never given the slightest hint. Part of me didn't even believe him. Was I that caught up in my thoughts of death and my intense discomfort sitting in Ember's studio, that I'd been oblivious? I wasn't sure. But I didn't want to think or talk about it right now. It was so disgusting that he wanted to kiss me, to grope me when we were standing right on top of a woman's murdered body. Her decaying hand was right there! "She's dead! And that's what you're thinking about?"

"I said I'm sorry."

I pulled my phone out of my pocket.

"I don't know if we should call the police yet," he said.

"Are you serious? Why not?"

"Shouldn't we tell the others first? They're going to be … what about Jade?"

I didn't want to tell the others first. One of them—Colin or Ember, but maybe Hendrix, or even Olivia or Avery—was a killer. Why would we tell them before the police had a chance to get here and watch their reactions as they found out their crime had been discovered?

At the same time, Bryce was right.

What about Jade?

It was going to be the worst day of her life, a horrifying moment she would never forget. It was cruel to make her hear about it from a police officer. It was beyond cruel to think about the clinical detail with which they might deliver the news. They wouldn't confirm it was Grace for ages. Maybe weeks or longer. They would say cold, anonymous, dehumanizing things to Jade about *the body*.

They probably wouldn't let her anywhere near her daughter's grave. It was possible she wouldn't *want* to be anywhere near the grave, but what if she did?

It was also possible she still wouldn't believe me. What was there to show her but a decaying woman's hand? Would she recognize it as her daughter's? Or would the denial root itself more deeply than ever? Would she be so sickened and shocked that she wouldn't even look, or in looking, she would *know* without a doubt that it couldn't possibly be the hand of her beautiful young daughter?

"I don't think they should know." I spoke slowly. Carefully. Still thinking as the words came out of my mouth. I hardly wanted to be talking to him at all. "But maybe I can bring Jade out here without them knowing."

"I don't understand your big rush to call the police. We could—"

"If you think I'm going to help you dig up her body. No. We need the police. Now. As soon as I tell Jade."

He took a tentative step closer to where I was. "Why don't you—"

"If you take one more step closer, I'm going to scream. So back off."

He moved away. He looked defeated and slightly worried.

"I don't understand why you don't want to call the police. They need to figure this out. They need to remove her body."

He was quiet for several seconds. Finally, he said, "Ember isn't going to like it."

I stared at him. Sometimes it seemed as if he was almost afraid of Ember. Maybe he knew in his heart that she had killed them. Maybe he'd known that all along.

54

NOW: MORGAN

*G*ently inviting Jade to come to the cactus garden to see the gravesite I'd uncovered turned out to be a waste of time and breath and energy. She was horrified that I'd found part of a woman's body.

"If you even *know* it's a woman," she said. "I do not know how you could even tell." She squeezed her eyes shut and twisted her lips into an expression of revulsion. "After being in the ground, and with … decay … and, everything." She shuddered violently and somewhat dramatically. She acted as if she were talking about a TV show, not an actual body lying unprotected in the ground several hundred feet from where she sat on the soft, cream-colored leather couch in the living room.

She didn't believe I could possibly determine whether it was the hand of a *young* woman.

"It could belong to an indigenous person who died in this area centuries ago," she said.

She certainly didn't believe it had anything to do with Colin or Ember. She reluctantly agreed the police *probably* should be called, but Colin and Ember should be the ones to make that decision and place the call.

"Don't you want to see it first?" I asked. "So you can—"

"Absolutely not."

"But what if it's—"

Tears filled her eyes. "Why are you trying to hurt me like this? It's hard enough that I haven't heard from Grace for all this time. I don't want to start worrying she's dead. Please don't do this."

"We need to call the police," I said softly.

"Call the police about what?"

I turned quickly at the sound of Colin's voice. I felt betrayed that nothing in Jade's expression had made me aware he was standing behind me, listening to our conversation. I'd hoped to give Jade a private moment to see what I'd found, to see if she might recognize her daughter's hand, as horrible as that sounded, as awful as it would be. But she would at least have a moment to go out there alone, with the support of someone who cared about her.

"I—"

"Apparently, Morgan was digging in your garden." Jade raised her voice to drown out anything I might say. She spoke in a rapid, excited tone. "And she found part of a human hand. She—"

"Not part—" I said.

Jade's voice grew louder. "She found a human hand. I explained that given the age of the building where Ember's studio is, it's probably a burial ground from—"

"A hand?" Colin walked into the room. He folded his arms across his chest. "Why were you *digging*?" He gave a short laugh. "Where, exactly, was this?"

I got up off the couch. "We need to call the police."

"We're not calling the police until you show me what you're talking about." Colin glanced at Jade. "That building was preserved from the 1870s. So I think Jade makes an excellent point. Let's go take a look. I think the first thing we need to do is get an archaeologist out here."

"We don't need an archaeologist," I said. "It's not just bones. It's …" I felt a wave of nausea pass through me. I placed my hand on my stomach, trying to calm my sick feelings. "It has skin and … I don't want to describe it. But we need to call the police."

Colin held up his hand. "Calm down."

"I'm calm."

"You don't look calm. And you definitely don't sound calm."

I took a step toward him. He was not going to intimidate me. "I found a human hand. I can show you where it is, but then I'm calling the police." I started toward the glass doors.

"I'm taking you at your word, but I disagree that the first step is calling the police," Colin said. "As I already told you, first, we'll get an assessment from an archaeologist."

"These aren't bones from two hundred years ago," I said.

"You're an expert?"

"There's *skin*. And … it looks …" I closed my eyes. "It's decayed."

"This is the desert. Decay happens differently under intense heat and dry conditions."

"This isn't old. I'm sure of it."

"We aren't going to create a circus with the police before we know what we're dealing with." He gave me a chastising look. "You don't seem to understand what happens when someone with a name like Ember West finds herself in the news. We need to protect her."

I laughed. "There's a dead woman's hand, and most likely, the rest of a dead body buried right outside her studio. And all you care about is PR?" I pulled my phone out of my pocket.

Colin turned abruptly and walked out of the room.

"Morgan." I ignored Jade's pleading voice and unlocked my phone. I tapped to open a browser to search for the Palm Springs police department.

"Morgan, please. Sit down so we can talk for a minute."

I stared at my phone, waiting for the search window to open, but it remained blank. I looked at the top of the screen. There were no cell connectivity bars, no WiFi bars. Only the SOS letters were displayed.

"There's no signal," I said.

"Please sit down," Jade said.

I turned to face her. "Why aren't you upset that there's a dead body in their garden?!"

"It's not a body. It's a hand. I just think you're overreacting a bit. Let's find out what we're dealing with. There's no emergency here."

I closed the browser window and opened another, knowing it was futile. I locked and unlocked my phone. I went to the settings and tried reconnecting the WiFi. "He disabled the cell booster! And the WiFi. I can't get a signal at all."

"Can we please let Colin handle this? He'll call the right people. I know you don't like it, but they need to worry about PR. And he probably wants to call their attorney."

I stared at my useless phone. Obviously, I wouldn't be calling anyone. Not even Tyler. I was trapped here. For all I knew, Colin would dig up the rest of Grace's body and move it to a place where no one would ever find it.

55

NOW: MORGAN

I left Jade alone on the couch, her hand resting on the cushion where I'd been sitting, as if she thought I might view it as an invitation to return for a deeper conversation. One in which she would persuade me that the hand I'd uncovered belonged to someone who had died before any of us were born.

I went into our room, took a long hot shower, and dressed in jeans and a tank top. I dried my hair and put it into a loose knot on top of my head. I didn't bother with makeup. I couldn't see the point.

Feeling cleansed of dirt and the touch of Bryce's hands on my body, as well as what I'd seen protruding from the earth, promising that more decaying flesh lay just below it, I went searching for a mug of strong coffee and something light to settle my stomach.

Bryce and Colin were in the kitchen. Colin was talking rapidly about taking things one step at a time. "After the archaeologist has made an assessment," Colin said, "we'll contact the police. Absolutely. They'll need a warrant first, of course."

Bryce stared at him. "But it looked—"

"We need an expert opinion, Bryce."

"The police are experts," I said.

"I don't want trouble because I disturbed a sacred burial ground," Colin said. "Ember does not need that kind of publicity."

"I'm not stupid," I said. "I know what old bones look like, and I know what a decaying corpse looks like. You don't have to be a forensics expert to know the difference between history and murder."

Colin scowled at me.

"It's so upsetting," Bryce said. "All this time, I really thought Derek killed himself. But now …"

"Don't start that," Colin said. "Ember doesn't need this. You need to be on her team. One hundred percent. You know that."

"But two bodies? In her *studio*."

"This is not in her studio," Colin said. "And the archaeologist might—"

"But right outside her studio. Almost on the doorstep. I was thinking about that when we were digging," Bryce said. "And if it is Grace, which makes sense … when you think about how she just vanished into thin air."

"She didn't *vanish into thin air*." Colin's voice was high-pitched, mimicking Bryce as if he were a small child making up fairy tales.

"I'm just saying. Ember is so passionate. So driven. We all know that. And Hendrix really capitalized on Derek's death. Maybe Ember thought …" Bryce glanced at me. "It sounds so awful. But she would do anything for her art. You know that, Colin. We all know that. She loves her work to the point of insanity."

"Stop it!" Colin shouted. "You're supposed to be her biggest supporter. She trusts you and relies on you to understand her vision. I forbid you to talk like that. Especially when she's not here to defend herself. She would never …" He gave Bryce a dark look. "My wife is not capable of murder. It would never even cross her mind. Whatever Hendrix did was marketing and crass commercialism. Sure, it worked. There's a sick vein in humanity. We're attracted to the unknowns, the latent fear of death. It doesn't matter. Ember is an artist. She's gentle and kind and spiritual. She's not violent."

He paused, breathing hard, looking as if he were trying to control his body, making sure he didn't strike out at Bryce with his fists. As if to prove my impression accurate, he folded his arms across his chest, curled his hands into fists, and tucked them under his biceps. "If you consider people in our circle who are capable of violence, who have a reported history of violence, maybe we need to take a look at your schizophrenic brother."

"My brother has—"

"He's already been charged with one murder. How many times was that woman stabbed?"

"Adam didn't kill her! That has nothing to do with this!"

"We all know how the legal system works. Didn't kill her, or had the best legal team money can buy?"

"That's not fair!" Bryce's face was red, looking as if his blood was pumping so hard it might start spilling through his long, light hair. "He only got legal help to make sure he got justice. But he didn't do it! The police blamed his mental health issues because it gave them an easy answer. No thinking required."

"Holding the weapon. Blood all over him." Colin snorted.

"He. Didn't. Kill. Her." Bryce hissed. "And you know that."

"Do I?"

"Yes."

"But I don't. And he lives alone. No one to supervise him taking his medication. And when he doesn't take it, all bets are off. Right?"

"You don't even know him. You don't know anything about him."

"I know enough. So how about we stop with the wild accusations? My theory is a lot more grounded in history and fact than yours is."

Bryce looked like he was going to be sick. He turned and walked out of the kitchen.

I desperately wanted a cup of coffee, but I was afraid to move.

Colin looked satisfied, as if he'd solved Grace's murder and there was nothing else to be concerned about. All the police needed to do was remove her body, find Bryce's brother, and arrest him.

"Why do you have her bra? With blood on it?" I asked. "If you think Bryce's brother killed her?"

"We don't even know if there's a body out there. You found a hand," Colin said. "So as I said, let's take this one step at a time. And we still don't know the age of your … finding."

"You didn't answer my question." I couldn't believe my boldness. If he'd killed her, what might he do to me? I would be in the house with him that night. "Why did you turn off the cell phone booster? And the WiFi?"

"Because this is my home and we need to follow the right procedure to protect my family. We need an archaeologist. We need to contact our attorney, and we need to engage Hendrix. There's no emergency requiring the police right now."

I stared at him, trying to read his expression, wondering if he was the most entitled person I'd ever encountered, or if he was scared out of his mind, or if it was something else.

Would he, or Ember, really do something to hurt me? Everyone would know. Or was he right about Bryce's mentally ill brother? When Bryce had mentioned his brother's health issues, he'd led me to believe it was something affecting his body, not his mind. What was Bryce trying to hide from me? Maybe he knew exactly where Grace was buried. Maybe I hadn't accidentally dug up her hand after all, but had been subtly and elegantly led to that spot by Bryce. I tried to recall how the morning had unfolded, but now it had all become a dreamlike blur.

I pressed my hand against my throat, not sure what to think, not sure if I should be afraid or if I was overreacting.

"I found the bra in Ember's studio," Colin said. "I didn't know who it belonged to and I … it just seemed best to keep it, and to make sure it was in a secure place. That's all. I was looking out for Ember. I always am." He turned and walked toward the doors leading to the patio.

I guessed he'd worked up his courage enough to go look at the hand lying half buried in his garden.

56

BEFORE: BRYCE

*I*t was one of the best days of my life when I heard the judge read the jury's verdict in my brother's trial for second degree murder—*Not guilty.*

He had an excellent lawyer. A lawyer who didn't come cheaply. He had a team of paralegals and other staff who gave Adam the best defense possible. They were able to create reasonable certainty that my brother had never seen that poor woman in his life. Not until the moment he'd tried to rouse her from death. That meant there was no logical motive for murder. They created tremendous doubt around the prosecutor's speculation about what Adam *might* have done. They left the jury believing Adam didn't have blood on him for any other reason than what he'd said repeatedly—that he'd tried to help by removing the knife.

His legal team brought in a panel of experts to testify about the nature of Adam's diagnosis and the specifics of how it presented in his case. There were flaws in the way the police handled his initial interview and mistakes in their handling of the weapon.

The attorney had told me when we first met that Adam's case wasn't difficult.

Still, I'd worried.

I'd spent months lying awake at night, picturing my brother in a prison cell, succumbing to despair. I pictured my slender brother with his surprised, slightly wounded, and confused brown eyes staring into the darkness. I imagined him squeezing his eyes closed in fear. I imagined him listening for every sound, terrified of the man sharing the cell with him.

I pictured him at meals, gagging down food cooked without any care for texture or flavor and minimal concern for nutrition. I saw him wasting away, retreating further into his mind as the neural pathways were overrun by his wild thoughts as he figured out ways to hide his medications and flush them down the toilet. Or worse, I imagined his medications poorly managed and his bright, curious mind dulled a little more every day until he resembled a zombie.

His mind would be transformed until he was nothing but the product of the chemicals they pumped into him, the drugs taking over his personality, altering his thoughts and quieting them to the point of numbness. All that would exist were the pharmaceuticals telling him when to stand and sit, when to eat and respond to questions in the most perfunctory way imaginable. Adam himself would dissolve into nothing.

My mother wanted Adam to live in a group home. She thought he would do best in a situation where there was a caregiver to monitor his medications. Of course, she was right. I knew that. I couldn't be running over to his apartment every day, arguing with him about pills. I couldn't be driving him to medical appointments.

"I don't need a babysitter," Adam said.

"The caregiver isn't a babysitter," I said. "You'll have total freedom to come and go like any adult, it's just—"

"I have to be there on a schedule for drugs. It's a hard no."

"Adam, please. If you don't take your meds, shit happens."

"Shit always happens. That's life."

"Mom will feel better. I'll—"

"I'm not on this planet to make you and mom *feel better.*"

I rubbed my eyes. "I know. I know. I shouldn't have said it like that. I—"

"What part of *hard no* did you not understand?"

"Are you going to take your meds?"

"Absolutely."

"But before, you stopped."

"This isn't before."

I got it. I wouldn't want to be treated like I needed a babysitter either. He was an adult man. But after what he'd just been through. He was one bad situation, one *wrong-place-at-the-wrong-time* choice from it happening again.

"There would be someone to clean for you. I sure wouldn't mind living in a place where I had housekeeping services," I said.

"Then you should move into a group home."

"What if you get into another bad situation?"

"I won't go grabbing knives out of dead women anymore. Promise. Lesson learned." He laughed.

The tone of his laughter did not make me feel better.

"You promise you'll take your meds?"

"I promise, little bro."

"Can I set alerts on your phone for you?"

"I can set my own alerts."

"Do you want me to come by? At least every ... maybe once a week or so?"

"Just back off, okay? I appreciate everything you did, Bryce. Okay? Getting that lawyer saved me from a lot of bad shit. But now I'm free. And I want to live my own life. Got it?"

I got it.

I was glad he was acquitted. I was absolutely certain he was innocent. I had been since the moment I received his phone call telling me he'd been arrested. But I had very little certainty he was going to stick with the regimen for his medications. It made me feel helpless and uncertain. I hated that feeling.

57

NOW: MORGAN

I ended up sitting in the guest room with the door locked all day. Colin refused to turn on the cell booster or the WiFi, and Jade saw nothing disturbing about this. She said I'd made him so uncomfortable, he couldn't trust me. Apparently, he had a satellite phone that he'd used to get in touch with their attorney and an archaeologist. Both were scheduled to arrive the following day.

After that, the police would be called.

Jade thought this was a perfectly reasonable reaction. When I told her Tyler would be worried, she assured me I was wrong. He wanted me to relax and enjoy the experience and he wouldn't give it a second thought.

Jade had driven into Palm Springs for the day, taking Ember with her because she thought Ember needed to get away from the trauma of what had happened. They were spending the day at a spa, soaking in a hot tub, getting massages.

"We're going to enjoy a long, lavish but healthy lunch," she said. "Mostly lavish, with lots of champagne." She giggled, as if the dead hand protruding from the soil behind the house was nothing more than a prank. A plastic prop. Something that had nothing to do with them.

They'd invited me to go with them, so I suppose I wasn't truly trapped there, but I had no desire to join them in pretending everything was normal. I actually didn't want to get in touch with Tyler at this point. I would not lie to him, and I didn't see how I could explain what was going on. I would have to see it through alone. My only choice seemed to be staying and making sure his willfully blind mother was safe with these people.

All day, fear and wild speculation gnawed at me, destroying my appetite. I existed on nothing but a few pieces of fruit and lots of water. I curled into a fetal position on my bed, wishing I could shut off my brain as easily as my stomach had turned off its desire for anything beyond a few slices of peach or the occasional strawberry that went down and sat in my stomach like a piece of wet clay.

Maybe Colin had finally been honest with me. For whatever reason, he hadn't mentioned Bryce's brother until he was forced into it. He allowed me to think he, or his wife, had murdered two people. Then, suddenly, when Bryce was disloyal to Ember, he'd opened his mouth and told the truth.

Didn't mental illness often run in families? Could that be the case with Bryce and Adam? Bryce had turned out not to be the sympathetic, helpful person I'd thought he was. It disturbed me that he insisted he'd been drawn to me since we first met. I was certain I would have picked up on that at some point. But there hadn't been a whisper of attraction—not a glance or a flirtatious comment or an accidental brushing of his hand against mine. Nothing. I hadn't once caught him staring at me in that way or noticed him trying to maneuver himself to sit beside me.

What he'd done was beyond disgusting. Aside from pawing at me without bothering to find out if I felt the same, to do that while part of a corpse was lying a few feet away from us was so revolting, I felt my stomach heave every time I thought about it.

He'd been so eager to help me dig. He hadn't questioned that I was moving the rocks, hadn't wondered if I was leaping to conclusions. He'd agreed wholeheartedly with my belief that Grace was buried there, and he'd started digging in the spot where she was.

Maybe he'd known exactly where she was buried because his brother had murdered her and Bryce had buried her body to cover up his brother's crime.

Adam had already been arrested and stood trial for brutally stabbing a woman. Colin suggested he'd had a very expensive legal team. It's no secret that the more someone pays, the better chance they have of getting acquitted. It happens every day in every state in the country.

I honestly wasn't sure what I believed.

I *was* sure that I was scared.

Someone had murdered Grace and buried her body near Ember's studio. How hard would it have been for Bryce to hide her blood-stained bra in Colin's office? Although Colin had claimed he found it …, maybe they were all lying.

It didn't really matter.

Two of Ember's subjects were dead. I didn't want to be the third, no matter how much my logical brain told me that couldn't and wouldn't happen, not with Jade here, not with Tyler knowing where I was. But the fear was still there. My hands trembled and my heart raced, no matter how much I assured myself I was safe.

As it turned out, Ember's pampering extended past dinnertime, because the sun was going down when Jade and Ember finally returned to the house.

By the time Jade opened our bedroom door, I felt like a wild animal, trapped in a corner, my claws extended, starved, and ready to lash out at anyone who came too close.

"I think we should leave." The moment the words were out, I knew they were a mistake.

Jade sighed. "Ember and I had such a beautiful day."

"I'm scared."

She laughed as she approached the foot of my bed, where I sat curled up near the headboard. She settled on the edge of my bed, crossing her legs. She ran her hand over her pale pink skirt. "I'm really concerned about you, sweetie." She placed her hand on the bed as if she meant to grab hold of my ankle in a comforting gesture, but couldn't quite reach it and couldn't be bothered to move closer.

She pulled her hand back to her side. "I know finding that hand was upsetting. But I'm sure it will all be worked out with the archaeologist. You need to stop obsessing about everything. I'm not sure what's causing all this, and I'm so sorry if I haven't been as attentive as I should have—"

"Don't you realize what's going on here?" Her reaction stunned me. I wasn't sure if she'd sunk so deep into denial she was making up stories in her head, or if she was gaslighting me. Had Ember asked her to *manage* me?

"I don't know if it's the pressure of sitting for a portrait, which everyone has explained can be grueling. Or if you're not used to the desert heat ..." She laughed softly. "But your behavior is so disrespectful. You've been insulting, and downright hurtful to some of my dearest friends. My family."

"I know, but ... you have to realize someone was murdered here. Probably two people. And I don't think it's safe."

She stood.

"Colin and Ember are dealing with legal issues now that are going to cause them a lot of upset. I'm not walking out when they need me. Please try to get a grip. If you'd prefer to leave, I'm sure Tyler will be more than happy to come get you." She walked out of the room, leaving the door open behind her.

58

NOW: MORGAN

The door yawned open into the dark hallway. I couldn't hear a sound coming from anywhere in the house, and I had no idea where Jade had gone.

I crept out of bed and went to the open door and peered out. As far as I could see, there was nothing but darkness, lit only by two small nightlights. I stepped out of the room and walked slowly along the hallway, feeling the buffed wood on the soles of my bare feet.

When I reached the entryway from where I could see the entrances to all the other rooms, everything was dark except for a standing lamp in the living room.

It was windy outside, and the air was blowing through the open bifold doors. I crossed the room quickly, overcome with terror that a mentally ill man, someone driven to kill without knowing why, might be out there. He could be watching from the other side of the patio. The gates were locked at night, but the five-foot walls weren't impossible to scale.

Why was the house so quiet? The fairy lights strung across the patio that had been lit every evening were turned off.

I began closing the doors as fast as I could. After I'd secured the first two, I felt my heart beating so fast I was gasping for air. Was I locking a madman out, or securing the killer inside the house?

I whimpered slightly as I closed the third door.

"What's wrong?"

At the sound of Ember's voice, low and somewhat meek sounding in the semi-darkness, I whirled around.

"Are you okay?" She turned on one of the table lamps. "You look scared out of your mind."

"I…"

She moved toward me. "Why are you closing the doors? It's nice to have some fresh air coming into the house." Her voice was still soft, much kinder and less imperial than usual.

I didn't know what to tell her. I did not know who to trust anymore. Was Adam Cunningham a killer, with a brother who helped cover his crimes?

"Colin said Bryce has a mentally ill brother. That he was arrested for stabbing a woman and—"

"He was acquitted. He has nothing to do with this."

"But he—"

"Colin had no business talking about that. It has nothing to do with him, or you, or …" she waved her hand, then covered her mouth as if she were trying to keep words, or maybe vomit inside her body. Her shoulders heaved slightly and she let out a muffled sob.

"I think it's Grace," I said. "Buried out there."

"Maybe," she whispered through her fingers. "I just don't …" she moved her hand away from her face. "Let's open these doors." Her voice was strained. She placed her keys and cell phone on the table and moved around me, unlocking the first door and sliding it along the track.

The wind drifted into the room again, washing over me. It felt soothing, but I couldn't stop looking outside, wishing the strings of lights were turned on.

"I hope it's not Grace," she said, sliding open the second door. "It would be too awful. I thought she just couldn't ... I never understood why Derek killed himself right in my ..." Her voice broke. "In my studio! It's been almost impossible since then. Even though ..." her voice fractured again.

"Even though your career took off?"

She nodded.

"I told him sitting for a portrait was hard work. But it felt like he wanted to punish me. And I don't really know why."

"Unless someone killed him," I said.

She shook her head so hard, the loose knot of hair came undone and her hair tumbled down around her shoulders. She hurried to the other door and wrenched it open, lifting her face so the air could blow across her skin. "I can't do it. Sometimes, I don't think ..." There was a long, achingly painful silence. "I can't do it."

Her words echoed precisely the words Olivia had said were painted across the neck of Derek's unfinished portrait. The supposed *suicide* note—*I can't do it.* Maybe it wasn't a suicide note after all. Had Ember written them?

"Can't do what?"

"I can't do them justice. I can't do you justice. I can't capture your spirit, your soul. I just ... can't." She turned and rushed out of the room.

I stood in front of the open doors, feeling the wind whip through the room. It wasn't safe, standing there alone, still wondering who might be out there, but equally afraid of who was inside the house. I didn't even know where Jade had gone. Maybe she was cozied up having a heart-to-heart talk with Colin. Maybe she'd gone with him for a late night meeting with their attorney.

Staring out into the darkness, I felt totally exposed on all sides.

I can't do it.

The words danced in my head. I'd never seen Derek's unfinished portrait. I'd never seen Grace's. Bryce had interrupted me that day when I was looking for them. Were they still in the storage room, or had they been destroyed? And now, I was overcome with a desire to see my own unfinished portrait as well.

I had to see all of them, but mostly, I wanted to see the words painted on Derek's portrait. I wasn't sure why. How would I know if she'd painted them? And if she had, what did it mean?

All I knew was that I had to see those portraits.

59

NOW: MORGAN

*W*alking out to the studio was terrifying, but I wasn't going to wait until morning. If Colin continued with his charade of calling in an archaeologist, I might not be able to get into the studio. And he couldn't put off calling the police indefinitely. Once they arrived, the entire area would be off limits..

If I wanted to see those paintings, this was my only chance.

I was still barefoot because I didn't want to risk returning to the bedroom, running into someone else, and being prevented from going out there. The minute Ember had left the room, and I saw her cell phone and keys, forgotten on the table, I'd grabbed her keys.

Inside, the studio was the same comfortable temperature as always. It surprised me to know it was kept that way even at night. I left the lights off and hurried through the studio to the hallway leading to the supply room, her workroom, and the gallery at the back.

I went into the supply room and shone my light around. Filling the entire wall to my left, floor-to-ceiling, was a large cabinet with narrow drawers. I opened one and saw tubes of paint lined up in perfect order, all the ends rolled up neatly instead of squashed in the middle like some might have done. I opened another drawer, which was filled with palette knives.

The adjacent wall was occupied by another large cabinet. Inside were brushes, stacks of sketch pads, charcoal pencils, and boxes of other supplies. Next, I went to a waist-high rack that extended about four feet from the back wall, standing beneath a long window covered by shutters. The rack had thin wooden rods across the top. Canvases stretched on frames were stacked inside. There were at least forty canvases in the rack. I'd only made it through about ten of them before Bryce had interrupted me a few days earlier.

One by one, I began pulling out the paintings, just far enough to see the subjects. I had no idea what Derek looked like, but unless it had been painted over, the note on his neck would set him apart. So far, all the paintings I'd seen appeared to be unfinished. Many of the faces were amorphous, giving them a slightly ghostly appearance. It made me nervous about finding my own, because the paintings didn't look necessarily unfinished, but almost deliberately disturbing.

I'd only seen a few photographs of Grace, so I also wasn't entirely sure I'd recognize her portrait either. I hadn't expected to find quite so many unfinished. Had all the subjects in these paintings left before Ember could finish painting? They couldn't possibly be dead. Surely I would have heard about that.

I'd gone through fifteen or twenty canvases before I pulled out one that I knew without a doubt was Grace. Even with only a vague suggestion of her cheekbones and forehead, I recognized her. The color of her hair was almost identical to Tyler's. And her half-smile made me feel like I was looking at my fiancé. I hadn't realized they looked so much alike. I gasped softly, suddenly aware of the genius everyone raved about when they talked about Ember's work.

Still, I couldn't look at it for long. Like the painting in her gallery at the back of the studio, the eyes made me uncomfortable. They were flat and soulless. I wanted to cry. The deathlike quality of her eyes made the painting feel like a premonition of sorts.

I shoved it into the rack, hiding it behind another painting. I wondered if Jade had ever seen it. I wondered if she'd asked about it. She must have made at least a partial payment for it. Didn't the work, even in this state, belong to her? I tried to shake off the image of those eyes as my own eyes filled with tears. I wiped them away and began looking for Derek's portrait.

When I found it, the tears returned. He had the same deadened eyes. The words across his throat looked as if they'd been painted with a palette knife. They were more like cuts on the canvas, and therefore on the skin of his neck. Slashes of blood on his throat—*I can't do it.*

Surely it was the most obscure suicide note ever. Had he written it? Or were they Ember's words? I wanted to ask her, and I was determined that I would. I left the painting leaning against the rack and continued the search for my own, steeling myself to see my own likeness with eyes that looked like those of a corpse.

Then, I found it.

I thought I'd prepared myself, but I hadn't.

Staring into my face as if I were looking into a mirror, a mirror covered with fog that I wanted to wipe clear, was terrifying. I was so scared, I couldn't even cry. I felt the press of emotion inside my throat, descending into my chest, but the tears wouldn't come. My mouth opened as if I were about to scream. I pressed my hand over it, but I knew the scream wasn't coming either. It was too awful.

I felt as if I were looking into my own coffin.

I turned it to face the rack and took several steps away from it, looking behind me, feeling as if someone was in the room, about to twist a rope around my neck. But no one was there. All I heard was my own erratic breathing.

Standing alone against the fourth wall was an enormous old-fashioned roll-top desk. It had six huge drawers, three on each side. There was a tiny key on the chain that looked like it fit the desk lock. I inserted it and turned. I pushed up the roll top cover. Inside was an open laptop computer, locked with a password.

I opened the top drawer on the left side. It was filled with sketch pads. I took out the first one and flipped through it. Every page was filled with sketches of people's eyes. Some were just the iris and pupils, others had the entire eye—lids and lashes, some included the brow and surrounding skin. Pages and pages of eyes, a number of them stiff with oil paint renditions of eyes.

The other notebooks were the same. There were hundreds of eyes, maybe thousands.

Every single eye and partial eye had the same appearance—empty, blank, dead.

Clutching one of the notebooks of glazed, empty eyes, the cover closed so I didn't have to look at them, I turned to the drawers on the right for a quick check, expecting more of the same. Instead, I found expandable file folders with elastic straps. On the outside of each folder were dates and names. One folder listed Derek's name, another included Grace's name in the list. Inside were 8x10 photographs of eyes. They all had timestamps in the upper right corner, as if they had been pulled from a video clip.

Reaching beneath the stack of folders, I lifted all of them out. The last one had my name printed in black ink. Inside were several photographs of my eyes.

I heard a sound from the computer. I turned as it made another sound—a door closing quietly, but with the distinct click of a latch. I inhaled sharply. There must be a security camera in the studio that I'd never noticed. It must have been so tiny it couldn't be seen from the armchair, blocked by one of the hanging plants. It was clear the feed into the computer had just captured the sound of the door opening and closing.

60

NOW: MORGAN

I backed into the corner between the desk and the rack of canvases. Somehow, I felt safer pressed into that small space, although in reality, I was trapped.

The building was silent now, but I knew someone was in there with me. I waited, taking soft, shallow breaths.

A moment later, Ember was standing in the doorway. "You don't belong in here."

"I—"

"You stole my keys."

"They were on the—"

"Get out."

"What is all this?" I held up the notebook, opening it to show her the eyes, gesturing toward the desk.

"My work. It belongs to me. It's private and you have no right to be here."

"Why do they all look dead?"

She rushed across the room and grabbed the notebook. I hung onto it, twisting away from her. She clawed at me, raking her nails down my arm, tearing my skin. Tiny drops of blood bubbled out. "Get away from me!"

She grabbed at the book, pulling it so hard, she yanked me toward her. I fell against the desk, jamming my hip into the corner. I cried out at the sharp pain and she kicked my shin.

"Give it to me. It belongs to me! You shouldn't be looking at it."

"I want to know why they all look dead. Is that what you do? Paint dead people?"

"Stop! Stop talking about it!" She was screaming now, her lips wet with saliva. "You know nothing about it!"

She yanked hard on the notebook, forcing the edges of it to dig into the palms of my hands, but I hung on tightly. Tears filled my eyes as I tried to fight off her kicks. I couldn't kick back with my bare feet, and I couldn't grab at her or hit her and keep control of the notebook at the same time. Letting go of it meant I would never find out why she was so afraid of me seeing it. "Why are you so upset? Why can't I see your work? Why wouldn't you show me my portrait? It looks awful. It—"

"Because it's not finished! You can't look at something half finished and make a judgment. That's why you don't belong in here." She shoved me toward the door. I tripped on her long skirt and fell to my knees. As my kneecaps slammed into the floorboards, pain shot through my legs.

She kicked my ankle, then grabbed a fistful of hair, yanking my head back. "Give it to me right now."

My head was pulled back at such a sharp angle it was difficult to breathe. I couldn't talk, but I wouldn't let go of the notebook. I wasn't sure what I planned to do with it, but if she wanted it that badly, I knew I had to have it.

She yanked harder, ripping several hairs from my scalp. I screamed.

"Just fucking give it to me!" She shoved me to the floor and grabbed the book, twisting it furiously, bending the cover, gouging the corners into my ribs as I tried to hang onto it.

"What are you so afraid of?"

"Nothing. I just don't want you in my work. These are sketchbooks. They aren't for public view. I want you out of here right now. And I want my book."

"These drawings look like that painting in the corner of your gallery. Is that what you're working on? Do you have some sick obsession? Did you kill Derek and Grace so you could practice? Or maybe Colin murdered them for you, I don't know. It's so disgusting. I can't—"

"Stop talking. Stop saying those things. You don't know anything."

We continued wrestling over the sketchbook, scrabbling across the floor, neither of us talking anymore, neither one of us getting the upper hand.

There was no way I was letting go of that book. I tried to wriggle closer to the door, shoving my knees into her hips as best I could, worming my way out of her clawing hands that seemed to be grabbing me everywhere.

Each time I felt as if I were about to break free, she threw herself on me again, pinning my legs to the floor and getting a better grip on the sketchbook. Even so, I could feel I was moving closer to the cabinet with its drawers of paint, closer to the doorway. I was getting tired, taking deep, gasping breaths, but so was she.

Soon, I would be in the hallway, and maybe then I could use the walls in that narrow space to get some leverage and force her off me.

She hung onto my belt now with one hand. With the other, she grabbed the bottom drawer of the cabinet and pulled it open. I saw something flash in her hand. She had a palette knife, the sharp tip gleaming in the overhead light. I screamed. I gave her one furious kick in her neck and felt the blade of the knife slice my ankle.

61

BEFORE: COLIN

*E*ver since I'd betrayed Ember in the worst way imaginable, I'd been doing little things to show her how much I loved her.

Ember didn't know I'd slept with Olivia. Rather, I didn't *think* she knew. Olivia swore she hadn't told her. We'd been incredibly discreet. But women are perceptive. And the perception of an artist is an order of magnitude greater.

Still, Ember hadn't done or said anything to suggest to me she knew.

But I felt that making these extra gestures would help me as well. It would remind me how much I adored my wife. She was everything to me. Those words bounced around inside my head like a cliché, but I felt them in the marrow of my bones. Ember was my world. I was disgusted with myself for letting my body take control, drowning out what was in my heart, smothering my soul for those few hours. Not once, but twice. It was like a punch in my solar plexus every time I thought about it.

Sometimes I wondered how I would live with that pain for the rest of my life. Knowing what I'd done, even if Ember never did.

On Sunday mornings, I left a small gift on the tray of her easel.

During the week, I would drop into one of the specialty or gift stores in Palm Springs and browse for something I thought would charm her. I tried to avoid art supplies. She was so particular about those, I didn't dare guess at what she might want or need.

I'd bought her earrings, bracelets, toe rings, a pair of fluffy socks, lingerie, candles, books ... anything I could think of. I tried to stick to small items because I planned to keep this up for the rest of our lives. Even the jewelry was simple—leather straps or plain silver hoops—nothing extravagant. Just small whispers that I loved her and was thinking of her, even when she was working on Sunday mornings.

I went into her studio before sunrise so that I didn't have to talk to anyone and explain what I was doing. I wanted to be sure the gift was there in case she decided to slip out to her workspace early, which she often did when someone was staying with us for a sitting.

She didn't like me taking her keys and going into the studio without her, but she'd given me long, lingering kisses to thank me for the Sunday morning gifts, so I figured she'd overlooked the trespass.

I put the key in the lock and opened the door. I was assaulted by a metallic smell, and then a sight that almost dropped me to my knees.

Grace.

Ember's current subject, Grace—our houseguest for the past week—was sprawled on the floor in a pool of blood so large and thick it was difficult to believe there was any left in her body. She was naked from the waist up, her eyes and mouth open, her arms flung out to her sides. A palette knife with a sharp tip lay nearby, caked with dried blood. Her shirt was near her feet, drenched with blood—so much blood.

I lurched to the doorway and rushed out. I stumbled to the garden and vomited a thin stream of liquid onto the ground. After I caught my breath, I kicked dirt over the mess and returned to the studio.

I knew Ember worked too hard. I knew she was obsessed with her work. Painting consumed her. It was all she talked about, all she thought about. She spent most of her waking hours in this space. It didn't matter if she was working on a commissioned portrait or not. She was a perfectionist. She was driven ... beyond reason.

I'd moved past the point of blaming her for pushing me into that thing with Olivia. It wasn't blame, exactly, but if her work hadn't consumed her the way it did, my betrayal probably wouldn't have happened. Ember lived for her work. There wasn't space for me in her mind and, at times, in her bed.

But I took responsibility. When you love someone, you either accept the darker side or you part ways. I'd come to see that, and so I knew the betrayal was on me.

Her mood had been dark and brooding ever since Derek hung himself in her studio.

She'd been thrilled by her success, but terrified, and horribly upset by the morbid aspect. She was angry at the way Hendrix had manipulated her collectors and the people who'd been drawn to her work after the suicide, as if she had some kind of power over life and death.

I knew she'd been struggling with Grace, feeling as if the work wasn't going well, feeling as if she couldn't capture the woman's essence. She felt animosity from Grace. She'd said it was *complicated*, whatever that meant.

But *this* was what it had come to? Cutting up her subject ... with her palette knife?

I felt the bile rising again.

I knew what I had to do. Before anyone woke.

As I dug a grave in the back corner of the garden, behind the privacy of walls that had been designed to offer a space for contemplation or quiet conversation, I tried to imagine what Grace might have done to provoke Ember into such a rage. It wasn't difficult lately.

Ember was short-tempered. That phrase was laughable in its

understatement. She'd flown into such rages at her sister, and once, even at Avery, that I found myself forced into the role of peace-maker. I'd seen her throw expensive glassware, and once, a figurine that was given to her by her grandmother, not even expressing regret when it shattered into a thousand pieces.

It seemed to be getting worse, and I couldn't figure out what was causing so much anger. She had everything. She claimed to adore our son, although she rarely had time for him since he'd started to leave childhood behind. She professed love for me on a regular basis, but she ran hot and cold—sometimes passionate when we made love, other times staying in her studio long into the night for weeks on end. At times, she seemed to hardly notice that I even had a career of my own, that I existed at all outside of her orbit. She canceled plans with our friends at the last minute, and other times she wanted to throw lavish parties with little planning.

Digging in the hard soil was backbreaking work, but I needed to move faster. The stars were fading and dim light was starting to spill over the horizon. Once I'd moved her body into the ground, I had a tremendous amount of cleaning up to do.

When I finished, it was daylight. I was sweating as if I'd run a marathon in the desert heat.

I opened all the windows in the studio and turned on the ceiling fan.

Then, as I stepped behind the easel to place the gift I'd brought for Ember, I saw Grace's blood-stained bra. I stuffed it into my pocket, left the gift in its place, and went outside. I stood on the patio taking deep, gulping breaths of fresh air.

It was the strangest, most inexplicable thing I'd ever done. That any man had ever done, perhaps.

A normal man would speak to his wife about it. He would ask her *why* she'd brutally murdered the subject of her portrait. He wouldn't simply bury the body and carry on as if nothing had happened. He wouldn't return to the guest room later and collect the woman's things, disposing of them in an anonymous dumpster, destroying her cell phone, fabricating a story about a woman who had suddenly decided to do some extensive traveling so she could *re-think her direction in life.*

But my mind was shattered, and therefore, numb. I couldn't seem to form any coherent thoughts. I honestly didn't know what to say. I didn't … maybe I was as obsessed as my wife. She'd let her art take over her mind, and possibly her sanity. I had let my devotion to caring for Ember and supporting her art take over my own sanity.

She possessed me.

At the time, in my panic and shock, it was the only thing I could think of to do.

Afterwards, there didn't seem to be any way back.

I waited every day for her to ask me about it, but she never did. And that drove me to the edge of madness.

62

NOW: MORGAN

*W*arm blood flowed down the side of my ankle from the cut. I could feel it trickling along my Achilles tendon. The pain was like a sharp sting that burned, then subsided, then flared again, bringing tears to my eyes. Running would be almost impossible.

Ember must have sensed some of the fight had gone out of me, because she made a renewed effort to pry the sketchbook out of my hands. She scraped at my knuckles, drawing blood there, too.

"Why are you so afraid of anyone seeing your work?"

"You don't know anything. You don't understand the process."

"What are you so scared of?"

"I'm not scared. I'm angry. You're violating my work. You're violating me!"

"You're lying. You're absolutely terrified. It feels like you're trying to kill me, that you would ..." I started to cry. Maybe I needed to let go of the book. Would she kill me for it? She was hanging onto my leg with a grip so tight I was losing the sensation in my foot. She hadn't cut me again, but she was holding the palette knife close to my face and I had no idea what she might do with it.

"You had no right to steal my keys and come in here, digging through my things. You better never breathe a word of this to anyone. Or—"

"Breathe a word about *what*? I don't know what you're—"

"About anything. Anything you've seen, any of my work."

"I don't … what are you *talking* about?"

I heard the security camera feed on the computer capture the sound of the studio door banging open.

"Ember?"

"Not a word!" Her voice was low. She pressed the sharp tip of the knife against my cheek.

"I heard someone scream," Colin's voice was raised, anxious, as his footsteps thudded across the wood floor of the studio. "Are you okay?"

A moment later, he was standing over us.

Ember had moved the knife away from my face so fast, I didn't think he'd seen it.

"What's … what the hell happened?"

Ember let go of my leg and stood. She held out her hand as if to help me up.

Colin reached down and placed his hands under my arms, lifting me to my feet. "Let me help you into the studio so we can look at that cut. What *happened*? What were you …" He glanced wildly around the room, searching for the object she'd used to inflict a cut that would draw so much blood.

"It was an accident," Ember said.

Colin let out a quick burst of cynical laughter.

"She wouldn't give me my sketchbook." Ember pointed to the book I was still clutching to my chest as if it would save me, a shield protecting me from the point of her palette knife.

Colin held onto my arm, letting me lean on him as I limped down the short hallway to the studio. My head spun, not only from the shock of what had just happened and the woozy awareness of blood continuing to drip from my ankle, but because the man I'd thought might want to hurt me was now tenderly looking after me.

He settled me in the chair, then stepped into the hallway, entering the bathroom. I heard the water running, then he returned with several hand towels. He used a damp towel to wipe away the blood and wrapped a clean one around my ankle. "It needs to be washed thoroughly, but let's try to slow the bleeding first. I think it's mostly superficial."

I nodded, whimpering slightly at the pressure of the fabric on my sliced, raw skin.

"What's in the sketchbook that's so important?" Colin glanced at Ember.

I flipped open the sketchbook to show him.

"It's *my* work," Ember muttered. "She has no right to look at it."

"So you *sliced* her ankle?" He placed his hand across his forehead, closing his eyes. He took a deep breath. "Were you trying to …"

"I wasn't trying to kill her, if that's what you're thinking," Ember said.

"That's not what it looks like. That knife is sharp. And Grace …" His voice broke as he said her name.

"What?" Ember's voice was shrill. "Is that what you think? Is that who you think I am? You think I murdered one of my subjects?" Her voice rose and her eyes filled with tears.

"What else could I think? I came in here to leave your gift that morning and I found her. There was blood everywhere, and one of your palette knives was right there."

Ember lunged at him, shoving him away from the chair where I sat, toward her easel. He fell against it, causing it to tip precariously before she grabbed it. Colin stumbled away from her. "After Derek, after the way Hendrix used his death. And you went along with it … I don't know. I didn't know what to think."

"What … so you … what did you do?"

"I buried her. I didn't want to lose you." He was half crying now, covering his face with his hands.

"And you didn't even talk to me? You thought I was a killer, and you buried her and cleaned up everything and you never said a word to me?!" She was sobbing so hard it was painful to listen to.

"Who killed her?" Colin said. "And Derek. Who would do that? Who would want to hurt you like this?" He looked ill. His face had turned so white I thought he might pass out. I started to get out of the chair, but then his color returned slightly. "Could Olivia …?"

Ember shook her head. "No." She went to her easel and stepped behind it. She ran her hand down the side, letting her fingers rest on the tray.

After a few moments of silence, she left the room. I heard a desk drawer being open, followed by the thud of sketchbooks and folders being tossed on the floor. Then, I heard the sounds of thick paper as it was ripped in half, punctuated by Ember's grief-stricken sobs.

Colin left the room. I stood and followed, limping slowly after them.

Ember stood a few feet from her desk. She was holding the photographs of the eyes, ripping them into long strips, tears running down her face. The only sound was the tearing of paper.

Colin watched, doing nothing to stop her. He looked confused, but he seemed willing to wait for her to explain what was so upsetting about the photographs, what was going through her mind as she tore everything to pieces.

After she'd ripped nearly every photograph in two, she stood there, her shoulders slumped, her hair covering the sides of her face. "I know who wants to destroy me. And now he has. You or I will go to prison for Grace's murder. That, or I can destroy my career myself."

She collapsed onto the floor on top of the shredded photographs.

63

NOW: BRYCE

*T*he police came with a warrant at seven-thirty Tuesday morning.

I was awake, but still in my sitting area, drinking a latte from the espresso machine in my suite. I saw the blue and red lights. I wasn't sure why they thought they needed lights. And I really wasn't sure what was going on when I saw how Colin and Ember rolled out the red carpet for them.

There was a dark blue sedan, two patrol cars, and a white van. A team of four people climbed out of the van, ready to dig up the garden from the looks of their attire and gear. I expected they would soon be poring over the studio and the house for evidence. The rest of them were loaded with questions for the people who lived in the beautiful, tranquil Spanish villa belonging to Colin and Ember West—the soon to be infamous portrait artist.

I didn't have a good feeling about the mood in the house.

Colin hadn't said another word about an archaeologist. The body in the cactus garden had become known as Grace, and Jade was curled up on the sofa in the living room, weeping. Olivia sat beside her, offering comfort when Colin couldn't be near her.

Colin and Ember were acting like young lovers, whispering and touching each other, giving one another constant reassuring glances. Morgan was sublimely calm.

Something had changed. Dramatically. But no one had explained anything to me.

As the police settled themselves in the lounge area of the kitchen to begin conducting their interviews, I pulled Morgan into the corner of the entryway. "What's up with Colin? It sounds like he's done a complete about-face."

She shrugged.

"You convinced him it's Grace?"

"It's obvious, isn't it?"

"It is, but he didn't believe it."

"He does now."

Her answers were non-answers. I gave her a curious look. She gave me a grim smile. I wasn't sure if she was trying to comfort me or she just wanted to get the hell out of there.

Colin and Ember's attorney was there. I wondered if I should have one. It hadn't occurred to me until that moment. I wasn't like them. I didn't have an attorney sitting in the wings that I could call before business hours, expecting him to drive forty miles into the desert to hang out for a few hours whenever I needed him. In fact, I'd only spoken to one attorney in my life, and that was the one Ember referred me to. The one who had defended Adam against his murder charge.

All the interviews were brief—no more than ten minutes each. Avery's was even shorter, maybe three minutes. That made me uncomfortable. I had the feeling Colin or his attorney, or Ember, or Morgan ... someone had already talked to Detective Acosta before she arrived with her warrant.

My interview was last.

Detective Acosta and Officer Lewis were seated on one of the sofas in the lounge. I was facing them, feeling ganged up on.

"What was the name of the attorney who defended your brother,

Adam Cunningham against his murder charge?" Detective Acosta asked.

"My brother has nothing to do with this."

"Please answer the question."

"Greg Thatcher. But he—"

"And who paid Mr. Thatcher's bill?"

"Why does that matter?"

"Who paid Mr. Thatcher's bill?"

"Ember."

"Why?"

"Because ..." I didn't like where this was going at all. It was clear they'd talked to Ember. And not just during the ten minutes they'd spoken to her while I was sitting in the living room during the previous hour. There had obviously been a late-night conversation. Had she told them *everything*?

"Why did Ember West pay your brother's $578,000 legal bill?"

"I was her student and she ... I thought ... I was ... she offered ..." Shit. I had no idea what to say. And I'd already fucked it up by throwing out a bunch of words that made me sound nervous, as if I were trying to figure out what I wanted to say—the sure sign of a lie.

"Just tell us why she paid your brother's legal fees."

"I couldn't afford them." There. KISS—keep it simple, stupid. I smiled.

"That was very generous of her."

I shrugged.

"How were you planning to pay her back?"

I was probably going to lose. I wasn't sure why I was prolonging my agony.

"Why did she pay his bill, knowing you couldn't pay? Or, we can save some time. We can stop asking questions and you can explain your arrangement with Ms. West," Detective Acosta said.

"My arrangement."

"Arrangement. Agreement, whatever you want to call it. We already know the details."

"Then why do I have to explain it?"

"Because we want to hear it from you. And then we have a few questions."

I hated that she kept saying we. The other cop hadn't said a word.

"I was her student, and she was struggling to make a go of it at the time. She saw that I was really good at painting eyes. Capturing the subjects' personalities. And she couldn't do it for shit." I laughed. She still couldn't. Thousands of sketches and oil renderings, and still … nada. Maybe it took a certain talent, a different kind of talent, to make the human eye look dead like Ember did. But no one wants a portrait like that.

No matter how many times she touched her subjects' faces, poked at the bones around their eyes, tried to get the feeling of them into her own marrow, she couldn't reproduce what she saw. It was one hundred percent true what I'd told Morgan, and the others. No one grasped the passion, the hours of sweat and agony that Ember poured into her work. The endless dark nights spent sketching and painting, trying to capture the essence of a person's soul, that spark of life.

Ember couldn't do it. She simply couldn't do it. She was a genius with their mouths and smiles, the shapes of their faces, their posture. But she couldn't put life into their eyes to save her own life.

"She said if I came to work for her, she would pay for my brother's defense. One of the best criminal defense attorneys in Southern California. I would paint the eyes in her portraits. I would keep her secret and she would have a stunning career. She really is a talented painter, but the eyes … she just can't seem to get them right. It's become a thing. As if she's blocked or something. Now, it seems like the harder she tries, the more it eludes her. It's basically driven her insane, if you want my opinion."

"We didn't ask for your opinion, and she appears to be quite sane."

I didn't agree, but I was already sinking into a pit. It was better to stop talking. Maybe there was still hope for me. Committing fraud wasn't the same as murder. And lying isn't the same as keeping secrets. Keeping things to yourself is simple. Telling an outright lie is a little more difficult. But not saying anything? I've always found that easy.

"That's fraud," Officer Lewis said.

"For her more than me."

Neither of them said anything, so score one for me. Maybe. It probably didn't matter.

"And how did you find opportunities to paint their eyes without Ms. West's subjects knowing?"

"There's a camera hidden behind one of the hanging plants in her studio. We recorded the sessions, we asked them to sit without blinking and then captured stills off the video. It was crude and challenging. But I'm pretty good. I also did some sketches while she was working. The subjects assumed I was taking notes."

"You think well of yourself."

"It's a fact. I'm pretty good. Why do you think she sells so many paintings at those prices? Because the eyes in her portraits are utterly captivating. She's in a class by herself. And that's because of me." I smiled.

They didn't smile back.

"And you were tired of this arrangement. You wanted your freedom. You wanted your own career. But you don't have $578,000, even though Ms. West pays you a very good salary. So you thought the deaths of her subjects would damage her career."

"Is that what she thinks?"

"Is that what happened?"

"I have no idea."

"Did you hang Derek Shaw in Ms. West's studio?"

"No."

"Did you stab Grace Gibson with one of Ms. West's palette knives?"

"No."

"Mr. West found Ms. Gibson dead. He buried her body, which makes him an accessory to murder, but he claims he didn't kill her."

"And he's blaming me?"

"Did you kill her?"

"I said, no."

"Did you kill Derek Shaw?"

"No."

"Did you kill Grace Gibson?"

"No."

They asked me the same two questions twenty more times. I counted. I don't know if they thought they were wearing me down, if it was some kind of mental trick in which they thought I might get bored or confused and eventually say, yes.

Finally, they said our interview was over, for now.

They said they would be speaking to me again. I wasn't to leave the area. I was encouraged to have an attorney with me the next time, if I wanted to. I told them I didn't see the need for an attorney because I hadn't killed anyone.

Telling an outright lie was getting easier.

64

NOW: MORGAN

*J*ade and I were sitting in the garden near the hole where Grace's body had been removed.

I'd suggested we sit somewhere else. There were so many beautiful spots with solid, breathing, unyielding cacti, the reflecting pool, stone benches shaded by flowering trees, exotic oversized pottery. But Jade wanted to sit here, by the rubble and the shallow hole that had been hastily carved out for her by Colin in the midst of his tormented fear that his wife was killing the subjects of her artwork.

It was shocking to me that Ember had so quickly forgiven him for thinking such a horrible thing about her. Of course, there was more she didn't know that she had to forgive him for. If she ever found out, would she be willing to forgive?

Knowing what had unfolded in their marriage made me wonder what kinds of things Tyler and I would face over the years. Nothing even close to any of that, obviously. But difficulties, and probably times when we distrusted each other, misunderstood, or hurt the other.

How would we work our way through those times? I'd never

considered it before. I'd blissfully assumed we would always be as open and honest and wildly in love as we were now. It was times like this when I wished, more intensely than ever, that my mother was here to ask these questions. My girlfriends didn't know. And now I realized that no matter how much I longed to have a motherly relationship with Jade, I could never bring up questions like these. She wasn't *my* mother. She was Tyler's.

So what did I want from her? Maybe all the wrong things.

I couldn't replace the daughter she was grieving for and she would never replace my mother. I wasn't sure why I'd ever imagined she could. The idea was terribly disrespectful to my mother now that I saw it so clearly, as if my eyes were open for the first time.

I placed my hand on Jade's shoulder, hoping to comfort her.

"I can't believe she's gone," she whispered. "Almost worse, I can't believe I didn't *know*."

I rubbed her shoulder.

"I didn't believe you. I thought you were being hysterical. I thought I would *know* if she was dead. I thought I would *feel* it somehow, that I would be aware of her absence from the earth." She started to cry, her shoulders shaking under my hand.

I didn't know what to say, so I said nothing.

The police hadn't made an arrest.

They'd asked Colin, Ember, Avery, Olivia, and Bryce to come in for lengthier interviews. Detective Acosta had backed away from her initial eagerness to agree with Ember's insistence that it was obvious Bryce had murdered Derek and Grace.

Ember was certain that Bryce wanted to destroy her reputation, and thus, her career. Out of bitterness. In a desperate attempt to free himself from his obligation to her. If that was the truth, he'd failed. He still owed her more money than he'd been able to save, despite the attractive salary and her provision of room and board. He owed her a lot more than he could ever hope to earn now that his reputation in the art world was also irrevocably damaged.

He'd assured me he would recover. He'd done nothing wrong. He certainly hadn't *murdered* anyone! Ember had been holding him hostage. She'd offered to pay for his brother's defense out of kindness, then demanded that he either pay her over half a million dollars in legal fees, or agree to her unethical and degrading terms. His only choice was to become the secret to her success. And so he'd spent years capturing the eyes of her subjects, adding the magic to her portraits that brought her critical acclaim, skyrocketing sales of her work, and fabulous wealth.

Now, he was packing his things, preparing to leave Ember's home that afternoon. The police had no evidence he'd killed anyone, but Ember didn't need evidence. She was certain.

Jade and I planned to leave the following morning.

"I should have asked more questions," Jade said.

"Questions?"

"When Grace told me she'd broken up with Michael. She said *things* had happened. That she'd had a very intense encounter with a guy. And that it made her question whether she was ready for marriage. I didn't think anything about it. I didn't … I didn't actually connect it with something that happened here because she also said that being here in the desert without anyone she knew had given her a lot of time to think. I know …" A violent sob escaped from her. She pressed her hand against her chest. "But now …" She sat up straighter and lifted her chin, directing her attention away from the hole in the ground, staring up toward the top of the wall surrounding the garden and the sky beyond.

"Now …?" I asked.

"Well, Colin finding her partially undressed. I wonder what that was about. I wonder if Grace and Bryce … I wonder if that's how he lured her out to the studio at night. If there was something between them."

We sat there without talking for several minutes.

I thought about Bryce's awkward attempt to unclasp my bra, sliding his fingers around under my shirt. His declaration that he'd been attracted to me since he'd met me. He had not. It was a lie I'd felt viscerally. Had he said the same to Grace? Maybe he'd said it with more finesse. With more practice, in more fitting circum-stances.

65

NOW: MORGAN

*W*hen I asked Bryce to meet me in the cactus garden before he left, I didn't have a clear plan. The only thing I had was my phone in a deep pocket of my skirt with the recording app running. I wore a loose summery top that flowed over my hips, covering the pocket.

I was seated on a bench by the reflecting pool, which gave the illusion of offering a cool spot in the shade of a tree with white flowers.

By the time he showed up, the back of my neck and my scalp were damp with perspiration, partially from the heat, partially caused by my anxious heartbeat. It wasn't that I was afraid he might try to kill me. The others were in the house. I felt safe enough, although I still felt as if spiders were crawling up the backs of my arms and down my spine, lying in wait inside my tangled ponytail.

I was afraid I would stumble over my words and he would realize what I was doing. I'd end up chasing him away, with his secrets still locked inside his mind. As a result, Ember might eventually be arrested for Grace's murder due to the sheer weight of circumstantial evidence. It was ironic, considering that she'd paid a fortune to release Bryce's older brother from that very trap.

Colin would already be spending quite a few years, possibly decades, in prison for concealing Grace's murder. It was possible they might decide to stop believing his earnest insistence that he'd found her and buried her to protect his wife. A story that was likely only believable if you knew what their marriage was like, if you'd witnessed his utter and unquestioning devotion to his wife. A devotion that bordered on worship.

Still, despite all the time I'd spent feeling absolutely certain that Colin had murdered Grace, I was now equally convinced that I'd misjudged him. Knowing what Ember had required of Bryce, recalling his fumbling yet aggressive hands on my body, my gut had assured me I'd felt Grace's killer put his hand on my throat.

I couldn't keep Jade's godson out of prison, but I could keep him from being convicted of murder. I had to at least try to force him to expose himself, to give Jade the faint peace of mind that comes from knowing the truth.

Bryce was walking slowly as he came into view. His hands were in his pockets, his flip-flops slapping the bottoms of his feet, his hair damp and loose from a recent shower.

Instead of taking a seat beside me, he stood facing me. "What do you want?"

"Can you sit for a minute?"

"I'll stand, thanks."

"I just—"

"I'm supposed to be out of here, so you need to make it quick."

"Was that the truth? When you said you wanted me?"

He stared at me. He pushed a strand of hair away from his face. He turned his head slightly, looking toward the building that housed Ember's studio where he'd spent eight years of his life, painting eyes that evoked a sense of something like fear in Avery, but captivated thousands of collectors and led critics to call Ember a genius.

He looked back at me, but didn't meet my gaze. He seemed to be staring through me. "What does it matter?"

"Because I didn't know. And when you tried to kiss me, I was—"

"What's the purpose of this conversation? Because I need to get going."

"I know something you might want to know."

He narrowed his eyes. After a moment, his expression relaxed, and he smiled. "I doubt that."

"I do."

"What is it?"

"First, I'm curious. Did you hit on all of Ember's subjects?"

"No."

"But you hit on me. And Grace. Did you hit on Derek too? Everyone you wanted to kill?"

He took several steps away from me. "None of that's true. I didn't kill anyone."

"You hit on me. You said—"

"And I took no for an answer."

"You hit on Grace. I guess that's why she was—"

"I didn't hit on her."

"Jade said—"

"Jade doesn't know shit." He took a step closer to me. "And neither do you."

"Maybe I don't. Maybe Colin had it right. It was your brother. The police were too focused on collecting evidence around her grave and in the studio. They didn't think to look for signs of someone sleeping out here."

He lurched toward me and grabbed my upper arm, squeezing it hard, thrusting his face close to mine. "My brother has nothing to do with this. I told Colin that. I told the cops that. Nothing. He's never been anywhere near this place."

"Let go of me."

He released his grip.

"You could have unlocked one of the gates every night and let him in. Given him a place to sleep. Sometimes people with mental health issues don't like to take their medication. And when they don't, it's hard to find a place to live. He could have slept out here for months, years, and no one would have ever known. You let him in and fed him and gave him a place to stay and then he went and did that. Just like he stabbed that other woman."

His face was filled with rage. "I know for a *fact* he didn't kill anyone. He was never here. He—"

"You know for a *fact*? How do you know that?"

"I … because he wouldn't. He's not a killer. He didn't kill that other woman. He was acquitted."

"He had a very good attorney. A very, very expensive attorney."

"He never killed anyone."

"But you said you know for a *fact*. How could you know? For a *fact*? Because you killed her. Is this what you did when she asked you not to?" I grabbed his wrist. "Is this what you did to Grace? Like you did with me?" I slid his hand under my top and placed it over my breast. He tried to pull it away, but I had a firm grip, nearly as strong as his. "Is that what you did before you stabbed her?"

"I didn't touch her, she …" He yanked his hand out from under my shirt.

I let him go.

"But you were there."

"No, I wasn't." He backed away from me. "I'm done talking to you. You better not start saying things about my brother. You have no proof. You're just making things up. Everyone wants to blame him for every bad thing that happens because he has a mental illness. They act like he's a monster. He's not! He's the sweetest, most amazing guy I've ever known. You have no proof of anything and you don't know *anything*. And you don't know my brother."

When he was gone, I stopped the recording and saved the file. Then, I called Detective Acosta.

66

NOW: BRYCE

I was shoving my smaller suitcase into the back of my Jeep, wedging it between boxes, when I saw Detective Acosta's sedan heading up the long driveway. She pulled into the area in front of the carport where my Jeep was sitting, nose out. She positioned her car so it was impossible for me to leave my spot.

I was minutes from driving away. I wasn't sure if her aggressive move suggested she knew that, or if she was setting the stage for a different kind of interview, an interview where she turned the screws more tightly than she had before.

There was nothing to worry about. She knew nothing. Ember could fabricate whatever theory she wanted. So could curious little Morgan, but no one had proof of anything. If the detective wanted to play it like this, if she wanted to have yet another round of questions, thinking the repetition would wear me down, that was fine. All I needed to do was keep cool and keep my brother out of it.

After eight years of bowing to Ember's will, working to pay off a debt that was still on a horizon I couldn't see, making her famous to the point of reverence, I'd finally realized it was either her or me.

I could continue capturing the essence and vulnerability, the very souls of Ember's subjects through their eyes, or I could take their lives and make it look like Ember had gone insane. That she'd killed the people she was trying to immortalize.

But it hadn't worked out the way I'd planned.

Maybe hanging Derek had been a poor choice on my part. I'd chosen it because I hadn't wanted to deal with a lot of blood. I wasn't sure I had it in me to stab someone, and I certainly wasn't going to use a gun, which wouldn't have worked due to the noise. It just seemed cleaner to threaten him with a knife until the rope was around his neck. He'd gone along with my game, with my suggestion that in order to show fear, the vulnerability that made for the most depth in a person's eyes, he needed to experience genuine terror.

But Ember—I can only assume it was her—had to go and write that message on Derek's portrait. So the cops and everyone else leaped to the conclusion he'd hung himself. Not a single person, except Zoe, who they all wrote off as blinded by grief, even whispered the word murder.

And Grace. The aftermath of her death was a mind-fuck that made me feel as if I'd stepped into an alternate reality.

I thought I had it set up perfectly. Her body was in Ember's studio, just like Derek's. I'd worked up the courage to stab her, fortifying myself with a few shots of Colin's tequila beforehand.

Then, her body vanished into thin air. At least that's what it felt like, at first.

Sunday morning came and Ember went out to her studio as she always did. I didn't hear a sound. The screams I expected never materialized. She worked all morning, and we had a light lunch. No one said a word about Grace being absent. Everyone acted as if things were normal. The minute we finished eating, I went out to the studio. Her body was gone. The floor was spotless.

She'd truly vanished into thin air.

My heart was racing. An instant headache exploded as I tried to imagine what could have happened. Where was her body? Who cleaned up all the blood? Ember was calm and in an unusually good mood. Panic ricocheted through my brain like hailstones. The headache grew worse until I could hardly see out of my left eye.

Later that afternoon, Colin started going on about how Grace had abandoned her portrait. She'd left early in the morning, telling him she couldn't take it anymore. She'd split with her fiancé a few days earlier, which I'd already known. The breakup hadn't been a surprise. Not after all those invasive, mind-twisting questions Ember and I asked all of her subjects in order to distract them from the fact that I was sketching their eyes while Ember worked on the rest of the portrait. Not after I'd convinced Grace to take off her clothes to expose her vulnerability. Not once, but on three separate occasions.

Now, Colin told us, speaking as if he were reading a script, Grace needed time alone. She needed to get her head together. She was heading overseas, with no itinerary. Just like that.

It was clear he'd buried Grace's body and cleaned everything up. Or the two of them had done it together. I was never really sure.

The next year of my life was pure torture. I had to get out of there. It was worse than ever by an order of magnitude. I was losing my mind. Then. Morgan showed up. It was very close to home—killing another woman connected to Colin's godmother. But I liked the artistic pattern of it.

Detective Acosta got out of her car. Officer Lewis stayed seated in the passenger seat. Maybe she wanted to be sure no one moved the car, allowing me to escape.

"Let's go inside, Bryce. I have a few more questions for you," Detective Acosta said.

It seemed a little ballsy of her to assume she could commandeer part of Ember's house as her official interview room, but maybe she had permission. What did I know? Things seemed to be happening around me in an orchestrated fashion, led by a conductor I was unaware of.

"If it's okay with Ember," I said.

"Follow me, please."

She walked quickly toward the courtyard. I slipped my keys into my pocket and followed, obedient, but confident. I had this.

67

NOW: BRYCE

Seated at the dining room table, the doors closed, Detective Acosta placed her phone on the table between us. "I think you stabbed Grace Gibson with Ember's palette knife until she was dead."

I stared at her.

"Did you?"

"I've already told you, no. A hundred times."

"Why don't I believe you?" she asked.

"I don't know."

"It's very unusual that you've allowed us to question you three times without an attorney."

"Only the guilty need an attorney," I said, pleased to have the upper hand.

"You believed your brother wasn't guilty. Yet, you eagerly accepted Ms. West's offer to hire a highly regarded attorney to represent him."

I felt my jaw get so tight, I wondered if I would be able to move it to speak. "Why do you keep dragging my brother into this? He lives in Santa Clarita. He's never been within fifty miles of this place."

"You know that for a fact?"

"Yes."

"It's interesting that you're so certain about your brother's habits. Absolutely *certain*. You used that exact phrase when you told Morgan Hayes that you knew *for a fact* that Adam hadn't killed anyone."

"How do you know his name?" My voice was louder than it should have been. All I needed to do was stay cool. I tried lowering the volume, but I still sounded tense. "I don't think I used that exact phrase." I laughed, sounding very casual, I thought.

"You did use that phrase: *I know for a fact*." She tapped her phone. "Morgan had the foresight to record your conversation."

"She ... is that legal?"

"How can you know for a *fact* that Adam didn't kill Grace Gibson? Were you with him for the entire month of April of last year, which is when we estimate she was murdered, based on the decomposition of her body?"

"No. But I know he's never been here."

"How do you know this?"

"I just know."

"You made a very strong statement to Ms. Hayes. A definitive statement that there isn't any doubt in your mind that your brother could have committed this murder. I'd like you to explain what your thinking was that allowed you to make that statement."

"You have no reason to think my brother has anything to do with this. He was acquitted of that other murder and you're not allowed to accuse him of something just because—"

"There wasn't enough evidence to prove he'd murdered that woman, I agree. I reviewed his case. But I also think the circumstances were ambiguous. They never made another arrest. I don't think it can be proven that Adam did *not* kill her."

"He's innocent! Stop talking like he's guilty. You cops want to find the easy way out or something. Close your case. Find someone to blame when you can't figure it out. I don't know what it is." I glanced down at the table. My hands were balled into fists. I moved my arms, sliding them off the table and resting them on my legs. I leaned back in the chair, trying to take a deep breath, making sure I looked chill. Confident, but chill.

"How do you know for a *fact* Adam didn't murder Grace? Because you did?"

"No."

"I think that's a logical conclusion."

"It's jumping to conclusions."

"You've been trapped in this position with Ms. West. A virtual prisoner. You're incredibly talented—able to capture something indefinable in people's eyes. And Ember took all the credit for that. It's what made her work remarkable. It made her famous and quite wealthy."

"That doesn't make me a killer."

"You've worked in obscurity, making a decent salary, as I understand it. But how many years would it take you to earn over half a million dollars? It's been eight already. Most of your living expenses are covered, but the cost of caring for your brother isn't insignificant, is it? So saving up $578,000 takes some time."

I folded my arms across my chest and relaxed my shoulders. I gave her a stoic look. I was calm. I was cool.

"It might be another ten years before you save that amount. Possibly longer."

"What's your point?"

"There was no escape for you." She paused, rather dramatically. "Unless Ember's career was destroyed, right?"

"I still don't see your point."

"I think you do. We discussed it before. You killed Derek. And when his death was ruled a suicide, you stabbed Grace, hoping that Ember would be blamed. But Colin buried her body. What a shock that must have been." She laughed.

"Isn't it inappropriate for you to be laughing about a murder victim?"

She continued smiling.

"The body was found here, Bryce. We know her killer was someone connected with this property. The palette knife was wiped clean, which suggests it wasn't Ember. If she used her own knife, why would she wipe it clean? She would know her palette knife would implicate her."

"I didn't do it."

"To be honest. Most crimes are committed by someone with a history of violence. And in this case, that person is Adam."

"He doesn't have a history of violence!" I hadn't meant to shout, but she was acting like he was convicted. She had no right to do that. It's as if she didn't even believe the jury.

"He has a connection to someone in this house. He was only acquitted due to a lack of motive and clear evidence. He's someone we're going to want to talk to. Unless there's anything else you want to tell us."

"Because you're lazy?! Because you can't find anything? You have to find someone and if there isn't enough evidence, you're just going to ask the same questions over and over or start accusing someone just because he was treated like shit before. Just because he was accused of something he didn't do because he has a mental illness!?"

My voice was too loud. I was not chill, but I couldn't help it. Adam didn't need this. I couldn't afford another lawyer for him. If they talked to Adam, I had no idea what he would say. I could never predict what he would say. The only thing I could predict was that it would be something unpredictable and unexpected. No one would understand what he was trying to say, and that would make them think he was strange and scary and therefore capable of murder.

I could feel tears coming into my eyes. I couldn't let her see that. I couldn't.

"This shows how fucked up the world is!" Now my voice was so loud they could probably hear me in the other rooms if anyone was out there listening. "Someone tries to help a poor woman lying under a bench with a knife sticking out of her and he gets accused of murder. Ember says she'll help pay for his attorney because she likes me and I'm talented and she feels bad for my brother and then she turns me into a prisoner!"

"It must have felt awful," Detective Acosta said.

Now she was patronizing me. "That's how *nice* the sane world is. She doesn't deserve to be an artist!" I shouted. "She doesn't deserve all this recognition and fame. She can't paint for shit. I'm the artist here! I'm the one who could see into Derek's eyes and show who he was. I'm the one who got Grace to reveal who she really was. When she was sitting there almost naked, I *saw* inside her. It was the first time she really knew who she was herself. Her eyes were luminous!"

"And then you turned out that light," Detective Acosta said.

I touched my fingers to my face. It was wet with tears.

"Do you want me to interview Adam?" she asked. "Or do you want to tell me who killed Derek and Grace?"

"It's me." After I wiped the tears off my face, she read me my rights. Then she handed me a notepad and told me to write down everything I'd said, and all the things I'd done to Derek and Grace.

I wrote down everything she wanted.

68

NOW: MORGAN

It was difficult for Jade to pack her suitcase. In fact, it was difficult to get her to leave the back corner of the cactus garden where her daughter's shallow grave had now been filled. When I realized she wasn't going to be able to manage, I packed her things for her while she and Ember sat in the garden.

They leaned against each other, their heads pressed together— Jade's blonde hair bright against Ember's dark, unwashed strands. In some ways, Ember's grief seemed too poised to consume Jade's. I wondered if Jade was aware of that.

I'd expected Ember would be destroyed by the loss of her career, the thing she'd appeared to love more than any person or any object. But it hadn't been that way. Instead, she seemed relieved of a terrible burden. Her eyes had lost the haunted quality I'd noticed the first time I'd met her. They still looked tired, but they seemed less troubled. Now, they were filled with a different kind of grief than I'd expected, and strangely —love.

She was grieving the loss of a man who had loved her so deeply he'd covered up a gruesome murder, thinking he was protecting her. She was weeping for all the years she'd hardly noticed he was there, and now all the years she would be living alone in the gorgeous home he'd built for her.

Avery and Olivia seemed as if they were in a state of suspended motion. I was hopeful that once Jade and I were gone, they would help Ember find her footing. Maybe she would finally see them now that she wasn't blinded by the layers of deceit that had turned her into a monster of sorts.

Maybe.

I was hopeful, if only because she no longer seemed like a monster, and I could see how much Avery, especially, was hopeful that his mother would notice that he was only twelve, barely out of childhood, and he still needed her.

* * *

As Jade drove down the long, straight driveway, I turned to look back at the Spanish villa standing alone in the desert. It looked as desolate as when we'd arrived. I thought about its icy cold interior and the almost unbearable discomfort of having someone try to replicate me in oil paint on a canvas.

After a few moments, I turned forward to face the scenery ahead of us—wide, sweeping vistas where the crisp blue sky reached down to touch the earth. I thought about the home Tyler and I would build together. I was more certain than ever that I was truly, madly in love with that man.

Two weeks in the desert had brushed the clouds from the past out of my eyes. I could see so clearly now that all I needed was my best friend, my lover, the man who was my partner for the life ahead of me—not my muse or protector or someone to fill an empty space from my childhood. I no longer needed to create some fictitious life that I imagined I'd lost when my mother died.

There would never be a day I wouldn't miss my mother, but I didn't need a surrogate. I didn't *want* a surrogate. I didn't need to mold my mother-in-law into someone she wasn't. No one could ever fill the place left empty when my mother died, but that was okay. That place was for remembering her, as best as I could.

Ember never finished my portrait. I didn't want my eyes painted by Bryce, no matter how talented he was. And he was, indeed, remarkably talented. I saw what he'd done with my eyes. He'd captured something that I didn't even see in myself. But as Avery had pointed out, there was a slight hint of madness, if you looked at them from a certain angle.

At the same time, maybe we all have a hint of madness in us when we're in love, when we're consumed by passion.

69

BEFORE: BRYCE

*A*dam sat at the dining room table with his laptop open in front of him. He refused to use it in his bedroom anymore. His bedroom was at the back of the house, which meant it was too close to the neighbor's house. They were conducting surveillance on his computer activity. Adam had printed out thirty-eight pages, single-spaced, of dates and times when a computer in the house behind ours had pinged his computer.

When he sat at the dining room table, they were unable to access his laptop. Partially because there was a large mirror on the wall facing the dining table. When my parents weren't home, Adam covered it with foil, *to create a protective shield*, he said.

To keep myself from getting upset when Adam told me these things, I sat across from him with a sketchpad. He stared at me, his eyes wide, too wide, filled with an aching desire for me to feel the concern as deeply as he did. I propped my pad against the edge of the table, held the charcoal in my hand, and sketched his eyes. My notebook was filled with pages of Adam's eyes.

It calmed me, drawing his eyes, trying to capture every mood that flashed across the surface.

Drawing his eyes, trying to recreate a hundred, a thousand

emotions that tormented him, made me feel like maybe I could understand him. If I could get them all down on paper, maybe I would understand what was going on behind his wild-looking eyes. Maybe I would find something sane and rational in there.

It sounds crazy to say it.

Maybe I thought I could help both of us.

The only one I helped was me. I became a genius at drawing the human eye. Later, in my room late at night, I squeezed out oil paints to recreate on small canvases what I'd sketched with charcoal. I loved doing it and I couldn't imagine spending my time on anything else. After a while, I took art classes at the Junior College. Then I signed up for a private oil painting class with Ember West.

* * *

It's raining outside. The house is so dark it feels like evening. Adam and I are alone in the house. I'm supposed to be doing my Trig homework, but he's in the dining room again, covering the mirror with foil. When my bedroom door is open, I can hear him tearing foil and wrapping it over the mirror. It makes an awful sound, like someone tearing the walls off our house. I want to cover my ears with my hands.

I go into the dining room. "How are things?"

"You know how they are. But I'm trying to keep you safe, Bryce. I'm doing my best."

"I know you are."

"I'm not crazy."

I don't say anything.

He doesn't seem to notice.

He sits at his computer. He puts on his headphones. I know he's going to his chat groups. The groups that are considered sane, but say crazy things and make him feel like he's not alone. I hate it that he feels so alone in our family. That's why I try to hang out with him. I think he's going to feel alone in the world for the rest of his life. I hate thinking that, but it's probably the truth.

I open my sketchpad and start drawing his eyes.

I want the whole world to see what I see in his eyes. And they would every time I painted the eyes of another, a piece of my brother would be reflected there.

This incredible, complicated guy that has been there since the day I first opened my own eyes and saw the world. This guy—Adam Cunningham. My big brother. My brother that I love. And I always will. I'll do anything to keep him safe.

Other than that, all I want is to be an artist. And I will be.

ABOUT THE AUTHOR

Cathryn is the author of over thirty psychological suspense novels, including the ALEXANDRA MALLORY series featuring a sociopath you can't help but love. Readers have called the series "addictive".

The things that torment us in real life—obsession and revenge, guilt and envy and longing—are endlessly fascinating in fiction and she never grows tired of writing stories about characters struggling to overcome the worst.

Cathryn also writes ghost stories because who knows what lies beyond our senses—The Haunted Ship Trilogy and the Madison Keith series of novellas.

When she's not writing, she's usually reading, walking on the beach, or playing golf, going way out of her way to avoid hitting her ball in the sand or the water. She lives on the Central California Coast with her husband and her cat, Cleopatra.

www.ingramcontent.com/pod-product-compliance
Lightning Source LLC
Chambersburg PA
CBHW020942260626
47169CB00006B/1776

* 9 7 8 1 9 4 3 1 4 2 7 6 7 *